"Why did you kiss me?"

Annis sounded genuinely puzzled.

"Because I wanted to." Adam shifted a little, releasing her. He felt bereft without the touch of her hand. "And also because I was afraid that if I asked you first you would say that it was inappropriate for a chaperon to be kissed. And I would like to do it again."

"Oh, no." Now she took several decided steps back. "I am no easy entertainment for a rake."

"I hardly thought so, and I have told you I am no rake. I do not make a habit of kissing chaperons. In the main they are too old and unattractive." A flash of sheer masculine triumph went through him as he saw the struggle she had with her own feelings and desires. He waited.

Determination gave Annis strength to her tone. "I have a position to maintain, my lord, and I shall not compromise it further."

* * *

The Chaperon Bride
Harlequin Historical #692—February 2004

Praise for Nicola Cornick's books

Lady Allerton's Wager
"A charming, enjoyable read."
—*Romantic Times*

"Ms. Cornick has managed to pack a whole lot of
mystery and humor in this highly romantic and
fast-paced story and is nothing short of a
pure delight to read."
—*Writers Unlimited*

"The Rake's Bride" in The Love Match
"Through vivid detail, the author firmly establishes
time and place for her rollicking tug-of-war."
—*Publishers Weekly*

The Virtuous Cyprian
"…this delightful tale of a masquerade gone awry
will delight ardent Regency readers."
—*Romantic Times*

"A witty, hilarious romp through the Regency period."
—*Rendezvous*

Nicola Cornick

The Chaperon Bride

HARLEQUIN®

TORONTO • NEW YORK • LONDON
AMSTERDAM • PARIS • SYDNEY • HAMBURG
STOCKHOLM • ATHENS • TOKYO • MILAN • MADRID
PRAGUE • WARSAW • BUDAPEST • AUCKLAND

ISBN 0-373-29292-9

THE CHAPERON BRIDE

First North American Publication 2004

Available from Harlequin Historicals and
NICOLA CORNICK

Please address questions and book requests to:
Harlequin Reader Service
U.S.: 3010 Walden Ave., P.O. Box 1325, Buffalo, NY 14269
Canadian: P.O. Box 609, Fort Erie, Ont. L2A 5X3

Chapter One

June 1816

The coach from Leeds drew into the yard of the Hope Inn at Harrogate in the late afternoon and disgorged a number of passengers. Although it was still quite early in the season, the spa villages of High and Low Harrogate were starting to fill up with visitors coming to take the health-giving waters and on this occasion there were seven new arrivals. First to descend was a family of four: mother, father, a boy of about sixteen and a girl a year or so older, both with smiling faces and a lively interest in what was going on around them. Next descended an elderly lady wrapped up in a vast shawl and attended by a solicitous young man who might or might not have been her nephew. The other arrival was Annis, Lady Wycherley, carrying a small leather case and dressed in practical black bombazine and an unbecoming bonnet.

Annis Wycherley was not a newcomer to Harrogate, for she had been born near the town and had spent many happy holidays there with her cousins during the times that her papa had been on leave from the navy. The late Cap-

tain Lafoy had even bought a small estate out towards
Skipton, which Annis had inherited almost a decade before
and visited whenever she had the opportunity. She was not
in Harrogate as often as she would like, however. Her employment, as a chaperon to spoilt society misses, took her
to London or Brighton or Bath, although this latter was
considered rather *déclassé* these days, a shabby genteel
place that was not popular with the fashionable crowd.
Harrogate, with its romantic setting in the wilds of nowhere, its unpleasantly smelling but healthful spa waters
and its rustic northern charm, was fast becoming the new
Bath in the eyes of the *ton*.

Annis, espying her cousin Charles in the crowd thronging the inn yard, hurried across and gave him an affec-
tionate hug. He hugged her back, then held her at arm's
length, looking her over dubiously but with a twinkle in
his very blue eyes.

'Annis, whatever have you done to yourself?'

Annis gave a little giggle. 'Dear Charles, it is lovely to
see you too! I collect that your horror stems from seeing
me in my chaperon's attire? I always dress the part, you
know.'

'It puts years on you.' Charles gave the black bombazine
a bemused look and frowned at the bonnet. 'Lord, Annis,
it's wonderful to see you again, but I barely recognised
you!'

'You know that it is always a mistake to travel in your
best clothes. You end up either mud spattered or dusty.
Besides, as a professional chaperon I cannot look too elegant.'

'No danger of that.' Charles tried to hide his grin. 'Was
the journey good?'

'A little precipitate,' Annis said. 'I suppose that is why

the coach is called the Tally Ho? The driver certainly seemed to take that to heart!'

'I would have sent the carriage to Leeds for you, you know,' Charles said, gesturing to a smart black chaise that stood in the corner of the yard. 'It would have been no trouble.'

'There was no need,' Annis said cheerfully. 'I am accustomed to travelling on the stage.' She waved at the family of four as the landlord escorted them inside the inn. 'Dear Mr and Mrs Fairlie…Amelia…James…I shall hope to see you all at the Promenade Rooms before long.'

'You make friends easily,' Charles observed as the couple bowed and smiled in return.

'One must beguile the long journey somehow, you know, and they were a very pleasant family. Not like that young man over there…' Annis nodded across at the young gentleman who was helping the elderly lady up into a barouche. 'I am sure he is after her money, Charles. If I hear that she has passed away, I shall be most suspicious!'

'Annis!'

'Oh, I am only joking,' Annis said hastily, remembering belatedly that her cousin could be a bit of a high stickler. 'Pay no attention! Now you…are you well? And Sibella?'

'I am very well indeed.' Charles grinned. 'Sib is flourishing. She and David are expecting their fourth, you know.'

'I had heard.' Annis smiled, tucking her arm through his. 'She has been very busy whilst you and I, Charles, have let the family down sadly! You are not even married and I only look after other peoples' children!'

Charles laughed and patted her hand where it rested on his sleeve. 'Plenty of time for the rest of us. But it is fortunate Sibella did not come to meet you, Annis. She would have disowned you as soon as look at you!'

'Sibella is lucky in that she can indulge herself as a lady of fashion.' Annis looked around for her trunks. 'I am obliged to work for my living. Nevertheless I am grateful to you for swallowing the family pride and coming to meet me, Charles. I know I do you no credit!'

Charles laughed again. 'It was shock, that is all. I barely recognised you in all that frumpish black. You used to be such a good-looking girl...'

Annis gave him a sharp nudge. 'You used to be quite handsome yourself! Where did it all go wrong, Charles?'

Charles Lafoy was in fact a very good-looking man, as most of the female population of Harrogate would testify. Like his sister Sibella, he had the fair, open features of the Lafoys, the honest blue eyes and engaging smile. As lawyer to Harrogate's most prosperous merchant, Samuel Ingram, he had a prestigious position in village society. There was no shortage of inn servants queuing up to help his groom put Annis's luggage in the carriage. Everyone knew that Mr Lafoy always tipped most generously.

Annis Wycherley was almost as tall as her cousin, having a height unfashionable in a woman but useful in a chaperon, since it helped to assert her authority. Her eyes were hazel rather than the Lafoy blue, but she had the same rich, golden blonde hair. In Annis's case this rarely saw the light of day, being hidden under a succession of lace caps, ugly bonnets and ragingly unfashionable turbans. She had learned early on that no one took a blonde chaperon at all seriously; it could, in fact, be positively dangerous to display her hair, for it made gentlemen behave in a most inappropriately amorous manner.

The shapeless gowns in dowager black, purple and turkey red were all designed and worn with one intention in mind—to make her look older and unattractive. This was a necessity of her profession. Just as no one would take a blonde chaperon seriously, so would nobody entrust their daughter, niece or ward to a girl who looked as though she had only just left the schoolroom herself. Annis was in fact seven and twenty and had been widowed for eight years, but she had a fair, youthful complexion, wide-spaced eyes, a snub nose and a generous mouth that all conspired to undermine the sense of gravity required by a professional chaperon. Prettiness combined with poverty had always struck her as a recipe for disaster, so she did her best to disguise those natural assets she possessed.

'I thought that we would go straight to the house in Church Row,' Charles said, as they made their way across to his carriage. 'You will have the chance to settle in comfortably before Sibella calls on you this evening. When do your charges arrive?'

'Not until Friday,' Annis said. 'Sir Robert Crossley is escorting the girls up from London himself and Mrs Hardcastle accompanies them as duenna in my absence. I am persuaded that she will have licked them into shape before ever they darken my door!' She shivered a little in the breeze. 'Gracious, Charles, I can scarce believe that it is June. The wind off the hills is as cold as ever.'

'You have gone soft from living too long in the south,' Charles said affectionately. 'These charges of yours, the Misses Crossley—do they have a large fortune?'

'Big enough to buy half of Harrogate!' Annis said. She grimaced, remembering the interview that she had had in London with the Crossley girls before she had agreed to take them on. 'I fear that even that will not be sufficient to sweeten the pill of Miss Fanny Crossley's bad manners, however. The girl is as sharp as a thorn and only passably good-looking. She may well be my first failure!'

'I doubt it.' Charles grinned at her. 'Even here in Harrogate we have heard of the striking success of that matchmaker *par excellence*, Lady Wycherley! They say that you could catch a husband for any girl, be she ugly as sin and poor as a church mouse.'

'One or other, perhaps, but not both together!' Annis laughed. 'You are not hanging out for a wealthy bride, are you, Charles?'

'Not I!' Her cousin watched as the last bags were strapped onto the platform of the chaise. 'I do have a client who is looking, however. Sir Everard Doble, a very worthy but rather dull man with an estate mortgaged to the hilt. We shall arrange a meeting for him with your charges.'

'Dear Charles,' Annis said gratefully. 'I feel my task is already half done. And Miss Lucy Crossley, unlike her elder sister, is a sweet girl who should make a match easily enough amongst all the half-pay officers who seem to crowd the place. I do not imagine that either sister will make a dazzling match, but it should be possible to settle them creditably. So...' Annis sighed '...I may get them off my hands and then spend some time at Starbeck. It was the real reason that I accepted Sir Robert's commission to chaperon his nieces, you know. I wanted to spend some time at home.'

Charles frowned slightly. 'Ah, Starbeck. You know that I have not been able to keep a tenant there for the last few months and that the house is in a poor state? I need to talk to you about it at some point, coz.'

Annis looked at him sharply. There was something odd in his tone, a reluctance that made her heart miss a beat, for it boded ill. The small estate of Starbeck was a drain on her limited income and she knew that Charles thought she was a sentimental fool to hold on to it. He had administered the estate for her since her father died and he had been urging her to sell for several years. The house was tumbledown and swallowed money in constant repairs, Charles had been unable to find a tenant who would stay there for any length of time, and the home farm was so poor its owners could barely scratch a living. Since Annis had no money other than what she earned plus a small annuity, it was financial nonsense to continue to support Starbeck, and yet she did not want to let it go. She had had a peripatetic childhood following her father about the country from posting to posting and travelling abroad with her parents on several occasions. Starbeck was home, the only certainty she knew, and for that reason she did not want to lose it.

'Of course we may talk—' she began, but broke off as a green and gold high-perch phaeton swept into the inn yard, scattering the ostlers like nervous chickens.

'For pity's sake!' Charles flushed red in annoyance and skipped out of the way as the offside wheel almost ran over his foot. Annis tried not to laugh. Her cousin had always been slightly stuffy, the responsible one amongst the three of them. Perhaps it stemmed from the fact that Charles was the eldest, or more likely it was because he was the only boy and as such was now head of the Lafoy family. Whatever the case, he deplored frivolity.

The phaeton was gleaming and new and contained two occupants, a lady and a gentleman. The lady, a buxom brunette, was swathed in furs. She was laughing and clutching a saucy hat on her dark curls. Her vivacious brown eyes scanned the assembled company, rested thoughtfully on Charles's red face and dismissed Annis's plain one, before she took her companion's hand and jumped lightly down to join him on the cobbles of the inn yard. The landlord had emerged and was bowing enthusiastically, waving them towards the inn door.

'Ashwick!' Annis heard Charles say, under his breath. She cast him a quick glance. Once again there was an odd note in Charles's voice, one that she could not place. It was neither envy nor even disapproval, both of which might have been understandable from the country lawyer to the dashing peer of the realm. Annis knew of Lord Ashwick, of course; no one who had sponsored girls in *ton* society for the last three years as she had could fail to be aware of a man whose recent career consisted mainly of playing high and keeping low company. Adam Ashwick was a friend of such luminaries as the Duke of Fleet and the Earl of Tallant, who had scandalised the town with their exploits for years. Tallant was married now and had become disappointingly uxorious, but the gossips were still entertained by the activities of Sebastian Fleet and Adam Ashwick. It seemed extraordinary to find him in so out of the way a place as Harrogate.

The couple had to pass them to reach the inn door. Annis drew back against the side of the coach, having no wish to push herself forward for notice. To her surprise, however, Adam Ashwick paused in front of them and gave Charles the briefest of bows.

'Lafoy.' His tone was cold.

Charles's own bow was correspondingly slight. 'Ashwick.'

There was a silence that prickled with tension. Annis, looking from one to the other, sensed all kinds of undercurrents that she was at a loss to explain. Ashwick was watching Charles, an unpleasant smile on his lips, and Annis took the opportunity to study him whilst his attention was diverted.

At first glance, she did not consider him to be a good-looking man in the conventional sense, for his face was too swarthy, and its hard angles were too stern and uncompromising to be considered handsome. His eyes were wide set and a cool grey beneath straight black brows. Although he could only be in his early thirties, his thick, dark hair was turning silver, which added a certain distinction to his looks. He was above average height and had a sportsman's physique, but he was dressed with what appeared to be deliberate understatement, in tight dove-grey riding breeches and a pristine black coat that made his linen seem a very pure white indeed. Instead of Hessians he was wearing a fine pair of leather riding boots with turned-down cuffs. He had the appearance of a man of action rather than the dissipated aristocrat Annis had been imagining, and he exuded latent power. Annis could feel the effect. It was different from the confidence that Charles possessed as a successful professional man; Ashwick's authority was instinctive, unquestioned.

His cool grey gaze switched to her and Annis hastily lowered her eyes. She did not wish him to think that she had been staring. Adam Ashwick bowed again, with scrupulous courtesy this time.

'Madam.'

'My cousin, Annis, Lady Wycherley,' Charles said, with such obvious unwillingness that Annis felt her lips twitch. She was not sure if Charles's reluctance to introduce her sprang from disapproval of Ashwick's reputation or a more personal dislike. A split second later, she realised that Adam Ashwick was also considering the reasons for Charles's protective concern. As their eyes met he raised a quizzical brow and they were drawn into a moment of shared amusement. Annis broke the contact hastily, feeling a little disloyal.

She held out her hand politely. 'How do you do, my lord.'

'Your servant, Lady Wycherley.' Adam took her hand. She felt compelled to look at him again, then wished she had not. He was studying her thoughtfully, his gaze mov-

ing over her features with deliberation. There was a defi-
nite masculine interest in that appraisal and Annis recognised it with a shock. She felt a little shiver go through
her and withdrew her hand from his.

Ashwick's beautiful companion was getting restive at
the lack of attention. She pulled on his arm.

'Are you not to introduce me, Ashy, darling?' Her
French accent was slight and very pretty. She peeked up
at him under the brim of the dashing hat with the charm
of a wilful child.

Ashy! Annis thought, trying not to laugh at the diminutive. She caught Ashwick's eye again and looked quickly
away, for fear that he might read her mind again. She did
not seek such affinity with him.

'Margot, may I present Annis, Lady Wycherley, and her
cousin Mr Charles Lafoy?' Ashwick sounded pleasantly
indifferent now as though the moment of enmity with
Charles had never occurred. The lady nodded to Annis and
batted her eyelashes at Charles in exaggerated fashion. Annis felt slightly amused and rather more irritated. The
whole inn yard seemed to have stopped in order to stare
at the Beauty and Annis wondered, as she had on many
previous occasions, just why people were always drawn to
the obvious. She had lost count of the times that débutantes
with charm and fine looks were overlooked when something flashier came along. It was the same here. The ostlers
were gaping, the other travellers were staring in admiration
and some of the guests were even peering from the inn
window to admire Ashwick's fair companion.

'I am Margot Mardyn,' the lady said, with the air of one
making an important announcement. 'You have heard of
me, *non*?'

'Of course,' Annis said hastily, as Charles looked blank.
'I hear that we are will be privileged to have you perform

at the Theatre Royal this summer season, Miss Mardyn. My cousin and I shall be sure to attend.'

Margot Mardyn nodded, whilst smiling bewitchingly at Charles. 'I shall hope to see you after the show,' she said graciously to him.

She squeezed Ashwick's arm. '*Viens*, Ashy, I am cold. This "north" of yours is a shockingly barbaric place. Why, do you know…' she turned back to Charles confidingly '…at some of the inns along the way we were obliged to drink in the common tap? *Alors!* Along with all the hoi polloi! Come along, Ashy!'

Annis looked at Lord Ashwick and was taken aback to see that he was still watching her. He inclined his head and gave her a faint smile, which Annis found even more disturbing. She fidgeted with the seam of her gloves and hoped that her colour had not risen. Famously impervious to the good looks of eligible young gentlemen, she found it very odd that she should be drawn in this curious manner to a man whose style of life was so far removed from her own. Yet she could not deny it; the air between them was sharp with awareness. It was extremely disconcerting.

'I shall look forward to meeting you again, Lady Wycherley,' Ashwick said politely. 'I hope that you enjoy your stay in Harrogate.'

'Who was that?' Charles asked in a bemused tone as Ashwick steered his fair companion through the inn door and the excitement in the yard subsided. Annis, observing the rapt expression on his face as he watched Miss Mardyn's departure, sighed to herself.

'That was Lord Ashwick,' she said drily. 'I collect that you are acquainted with him?'

'Of course I know Ashwick.' Charles turned to her impatiently. 'His family have owned property around here for hundreds of years.'

'Of course.' Annis remembered this herself now. The Ashwicks had been part of the long and turbulent history of the Yorkshire moors for centuries, from the time that the first baron had served at the court of Charles II and had been given an estate in the back of beyond for his pains. Presumably Lord Ashwick was in Yorkshire to visit that very estate. Annis found herself wondering if she would see him again.

Charles was still looking over his shoulder in the direction that the couple had gone.

'Annis? Are your wits wandering? I meant the lady—'

'Ah, the lovely Miss Mardyn. She is a dancer and singer who has recently graced the stage at Drury Lane.' Annis looked at him sardonically. 'Charles, I should be obliged if you would help me up into the carriage. We have been standing here these ten minutes past and, as Miss Mardyn so succinctly observed, it is rather chilly.'

She waited until they were settled back on the fat red squabs of the Lafoy carriage, then added, 'I heard on the journey up that Miss Mardyn is to entertain us with *Harlequin's Metamorphoses, Escapes and Leaps.* Mr Fairlie was telling me about it and he was most excited. I believe the show will sell out, so you had better hurry to get your ticket.'

'That…child, a dancer?' Charles's mouth seemed permanently propped open. 'She cannot be above seventeen, surely?'

'Thirty-five if she's a day,' Annis said cheerfully, reflecting ruefully that men were always distracted by a pretty face and could never see what was under their nose, 'and hailing from the Portsmouth Docks rather than Paris, I hear.'

Charles looked appalled and fascinated all at the same time. 'Good God! And her connection with Ashwick?'

Annis gave him a speaking look.

'Oh!' Charles said.

'Well, it is entirely possible that Lord Ashwick was escorting Miss Mardyn as a favour for a friend,' Annis said fairly. 'When I left London the *on dit* was that she was the Duke of Fleet's inamorata. Who would have thought that such a bird of paradise would alight in Harrogate, of all places?'

'You are very free in your conversation, Annis,' Charles said, his mouth turning down at the corners. 'It must be the effect of London living. I hope you do not encourage your charges to listen to gossip.'

Annis laughed aloud. 'I am sorry if I offend your sensibilities, Charles. I had no idea you had turned into such a puritan!'

The coach trundled out of the inn yard and turned on to Silver Street. It was only a step to the house that Charles had hired for Annis in Church Row, but with her trunks it had clearly been impractical to walk. Annis leaned forward to look out of the window at the open ground of The Stray, bathed in the late afternoon sunlight.

'Oh it is quite delightful to be back! I do believe the last time was two years ago, and a flying visit at that. Tell me, Charles—' she turned back to look at him thoughtfully '—what is the nature of your quarrel with Lord Ashwick? I was not aware that the two of you knew each other.'

Charles shifted uncomfortably. 'I met him last year when his brother-in-law died. It is a little difficult, Annis.' Charles sighed. 'The late Lord Tilney, Ashwick's brother-in-law, was involved in a business scheme with Mr Ingram, but it failed and Ingram bought all his debts. When he died, Humphrey Tilney owed Ingram a deal of money. Ashwick agreed to pay the debt to save his sister from penury. The situation caused some difficulties.'

Annis raised her brows. Samuel Ingram, Charles's most powerful client, was a man who rode roughshod over all those who opposed his business dealings. She could imagine a nobleman of Lord Ashwick's calibre deeply resenting being in debt to such a man.

'What was this business venture?'

Charles looked gloomy. 'You probably remember it. It was in all the newspapers. Ingram and Humphrey Tilney were joint owners of the *Northern Prince*, the ship that went down carrying goods and money to the colonies eighteen months ago. There was the devil of a fuss.'

'I imagine there would be.' Annis frowned. 'Was there not a fortune in gold on the ship?'

'That is correct, and banknotes and silver and God alone knows what other valuables in addition.'

'Surely it was insured?'

Charles shifted uncomfortably. 'Yes, but Humphrey Tilney had overreached himself financially to fund his part in the enterprise in the first place. Under normal circumstances he might have recouped his losses within a couple of years but, as it was, he ended thirty thousand in debt. Ingram bought his debts up to help him rather than let him fall ever deeper into the hands of the moneylenders.'

'How charitable of him,' Annis said drily, thinking that a man such as Samuel Ingram seldom did anything out of the goodness of his heart.

Charles frowned to hear the note in her voice. 'See here, Annis, Ingram charged a very reasonable rate of interest—'

'And you wonder at Lord Ashwick resenting the fact!' Annis said, even more drily.

Charles subsided like a pricked balloon. 'That is the way that business works…'

'I dare say. I suppose there was no doubt that the ship

actually went down? Ingram has not compounded his sins by defrauding the insurers?'

Charles looked horrified. 'Devil take it, Annis, of course not! Of course the ship went down! For pity's sake, do not go around saying such things in public!'

Annis was startled at his vehemence. 'Very well, Charles, there is no need to roast me for it! I only asked the question. Speaking of Ingram, I read in the *Leeds Mercury* that there had been a fire at his farm at Shawes. Is foul play suspected?'

Charles gave her a very sharp look. 'Not at all. Why do you ask?'

Annis gave him an old-fashioned look. 'No need to pretend to me, Charles! I know that Mr Ingram is not popular hereabouts. I have read all about the arson and the threats to his property.'

Charles looked shifty. 'Yes, well, I will concede there has been a little local difficulty over the enclosure of the Shawes common, and there has been some discussion about rents this year—'

'You sound like a lawyer!' Annis said with a sigh.

'Well, so I am. And Mr Ingram's lawyer at that. It is my place to be dispassionate.'

'I would have thought that Mr Ingram would see it as your place to support him,' Annis said drily. 'That is what he pays you for.'

Charles blushed an angry red. 'See here, Annis, must you be so blunt? I'm astounded you ever find a match for those girls of yours if you are as outspoken with their suitors as you are with me!'

'Fortunately the gentlemen are marrying the girls and not me,' Annis said cheerfully. 'I do not seek to marry again, as you know, Charles.'

'Can't think why not. At least you would not need to work then.'

'Thank you, but I prefer to be independent. You know I dislike to be idle. Besides, I found that the married state did not suit me.'

'Not surprised if you spoke to John as plainly as you do to me!'

Annis locked her gloved hands together and looked pointedly out of the window. It was no secret that she and her elderly husband had been unhappy together, but even after eight years of widowhood the memory caused an ache.

'Sorry, Annis.' Charles sounded remorseful. 'I did not mean to offend you.'

'It is no matter, Charles.' Annis spoke briskly. 'You know that John had decided opinions about women and their place. Now that I am no longer required to respect those views, I fear I have become quite outspoken.'

'I suppose there are some men who like their wives to read the newspaper and have decided opinions,' Charles said dubiously.

'Are there? I have never met any of them.' Annis smiled. 'So perhaps it is fortunate that I do not look to marry.'

The carriage slowed before a grey stone house with neat sash windows, then turned through a small archway into a cobbled yard with stables along one side.

'There is a walled garden at the back,' Charles said eagerly, 'and I have engaged a couple of servants for you. You indicated that Mrs Hardcastle was to be housekeeper, so I imagine that she will wish to have the ordering of the household affairs once she arrives.'

'Of course. Hardy will soon have everything organised.'

Annis looked about her with approval. 'You seem to have done us proud, Charles.'

'There is a drawing-room and walk-in cupboards in the bedrooms,' Charles offered, still trying to make amends for his earlier insensitivity. 'It is all very modern. I am sure that it is just what you require, Annis.'

'Thank you.' Annis took his hand as she descended from the coach. 'There is a most pleasant aspect to the front.'

'And the shops are not far away.'

'I assume that it is a quiet neighbourhood and one suitable for the Misses Crossley? No undesirable alehouses or rowdy neighbours? I would not wish my charges to be subject to unsuitable influences.'

Charles had opened his mouth to reply when there was a loud tally-ho from the road and a green and gold phaeton shot past, its occupants shrieking with laughter. It turned neatly through the archway of the house behind. Annis raised her eyebrows.

'My new neighbours, I presume?'

'Oh, dear,' Charles said unhappily.

'Ashy dearest,' Margot Mardyn said sweetly, draping herself over the arm of Adam Ashwick's chair, 'whatever would your mama say if she knew that you had brought me here?'

Adam glanced up briefly from the *York Herald*. The diva's cleavage was inclining tantalisingly close to his nose. It was plush and pink, and smelled cloyingly of roses. Adam looked thoughtfully at it, then returned to his paper.

'Margot, my sweet, do go and sit down. You are blocking my light. I am sure that Tranter will be in with the tea in a moment.'

Miss Mardyn flounced away to lay herself seductively

along the sofa. 'Ashy...' her voice fell several octaves
'...you have not answered my question.'

Adam sighed and laid his newspaper aside. He knew
there was not the least chance of him finishing the item
until Miss Mardyn had partaken of tea and been delivered
to her palatial suite of rooms at the Granby Hotel. His
original intention to deliver her directly there had been
thwarted when one of his horses had thrown a shoe, necessitating the stop at the Hope Inn. After that, Margot had
insisted that nothing but tea in Church Row would soothe
her ruffled sensibilities.

'I am persuaded that Mama would be delighted to find
you here, Margot,' he said. 'She will be quite cast down
to have been out of town.'

'But now that we are here,' Miss Mardyn purred, with
a soft fluttering of her lashes, 'we might find a pleasant
way to pass the time, Ashy...'

Adam raised his brows. 'Indeed we might, sweet. We
could talk, and take tea and even...' he smiled at her
'...plan a trip to Knaresborough!'

Miss Mardyn scowled unbecomingly. She did not take
kindly to teasing.

'I had something so much more exciting in mind, Ashy!'

'Did you?' Adam murmured. 'I doubt that Seb would
appreciate it, my love, if I took you up on that offer!'

'Sebastian will never know,' the diva replied. She sparkled at him. 'Please, Ashy. I am most curious. I beg you
to indulge me. Lydia Trent says that you were *magni-
fique*—a stallion, *en effet*!'

'I am indebted to Miss Trent for her enthusiastic description,' Adam drawled. 'Alas, the answer is still no, my
sweet. Sebastian Fleet might not know, but I would know
that I had betrayed his friendship!'

'You men and your honour!' scoffed Miss Mardyn. 'Am I not worth it, Ashy?'

The answer, Adam reflected, was a decided 'no' but even he, renowned as he was for plain speaking, could hardly be so unchivalrous as to say so. He had been widowed for nine years and during those years he had sampled the favours of quite a few opera singers, actresses and dancers like Miss Trent, with the addition of several bored society ladies as well. Even so, he felt he could scarcely lay claim to the title of rake, for all that others awarded it to him. Despite Miss Trent's extravagant praise, sexual conquest was not even an activity that particularly interested him. There was something deplorably mechanical about the amorous liaisons of many of the *ton*, whereas he, having once experienced true love, was at heart a real romantic.

Six months before, the past had finally and unexpectedly caught up with him and put paid to any rakish tendencies for good. They had taken dinner at Joss Tallant's house that night, he, Seb Fleet and a number of other friends. Gradually the others had drifted away to the clubs and balls, leaving Joss and he partaking of a malt whisky and talking over times past and the time to come. At some point, late in the evening, Amy Tallant had come in, kissed her husband goodnight and warned him not to be too late to bed. From the look in Joss's eye, Adam had guessed that it would not be long at all until he was politely ejected from the house and Joss went hot foot to join his wife. And that was when it had happened. Adam had felt the most sudden and shocking jolt of jealousy and misery go through him like a sword thrust. It was not that he envied Joss his wife, serene and charming though Amy was. It was that for the first time in years he remembered the

warmth and intimacy and pure pleasure of marriage, and
he felt sick to think that he had had it and lost it all.

Joss had seen the stunned look in his eyes and, old
friend that he was, had challenged him on it. They had
ended up talking until the morning and finishing the bottle
of whisky between them. Adam had sent Amy a huge
bunch of flowers the following day with his apologies for
keeping her husband from her side. But the ache of loss
had not been alleviated and Adam knew he would never
find what he was looking for in the scented bordellos of
Covent Garden. He would not even try. The favours of
Margot Mardyn, so eagerly sought by so many men, were
not for him.

Miss Mardyn was aware that his attention had slipped
from her. She wafted over to the window and stood twitching the drapes and peering out inquisitively.

'*Alors*, Ashy, it is that so-proper Englishman we met at
the inn! I do so adore men like that—so prim, so correct.
It makes me want to tear off all their clothes and shock
them to the core!'

'I am sure that Lafoy would be delighted were you to
do that to him,' Adam rejoined drily. 'Do leave that curtain
twitching alone, my love. It is so bourgeois!'

But Miss Mardyn was enjoying herself too much to
obey him. 'I do believe they must be your neighbours,
Ashy. Oh, do come and look! The freakish cousin is with
him. Have you ever seen anything so ugly as that bonnet?'

Adam felt a rush of irritation that had nothing to do with
Miss Mardyn's constant chatter. Why he should feel so
protective of Charles Lafoy's cousin he had no notion, but
protective he was. When he had first seen Annis Wycherley at the inn he had thought her a drab creature of that
class that were instantly recognisable as governesses and
schoolmistresses, frumpish, proper, and dull. Then, when

their eyes had met and he had seen the decided twinkle in hers, he had realised his mistake. He had watched her during the conversation and seen her covert amusement at both Margot's affectations and Lafoy's discomfort. It argued a certain sophistication of mind that intrigued him, hidden as it was behind the chaperon's dull exterior. Yet she had also seemed an innocent, so much so that she was not quite able to hide the fact that she was not indifferent to him. It had charmed him—and he had wanted to see her again.

He could see her now, walking under the fruit trees at the bottom of the garden. The garden of his own house sloped down from the terrace to a narrow lane and the wall of the neighbouring garden backed on to it. Under normal circumstance it was not an arrangement that would have met with his approval. He was a man who guarded his privacy jealously, and the Harrogate town houses were too close together to suit him. He preferred his estate at Eynhallow—remote, unspoilt and not overlooked.

Adam watched as Charles Lafoy gave his cousin his hand to help her back on to the path. He disliked Lafoy intensely for his part in helping Samuel Ingram fleece his brother-in-law. Whilst he was able to accept that the sinking of the *Northern Prince* was nothing more than devilish bad luck, Adam still bitterly resented that Ingram had persuaded Humphrey into a partnership in the first place. Humphrey Tilney had been a weak man, easily led by the thought of making a fortune. Instead he had ended up losing one and bequeathing to his wife the uncomfortable role of Ingram's debtor.

When Humphrey had died the previous year and Adam had discovered the extent of his debts, he had felt honour-bound to pay them off and rescue his sister from ignominy. It had been a humiliating and infuriating episode. Ingram made no secret of his amusement at the deal and Adam hated him for it.

He could hardly blame Lady Wycherley for her cousin's sins, however. Finding out that she was a neighbour leant a curious attraction to what would otherwise have been a dull stay in Harrogate. Adam had originally intended only a short visit to his nearby estate at Eynhallow, but now he thought he might stay a little longer and find out about Annis Wycherley as well. It might prove interesting.

'Look!' La Mardyn was pointing at Annis now. 'What a shocking frump! I shudder, darling, positively shudder, to think that there are women like that in the world!'

'You are such a cat, Margot,' Adam said lazily. He smiled to himself as he saw that his fair companion was not sure whether to laugh or pout at his unflattering assessment of her character. Eventually she pouted.

'And you are so cruel, Ashy. I do believe that you are the rudest man in London.'

'Nonsense! There are plenty with manners far worse than mine. I merely speak as I find.'

'Then pray do not speak at all.' Miss Mardyn turned her shoulder. 'Or, if you must, tell me what you truly think of Lady Wycherley and her ugly bonnet.'

Adam sighed. He could see Annis walking slowly up the path and chatting to her cousin as she went. Certainly the black bombazine dress was unflattering, one might almost say disfiguring. It seemed to weigh her down and take the colour from her, leaving her drab and pale. On the other hand, he noticed that she had a slender figure that swayed with unconscious elegance as she walked. As for the offending bonnet, it was fit only for destruction.

As he watched, Lady Wycherley loosened the ribbons of the bonnet and, with one impatient gesture, flung it away from her. It bowled across the grass and came to rest under one of the trees, and Annis Wycherley laughed. Adam heard her. The late afternoon sunlight fell on her face, upturned to that of her cousin. She looked young and free and happy.

'Well, bless me,' Miss Mardyn said, forgetting her accent for once and sounding both older and irredeemably English, 'look at her hair!'

Adam looked again. Then he stopped. And stared. Loose from the bonnet, Annis Wycherley's long, blonde hair had come cascading down around her shoulders in a tumble of gold. It shone in the sun like a newly minted coin and framed a heart-shaped face that suddenly looked piquant and pretty.

'I'll be damned!' Adam found that he was smiling. 'What do you say now, Margot?'

'Why, I think that she must be an even greater fool to hide such beauty,' Miss Mardyn said acerbically. She had recovered her poise and now flounced away from the window. 'Such a thing is *incroyable*! She would make a passable courtesan with hair like that and a good figure. Not as attractive as me, perhaps, but all the same…'

'I rather think she disguises herself because she is a chaperon,' Adam said. He had never met Annis Wycherley in London, but he remembered quite well that she had a reputation for being able to settle even the most unpromising of girls. Now he could see that she had quite a lot of promise herself. 'No one is going to employ her as a companion if she outshines her charges!'

Miss Mardyn looked uncomprehending. '*Eh bien*, why be a chaperon if one can be a cyprian? I do not understand that, me!'

'No,' Adam murmured. 'I do not suppose that you do.'

He watched Annis Wycherley for a moment, then strolled back to his chair and picked up the paper again as

Tranter, the butler, came into the room, accompanied by a footman with the tea tray. There was an item about Samuel Ingram buying the lease to the local turnpike and building new tollhouses on the Skipton road. One of them would be near Eynhallow...

'What do you think of the current state of the turnpike trusts, my dear?' he asked Miss Mardyn, as the teacups were handed around.

Miss Mardyn bent a charming smile on the dazzled butler, then turned back to her host. 'I have no opinion on it, Ashy darling. You should know better than to ask me. Politics, economics...pah! The whole business bores me. I never read the papers.' She looked at him thoughtfully. 'If I had realised that you were turning into such a dead bore yourself, I should have agreed to play Cheltenham rather than Harrogate this summer. I hear the shops are better!'

Adam smiled. 'I do apologise for being such poor company, my dear. Perhaps you will find other gentlemen who please you more. Mr Lafoy, for example.'

La Mardyn dismissed Charles Lafoy with a wave of one white hand. 'Oh, the conquest would be fun, but after that is over...*pouf*...I expect he is as dull as ditchwater. Are there no other eligible gentlemen in Harrogate, Ashy? I must amuse myself.'

'I see that the Earl and Countess of Glasgow are here to take the waters this season,' Adam said, consulting the paper, 'though I fear the Earl may be a little infirm for you, Margot, and not very plump in the pocket to compensate. There is Lord Boyles—Boyles by name and by nature, I believe, so again, a gloomy prospect. Ah! Sir Everard Doble. He is a young man, and not ill favoured, if memory serves me. He might be a possibility.'

'Sir Everard Doble…' Miss Mardyn repeated. 'Well, we shall see, Ashy. And how will you amuse yourself?'

Adam's gaze fell on the paper again. 'Oh, I have plenty to occupy me, Margot. Estate business will keep me quite busy, I fear…'

From the garden came the sound of feminine laughter, spontaneous and infectious. Adam's gaze narrowed. He resolved that he would definitely find out more about Annis Wycherley. She seemed a most uncommon chaperon.

'That sounds lamentably boring, darling,' Margot Mardyn said, yawning widely.

'On the contrary,' Adam said, with a smile. 'I have the feeling that my stay could be very interesting indeed.'

Chapter Two

Tickets for Miss Mardyn's performance proved to be the most sought-after items in Harrogate, and it was a whole fortnight before Charles Lafoy could book a box at the Theatre Royal. Thus it was that, on a Thursday evening two weeks later, Annis sat in the theatre and reflected that acting as chaperon to two high-spirited girls at the same time was utterly exhausting. The Misses Crossley had taken to Harrogate society like ducks to water, and every day had been packed with outings and every evening with parties and entertainments. Indeed, a trip to the theatre was a rare luxury, for it allowed Annis to keep an eye on both girls at once and sit down at the same time. On this particular evening she was further blessed, for she had the pleasure of her family's company as well. Charles, Sibella and Sibella's husband David had all accompanied them to the theatre that night.

'That was very…entertaining, was it not?' she said, joining in the applause as Margot Mardyn executed her final spin and ran gracefully from the stage. 'Miss Mardyn is really quite talented.'

Annis caught her cousin Sibella's gaze. Sibella was an indolent blonde who had been an accredited beauty in her youth and still had the fair Lafoy looks, blurring a little into comfortable plumpness now. Sibella glanced towards the men and rolled her eyes expressively.

'I hear that dancing is the least of Miss Mardyn's talents!' she said.

Annis laughed. The sight of the shapely Miss Mardyn in her gauzy finery had transfixed the male members of the audience. Miss Mardyn might not be a particularly skilful dancer or indeed an above average singer, but no one in the audience cared a whit for that, Annis thought. Harrogate had never seen anything quite like her and the whole auditorium was buzzing with excitement. Annis could not help wondering whether it had been a suitable entertainment for the Misses Crossley. Perhaps the more provocative of Miss Mardyn's dance movements had passed them by. She hoped so.

She consulted her theatre programme. 'I see that there is an interval now. Would you care to stretch your legs, girls?'

'No, thank you, Lady Wycherley,' Fanny Crossley said pertly. 'Lucy and I shall do very well where we are. We are…admiring these country fashions…'

The two girls dissolved into giggles and Annis sighed inwardly. She knew perfectly well that the Crossley girls were hanging over the edge of the box so that they could assess all the young gentlemen in the audience and be admired in return. Miss Fanny, attired in a fussy dress of yellow silk that Annis privately thought much too old for her, was making waspish observations. Miss Lucy was agreeing eagerly. Miss Crossley and her echo, Annis thought. There was no malice in Lucy Crossley, for her elder sister had enough for two, but Lucy did so like to agree with everyone.

'Look at that strange gentleman there, Luce—' Miss

Crossley was pointing with her fan into the pit. 'Why, he is as scruffy as a scarecrow and I do believe the candle wax has dripped on his bald head! How absurd he looks!' She stifled a giggle.

'Quite absurd,' Lucy echoed dutifully.

'That is the Marquis of Midlothian,' Annis said. 'He is a most highly respected gentleman.'

During the first two weeks of the Miss Crossleys' visit, when Annis had been getting their measure, she had corrected Fanny's bad manners and barbed remarks. Now, in the third week, she had realised that there was little point in trying to improve the elder Miss Crossley. Fanny was vulgar through and through, and, unlike her sister, was disinclined to accept guidance. Indeed, any attempt to improve Fanny's behaviour often had the reverse effect, for she was like a wilful small child. As a result, Annis often held her tongue and concentrated instead on the large sum of money that Sir Robert Crossley was paying her to chaperon his tiresome niece. She simply hoped that she would not be tempted to strangle the goose that laid the golden eggs before the egg actually materialised.

'A marquis!' Fanny looked put out, then brightened. 'Oh, but as it is an Irish title one cannot be surprised that he looks all to pieces. I hear the Irish aristocracy are a ramshackle bunch.'

'They may well be,' Annis said, 'but Midlothian is a Scottish title.'

Fanny turned her shoulder to Annis and leaned towards Lucy again. 'Look at the shocking quiz in that purple feathered turban,' she said, in a stage whisper. 'I do declare she is the greatest frump in creation!'

Since Annis herself was wearing dowager purple and a turban that night, it was easy to see at whom Fanny's shaft was aimed. Lucy flushed an embarrassed pink, cast Annis an agonised look and muttered something unintelligible. Annis smiled at her reassuringly. It took more than a few malicious words from a slip of a girl to discompose her. Lucy was more upset than she was.

Annis turned her attention to the crowds milling in the pit and aisles. Everybody who was anybody took a box, of course, but during the intervals they all went for a stroll and greeted their acquaintances. Some even went out onto the green in front of the theatre to get a breath of fresh air, for on a hot summer night the temperature inside could become stifling. The general scene in the auditorium was one of immense, cheerful disarray now. Gentlemen were leaning over the green rails of the gallery and accosting their friends below. Ladies preened and fluttered their fans. Annis, watching, felt a warm pleasure to be back home.

'I see that the Ashwicks have taken a box tonight,' Sibella said, leaning forward to speak in Annis's ear. 'It has been so awkward this year past, Annis, for although Lord Ashwick had mostly been in London, the rest of the family have stayed at Eynhallow and frequently come to Harrogate. I have scarcely known what to say to them, for it is such a small town one cannot avoid one's acquaintance. Yet everyone knows of the difficulties between the Ashwicks and Mr Ingram, and I have felt so uncomfortable because of Charles's involvement...' Her voice trailed away and she looked unhappily at Charles, who was chatting in an undertone to David at the back of the box.

Annis patted her hand comfortingly. Sibella, like Lucy Crossley, wished everyone to be happy, but sometimes it was simply not possible.

'Charles has a job to do—'

'I know.' Sibella gripped her hand. 'I know he does not have the funds to do anything but work for a living. Neither of us inherited anything from our father. Yet I do not like Charles's job, Annis. Particularly when it obliges me to be polite to Samuel Ingram and his wife! Speaking of which, I do believe that they are coming this way…'

Annis followed her gaze. It was many years since she had met Samuel Ingram, but he looked very much the same. He was a tall man, stout and with the prosperous air of consequence of the self-made merchant. His waistcoat was just a little too ornate with its gold embroidery and a large signet ring shone on his right hand. Beside him, Venetia Ingram glowed like a rare jewel. Annis watched as Ingram solicitously escorted his wife through the crowd, a hand in the small of her back. He shone with pride, like a preening turkey cock. There were those who said that Ingram's only weakness was his young wife. When it came to the fair sex, Annis knew that there was no fool like an old fool, for she had taken advantage of that fact herself, when finding suitors for some of her charges.

'Who is that lady over there, with the old man?' Fanny Crossley said, and in her voice Annis heard all the cruelty and envy of youth. 'She is so very beautiful…'

'That is Mrs Ingram,' Sibella said. She caught Annis's eye and grimaced. 'Mr Ingram is not so very old, Miss Crossley—'

'I expect that he must be rich, to be married to such an incomparable,' Lucy Crossley said wisely, and Annis sighed. She could not rebuke Lucy for so accurate an observation. Money marrying beauty was, after all, the way of the world in much the same way as money married a title.

'Come along now, girls,' Sibella said, with surprising firmness. 'It will do you good to have a little exercise. Did you not know that if you sit still all the time you will become fat and then what will the gentlemen think of you? We shall go down into the foyer for a few minutes. David, if you would be so good as to give me your arm, you may take Miss Lucy on your other side. Charles, I know you would be delighted to escort Miss Crossley.'

Annis threw her a grateful look. Sibella was indolent to a fault, but she was kind-hearted and she was also sensitive. Sibella knew that Annis found the Crossley girls very tiresome at times, but she had put herself out to take the girls out shopping and introduce them to other young ladies and chaperons who might share the burden a little. Annis had been extremely touched by her cousin's kindness for she knew that given a choice, neither Charles nor Sibella would have come near the Crossleys girls with a barge pole. Unfortunately, she herself could not be so choosy. Her livelihood depended on chaperoning the nieces, wards and daughters of cits and minor gentry and she counted herself fortunate that most of them, unlike Fanny Crossley, were pleasant company.

'Luce, it is Lieutenant Greaves and Lieutenant Norwood!' Fanny, having espied some red-coated gentlemen in the gallery, turned to grab her sister's hand. 'You remember—we met them yesterday at the Promenade Rooms!' She frowned slightly. 'I do hope they have not taken seats in the upper gallery. They only cost a shilling each!'

'Lieutenant Norwood!' Lucy's face was suddenly poppy red. 'Oh, let us go down. Quickly! We shall miss them else!'

The two girls scampered out of the box like a couple of puppies and Sibella subsided into her seat again. 'You shall never teach those girls how to go on, Annis,' she said, watching as the Crossley sisters rushed out into the pit and waved energetically at the gentlemen in the gallery. 'Miss Lucy has possibilities, but is led astray by that hoyden of a sister, and as for Miss Fanny, the best thing you can do is to promote the Doble match as quickly as possible and get rid of her. How does it progress?'

'Quite well, I think,' Annis said. She had been disappointed that Sir Everard Doble had not been able to join them at the theatre that night, for his courtship of Fanny was advancing, based on the need for a fortune on his part and the desire for a title on Fanny's.

'The problem with Fanny is that I fear she may go off at a tangent at any moment and ruin the whole plan. If she sees someone she likes better…' Annis looked over at the officers, who were strolling down from the gallery to greet the girls. 'Lieutenant Greaves looks very dashing in his regimentals, I know, but he has not two pennies to rub together and is a sadly unsteady character into the bargain. It is a shame that he is such a great friend to Barnaby Norwood, for I wish to encourage the one and discourage the other! Lieutenant Norwood has taken quite a fancy to Lucy, I think.' She started to her feet. 'You know, Sib, I had better go down and keep an eye on things. I do not trust Fanny at all.'

'I will go,' Sibella said resignedly, struggling up again. 'Come, David, you may escort me down and content yourself with the thought that you are doing Annis a splendid favour. You might as well come too, Charles, in case we need the extra authority!'

Once left on her own, Annis sat back and closed her eyes. She let the hum of the crowd wash over her. Normally she enjoyed the theatre, but tonight there were too many other things going on. She had the feeling that if she gave Fanny an inch, the little hoyden would take a mile.

She opened her eyes abruptly, feeling a prickle of awareness, a sudden conviction that someone was watching her. The crowd in the theatre was dissipating a little now and Annis caught a glimpse of Charles, talking to someone behind one of the tall ornamental pilasters. His companion moved slightly, and Annis saw that it was Della Tilney, Adam Ashwick's sister, a vivacious, dark-haired beauty who always looked supremely elegant. Annis frowned slightly. It seemed curious that Charles and Lady Tilney should be on such good terms when he worked for Ingram and she was the widow of the man Ingram had ruined…

A second later she forgot all about Della Tilney when she realised that Adam Ashwick was looking directly at her. He was leaning against a nearby pillar and he did not look away as she caught his gaze. Annis saw him incline his head slightly to acknowledge her then start moving towards her, cutting a path through the crowd with an easy authority. He did not take his eyes off her the whole time.

Annis felt a little flustered. She did not understand why Adam Ashwick should have this effect on her and it only made her more disturbed that he should do so. She fidgeted with her fan, smoothed her skirt and looked away in an attempt to calm herself, hoping that Lord Ashwick might in fact have some other destination in mind. Sibella and David had joined Fanny and Lieutenant Greaves now, breaking up their cosy tête-à-tête whilst leaving Lucy and Barnaby Norwood together. Annis smiled her appreciation at Sibella's tactics.

'And serve you right, you little minx!' she said aloud.

'Good evening, Lady Wycherley.' Adam Ashwick's voice came from behind her, smooth and betraying a hint of amusement. Annis jumped and spun around in her chair. So he *had* been intending to seek her out. The thought made her go quite hot all over.

'Lord Ashwick. How do you do?' She forced a polite smile. 'I do apologise. I was not… I did not… I was not addressing you.'

'I guessed as much.' There was a glimmer of a smile in Adam Ashwick's eyes. He gestured to the chair beside her. 'May I?'

'Oh, of course!'

Annis had assumed that he would not be staying and now felt surprise and another emotion she could not quite place. She did not look to be distinguished by Adam Ashwick's attention and to be so set her a little on edge. It was something to do with the speculative interest she saw in his eyes, an interest he made no effort to hide. When they had met at the inn she had felt a curious tug of affinity with him and it was the last thing that she had expected or wanted. She was accustomed to living without male companionship and after an unhappy early marriage had no intention of changing that state. Yet it was disconcerting that, for all her seven-and-twenty years and her relative experience, there was a man who could disturb her equilibrium.

'I hope that you are enjoying your return to Harrogate, Lady Wycherley,' Adam said lazily. 'I understand that it is several years since you were here?'

'Indeed it is, my lord.' Annis smiled. 'I shall always think of this as my home even though I have spent so much time away. It is pleasant to be back here. Do you find it so?'

Adam smiled back. 'I find Harrogate enjoyable enough for a short space of time.'

Although they were talking quite conventionally, Annis was acutely aware that Adam was watching her intently. It was as though he was making the first moves in a game—a game he showed all the signs of pursuing. Annis caught her breath at the thought.

She raised her brows coolly, determined that his appraisal should not discomfort her. 'You do not appreciate the Yorkshire countryside, my lord?'

'Oh, the countryside is extremely beautiful. It is the society of a small town that I find somewhat restrictive. The same company, the same balls and parties night after night...'

'Rather like London during the Season, in fact,' Annis said, with just a hint of asperity in her tone.

Adam laughed aloud. 'You put me neatly in my place, ma'am! Yes, I suppose the Season in London does bear a striking resemblance to the Season anywhere else, be it Brighton or Harrogate. It is simply on a grander scale—and I have my own friends and entertainments.'

'So I hear!' Annis said sweetly. She saw that he was not offended by her directness; on the contrary, the laughter lines deepened about his eyes and there was amusement in their grey depths. She imagined that it would be very difficult to discommode Adam Ashwick. He had far too much experience.

Annis shifted slightly in her seat, wishing that she did not feel quite so hot. It was a humid night and, with the candles, the heat was almost overpowering. Then there was her purple turban, which was making her head itch and ache. First the black bombazine and now the dowager purple, Annis thought ruefully. It was a very long time since she had wanted a man to see her in anything other than her drab chaperon's clothes. Now though, Adam Ashwick's cool grey gaze was fixed appraisingly on her face and Annis was vain enough to wish that she were appearing to slightly better advantage. It was a novel experience for her to want a man to admire her and it was contrary to every sensible precept that governed her actions.

'You are often in London, are you not, ma'am?' he

asked. 'How comes it that we have never met there before?'

Annis gave him a very straight look. 'It is hardly surprising that we have not met, my lord. I believe that you do not attend débutante balls and I never attend events of any other sort.'

'Then that is one advantage that a small town confers,' Adam observed. 'Here we may all meet and mingle together. A decided benefit, Lady Wycherley, for otherwise I might never have met you.'

Annis laughed, refusing to be flattered. 'You are very apt with your compliments, my lord.'

The smile deepened in Adam's eyes. 'Do you imply that I am not sincere? I assure you that you are quite mistaken.'

Annis flicked him a look. His whole attention was focussed on her in a manner that was decidedly disconcerting. She looked away.

'Oh, men offer compliments when it suits their purpose! I could not have worked as a chaperon for so many years without realising that fact, my lord.'

Adam grimaced. 'You are a cynic, ma'am, as no doubt a chaperon should be. I expect it helps you sort the genuine suitors from the rakes when you are trying to make a match for your charges.' He leaned back in his chair and fixed her with a challenging look. 'Let us test your assertion. What is my purpose tonight?'

Annis frowned a little. 'I beg your pardon?'

'You said that men offer compliments when it suits their purpose. So what was my purpose in complimenting you?'

Annis looked away, vexed to realise that she was blushing. She had the feeling that she was straying towards dangerous ground here and was not going to be lured into offering a view. She gave Adam a reluctant smile.

'As to that, I have no notion.'

Adam shifted slightly. 'I think that you do. You suspect that I want something and am therefore making myself agreeable.'

Annis laughed. 'I apologise. I was judging on past experience, my lord. Most gentlemen try to charm the chaperon if they are interested in her charges. Perhaps you are looking to marry and are wanting an introduction to the Misses Crossley, Lord Ashwick?'

Adam kept his face straight. 'I thank you, but no. *They* do not interest me. You, on the other hand, Lady Wycherley, are a different matter.'

Annis kept her lips tightly closed and vowed to make no more unwary comments that evening. Adam Ashwick was altogether too quick to take her up on them. And Adam, who evidently knew to a nicety when to leave matters in his dealings with the fair sex, smiled slightly and turned the subject.

'Did you enjoy Miss Mardyn's dancing tonight, ma'am? I am not entirely sure that Harrogate was quite ready for the experience.'

Annis smothered an unexpected smile. 'I found it very imaginative, my lord. I can see why Miss Mardyn is so popular.'

There was an answering smile lurking in Adam Ashwick's eyes as he took in all the things that Annis had carefully omitted to say.

'I believe that we have *The Death of Captain Cook* after the interval,' he said. 'That should be something of a contrast. Will it be melancholy, do you think?'

'Almost certainly,' Annis said cheerfully. 'If your taste runs to something more classical, my lord, you might wish to return next week, for I believe Mr Jefferson will be appearing in *Hamlet, Prince of Denmark*. Or is Shakespeare too sober for you?'

'On the contrary, I like a good tragedy,' Adam said easily. 'However, I am not entirely certain that I shall be here next week. I have business at Eynhallow, my estate towards Skipton, and shall be back and forth to Harrogate during the next month.'

'Of course,' Annis murmured. She had forgotten that the Ashwick estate bordered her own land at Starbeck. Starbeck could scarcely aspire to be called an estate, for it was too small, and almost entirely surrounded by its more powerful neighbours. There were the Ashwicks and then, of course, there was Samuel Ingram's property at Linforth.

'I understand that your cousin has property in the same direction,' Adam continued. 'That charming little house at Starbeck is his, is it not?'

Annis smiled slightly. 'Starbeck is mine, my lord,' she said, aware of the hint of pride that crept into her voice. 'Charles administers the property for me, but it belongs to my branch of the Lafoy family.'

For a second Adam looked surprised. 'Does it, indeed? But I thought—' He broke off, a hint of speculation in his eyes.

Annis raised her brows. 'What did you think, my lord?'

'Why, merely that Starbeck belonged to Mr Lafoy rather than yourself.' His voice dropped. 'It is pleasant to think that I am not entirely surrounded by hostile forces.'

Annis laughed, despite herself. 'I am sure that it cannot be as bad as that, my lord.'

'I assure you that it is.' Adam's gaze was resting thoughtfully on Samuel Ingram as he chatted to an acquaintance in the theatre pit. He turned back to Annis. 'You cannot have failed to hear of my…dispute with Mr Ingram, Lady Wycherley, so I do not scruple to mention it. May I hope that you are more sympathetically inclined than your cousin?'

Their eyes met and held. 'You will find that I am most independently inclined, my lord,' Annis said coolly. She had no time for Samuel Ingram, but she did not want Adam Ashwick casting her as an ally against Charles.

Adam nodded. 'I imagine that is the best I can hope for?'

'I believe so.'

'Then we understand one another.' Adam smiled at her. 'You seem a most unusual chaperon, if I may say so, Lady Wycherley.'

Annis gave him a cool look. 'From what perspective, my lord?'

'Well, most chaperons do not own their own estates. One has the impression that they have to work for a living, whereas you, Lady Wycherley...' Adam gave her a thoughtful look '...you give the impression of choosing your profession. As I said, it is unusual.'

Annis laughed. 'Oh, I have to earn my living, my lord! It is true that I enjoy my work most of the time, and that I prefer to be busy rather than to wither away as some kind of genteel poor relation, but—' she shrugged '—it is not truly a matter of choice.'

'I see.' Adam did not seem put out to discover her lack of funds but then, Annis thought, if he had ever seen Starbeck he would know that she was scarcely flush with money. 'One gets the strong impression that you value your independence, ma'am.'

Annis was a little startled. She had not been aware that she had given away so much about herself. Normally she was remarkably guarded in speaking of herself, particularly to strangers. Particularly to gentlemen of Adam Ashwick's reputation and experience, who saw far more than they were told.

'I value my independence almost above all things, my

lord,' she said slowly. 'And being a chaperon is vastly
superior to being a governess or schoolteacher, you know.
I may choose when I work and whom I chaperon. I travel
and meet people—' Annis broke off, thinking again that
she was offering far too much personal information and
wondering why she was telling him such a great deal. It
did not help that Adam was giving her his undivided attention, watching her animated face with a faint smile on
his lips. She fell silent in something of a confusion.

'As I said, you are a most unusual chaperon,' he murmured.

Annis rallied. 'Do you know many chaperons in order
to make such a comparison, my lord?'

'No, I concede that I do not know many at all.' Adam
was watching her with a lazy amusement that made Annis's skin prickle. 'As you correctly surmised, ma'am, I
move in vastly different circles.'

'I imagine that most chaperons can only be grateful for
that, my lord,' Annis said tartly. 'One must be constantly
vigilant for the safety of one's charges and a gentleman
who is not interested in matrimony might be pursuing them
for a wholly different purpose!'

Adam laughed. 'My dear Lady Wycherley, I am not
interested in marrying your charges, but I equally uninter-
ested in endangering the virtue of innocents! Only the most
hardened of rakes would be so inclined!'

Annis nodded. 'I see. You make a distinction between
yourself and such gentlemen, Lord Ashwick?'

Adam raised his brows. 'Certainly I do. I am no rake,
although I see by your expression that you remain unconvinced, ma'am!'

Annis's lips twitched. 'I imagine that it matters little to
you what I think, my lord. We shall not be having much
conversation in the future.'

'How so?'

Annis gave him an old-fashioned look. 'Must I spell matters out, my lord? I am a very *proper* chaperon with two young ladies to look after. You are…' She paused.

'Yes? I am…what?'

'A gentleman that I would warn my charges to avoid. I am therefore unlikely to set the bad example of courting your company myself.'

Adam burst out laughing. 'My dear Lady Wycherley! You are harsh towards me. And most direct.'

'I beg your pardon.' Annis steadfastly held his gaze. 'I always feel that honesty helps one to avoid misunderstandings later.'

'I will grant you that, although I deplore your poor opinion of me, ma'am.' Adam was still smiling. 'Perhaps if we had met when we were younger you would not be so wary of me. Indeed, I am surprised that we did not meet, given that we shared a childhood in this very place. I remember your cousins well from my youth.'

Annis smiled. 'Everyone remembers Sibella, my lord.'

'Of course! The incomparable Sibella Lafoy! My brother Ned was heartbroken that she preferred David Granger to him. But where were you, Lady Wycherley?'

Annis looked away. 'I was not brought up near here, my lord. My father was in the Navy and my family travelled a great deal. I visited Starbeck but rarely.'

'I see. And when you were married? Did you live in London then, ma'am?'

'No.' For the life of her, Annis could not prevent a slight shiver. 'We resided in Lyme Regis.'

She turned away and made a business of looking for Lucy and Fanny in the crowds milling below. Both of them were firmly under Sibella's supervision, though Fanny was still casting enticing glances over her shoulder at Lieutenant Greaves. Despite the fact that her attention was diverted, Annis could tell that Adam Ashwick was still watching her.

His gaze was steady and perceptive. After a moment he said gently, 'I am sorry. Have I said something wrong?'

Annis looked back at him, then quickly away. There was no coolness in those grey eyes now, only a searching look that was as disturbing as it was observant. She fidgeted with her fan.

'No, not at all. Of course not! It is just… I am sorry…' She floundered, hearing the arch brightness in her own tone. That would convince him of nothing other than the fact that she was disturbed by something. She sounded as socially inept as a schoolgirl. Taking a deep breath she looked him in the eye. 'I beg your pardon. It is simply that I do not talk about my marriage.'

'Why not? Were you very unhappy?' Adam's tone was soft.

Annis blinked. She was not accustomed to such plain speaking, especially with a man who was virtually a stranger. Yet something in his own directness called an answering candour from her.

'Yes, I was. Which is why I do not like to speak about it, sir.'

She thought that he would let the matter drop, but Adam touched the back of her hand lightly. 'I am sorry to hear it, ma'am. Forgive my impertinent questions. When I want to know something I tend to be blunt.'

Annis forced a smile. 'Please do not apologise, my lord.' She frowned a little. 'I am simply uncertain of how we come to be speaking on matters of such intimacy when we are barely acquainted.'

Adam smiled at her. Annis watched the lines deepen

about his eyes again and felt a strange pang deep inside her.

'Natural affinity, I suppose,' he said softly. He touched her hand again, the lightest of touches. ''I shall always be happy to speak with you on any matter you choose, Lady Wycherley.'

'Annis!'

Annis tore her gaze away from Adam and swung round abruptly. Charles Lafoy had returned to the box and he looked to be in a very bad temper. Annis suspected that this was due in part to the Misses Crossley, who were chattering like a pair of magpies as Sibella ushered them back to their seats, but it was also indubitably the result of finding her deep in conversation with Adam Ashwick. To her own annoyance, she felt herself blush.

Adam got to his feet in unhurried fashion. There was a mocking glint in his eye. 'Evening, Lafoy. Granger, Mrs Granger, it is a pleasure to see you again…' He bowed to Sibella before turning back to Annis. There was a decided twinkle in that cool grey gaze now. 'I have enjoyed consorting with the enemy, ma'am. We must do it again some time…'

'Good night, my lord,' Annis said repressively.

Adam smiled at her and withdrew.

Sibella sighed, a little wistfully. 'Oh, he is as charming as they said he was…'

Charles slid into Adam's vacated seat. 'Annis, what the devil were you about, flirting with Ashwick of all people?'

Annis kept her own voice low. 'I am sure that one may greet an acquaintance without fear of censure, Charles. As you know, I never flirt.'

'Yes, but Ashwick!' Charles ran a hand through his fair hair. 'He is a loose fish. Gambling, drinking, women…'

'Show me a man who isn't,' Annis murmured. 'Or one who has not indulged at some point in his life.'

Charles looked disapproving. 'You might at least have some regard for my own situation, if nothing else! Ingram cannot approve—'

'Fortunately I do not have to be governed by Mr Ingram's approval.' Annis smoothed her skirts and threw her cousin a warning glance. 'You refine too much upon this, Charles. Lord Ashwick is a neighbour and was only doing the pretty. Now, the second act is about to start. May we call a truce?'

The rest of the show was quite spoilt for Annis, who hated to quarrel with either of her cousins. *The Death of Captain Cook* proved to be a melodramatic tale of tragedy that was ruined anyway by Fanny and Lucy Crossley chattering incessantly. Charles stared ahead with a frown on his handsome brow, completely ignoring the play. When Annis followed his gaze she saw that he was looking across at the Ashwick box, but he was looking not at Adam but rather at the serene countenance of Della Tilney, illuminated by the pale candlelight. When he noticed Annis's regard, Charles immediately looked away.

It was a subdued group that assembled in the foyer to take their coaches home. Fanny and Lucy Crossley were quite worn out with flirtation and gossip, Sibella, who was increasing, looked fatigued and leaned heavily on David's arm, and Charles was still preserving an abstracted silence. As Annis shepherded the girls up into the coach, she spotted a closed carriage pulling away from the side entrance to the theatre. The light from the coach lamps fell briefly on Margot Mardyn's pretty little face before she twitched the curtain back into place. Annis felt flat and cross at the same time. No doubt Miss Mardyn was being spirited away to join Adam Ashwick somewhere. It was just like a man, Annis thought irritably, to be escorting his mother and sister out of the front door of the theatre whilst whisking his *chère amie* discreetly out of the back. It should not have mattered to her, but unfortunately she found that it did.

Chapter Three

The morrow brought an invitation for Fanny and Lucy to spend a couple of days with their friend, Clara Anstey, under the auspices of her mother, Sibella's bosom-bow Lady Anstey. Given this unexpected break from her chaperonage duties, Annis decided to borrow Charles's carriage and make the journey out into the Dales to visit Starbeck. She had every intention of spending a few weeks there once Fanny and Lucy were off her hands, for she had no engagements until she returned to London for the Little Season. However, an advance visit to Starbeck would prove doubly useful; Annis wanted to assess the state of the house before she discussed its future with Charles, and she also wished to see what would be needed to make the house habitable for her stay.

It promised to be a hot day. The wind had dropped and the sun was already high above the Washburn valley. The grey stone villages dozed in the sunshine and higher up, the heather clad moors shimmered in a heat haze.

They stopped at one of Samuel Ingram's new tollgates on the Skipton road. At present it was simply a wooden hut and a chain across the road, but a group of men were working conspicuously hard on the construction of a neat stone house beside the road. Their factor, a bare-headed young man whose chestnut hair gleamed bright in the sunlight, was standing close by and keeping a wary eye on them. Annis recognised him as Samuel Ingram's agent at Linforth, Ellis Benson. Ingram tended to surround himself with the impecunious sons of the gentry, Annis thought wryly. Perhaps it was some manifestation of snobbery that he, a self-made man and son of a lighthouse-keeper, should employ those whose birth was so much better than his own.

Ellis saw her and his grim expression lightened in a smile as he lifted a hand in greeting. The tollkeeper came shuffling out of the hut to take their money and Annis leaned out of the window, recognising him as the former schoolmaster of Starbeck village.

'Mr Castle! How are you, sir?'

The tollkeeper raised one hand to shade his eyes from the sun. His parchment-grey face crinkled into genuine pleasure.

'Miss Annis! Well, I'll be... I am very well, ma'am. And you?'

Annis opened the carriage door and let the steps down. The sun felt hot on her face and she could feel the warmth of the road beneath her feet. She tilted the brim of her bonnet to shield her face, feeling grateful that today she had abandoned her chaperon's turbans for a straw hat and a light blue muslin gown.

'I am well, thank you, Mr Castle.' Annis shook hands with tollkeeper. 'I am back in Harrogate for the summer, you know, and shall be staying at Starbeck next month. But you...' Annis gestured to the tollhouse. 'What happened to the school, Mr Castle?'

A strange expression crossed the tollkeeper's face and for a moment Annis could have sworn it was guilt.

'I can't do both, Miss Annis. Besides, Mr Ingram pays me well to take the tolls for him. Nine shillings a week I'm making here.' He shuffled, turning back to the coachman. 'That's ninepence for a carriage and pair, if you please.'

There was a clatter of wheels on the track behind them and then a horse and cart drew up on the road beside the carriage. The carter and his mate jumped down and started to unhitch the horse from between the shaft. A richly pungent smell of dung filled the air. Mr Castle, who had been about to move the chain from across the road so that Annis' carriage could pass, gave an exclamation and hurried across to the cart.

'Now see here, Jem Marchant, you can't do that!'

The carter pushed his hat back from his brow and scratched his head. 'Do what, Mr Castle?'

'You can't unhitch the horse. Horse and cart is fivepence together.' Castle looked at the cart. 'Sixpence, as you've got narrow wheels.'

'Horse and cart are only thruppence apart!' the carter returned triumphantly. 'None of us can afford to pay Mr Ingram's prices. Daylight robbery, so it is.'

The aroma of manure was almost enough to make Annis scramble back into the carriage and put the window up, but she suddenly caught sight of what looked like a pile of bricks hidden beneath the manure and leaned over for a closer look. The carter's accomplice gave her a wink and shovelled some more dung over to hide it. Castle walked around the back of the cart and looked suspiciously at the load.

'What've you got here?'

'What does it look like?' The carter started to lead the horse towards the tollgate, tipping his hat to Annis as he went. 'Mornin', ma'am.'

'Good morning,' Annis returned. A small crowd of villagers was gathering now to see what was going on, appearing from the fields and lanes as though drawn by some mysterious silent message. A few came running up the path from Eynhallow village to see what was happening, whilst the farm workers abandoned their tools and hastened over to the tollbooth. It seemed to Annis as though they were scenting trouble and had come to watch.

The workmen, meanwhile, were leaning on their spades, the carter's mate was grinning, hands on hips, and Ellis Benson looked as though he thought he should intervene to support the tollkeeper, but really did not want to get involved. The carter unhooked the chain from across the road and urged the horse through.

'Tell you what, Harry Castle, you've made yourselves no friends taking coin from that Ingram. Bloody thief, that man is.'

Castle was sweating, the beads of perspiration running down his face.

'I'm only trying to make an honest shilling from an honest day's work, unlike you, Jem Marchant! What you got under that manure, then? Something you should be paying for, I'll warrant!'

'Why don't you look then, nosy?' The carter's mate stuck his chest out aggressively. 'Don't like to get your hands dirty, do you?' He spat out the straw he was chewing with deliberate insult in the direction of the builders. 'Incomers!' he said with disgust. 'Ingram 'as to bring men in and pay them over the odds to do his dirty work for 'im.'

A growl went through the ranks of the assembled workmen. Despite the hot sunlight the atmosphere seemed suddenly chill. The workmen were shuffling and looking as though they would like to use their spades on the carter

and his mate, and only a sharp word from Benson held
them back. The villagers were also angry, swaying like
corn with the wind coming up. Annis realised that at any
moment the whole situation could go up like a tinderbox.

She backed towards the carriage, wishing now that she
had not got down in the first place. The movement drew
the attention of the carter's burly mate.

'Ain't that Mr Lafoy's carriage?' He looked at Annis
with sudden suspicion. 'They're all 'ere today, ain't they?
All Ingram's vultures.' He took a menacing step towards
Annis.

'Now just a minute,' Castle said, the sweat dripping off
his chin as he looked anxiously from Annis to the crowd,
'this is Lady Wycherley from Starbeck, and no enemy of
yourn. She may be a Lafoy, but she's got nothing to do
with Ingram.'

It was enough to give the carter's mate pause. He tugged
his forelock a little bashfully. 'Beg pardon, ma'am. Dare
say you cannot help being Mr Lafoy's cousin.'

'Not really,' Annis said. 'It was something I was born
with.'

The carter tied his horse to a fence post and came bus-
tling up. He thrust his face close to Annis's own. 'All the
same, ma'am, you tell that Mr Lafoy that we don't like
turncoats up here in the valley. If he shows his face around
here, he'll be sorry—'

Ellis Benson started forward, obliged to intervene at last.
'How dare you threaten Lady Wycherley, man—'

It was the spark that set light to the tinder. Within a
second it seemed to Annis that the fists were flying as the
villagers pelted Ingram's workmen with stones and the
carter and his mate set about Benson and Castle with gusto.
Annis sidestepped the carter's wildly swinging right fist
and tried to gain the shelter of the carriage, but just as she

reached it a stone hit the Lafoy crest on the bodywork beside her head and splintered into pieces. Annis felt a sharp sting along her cheekbone and put up a hand in astonishment. Her fingers came away with blood on them.

There was a drumming of hooves on the road and the dust swirled up. Annis spun around. An arm went about her waist, scooping her off her feet, and the next moment she was on the saddlebow of a huge bay stallion, whose rider brought the dancing creature sharply under control with a single flick of the reins. The whole experience, so quick and so sudden, literally took her breath away; looking down from what seemed a great height, she realised that it had had a similar effect on the carter and his mate. Both had dropped their fists and were gaping up at her rescuer as though the hand of God had intervened.

'What the *devil* is going on here?' Adam Ashwick's incisive tones cut across the fight and brought all the men there to their senses. They fell apart from each other, panting heavily, hanging their heads, dropping the stones and shovels that had served them as weapons. Castle put up his sleeve to staunch the blood running from a cut on his forehead. Benson, who seemed to have had the best of the fight owing to a promising amateur career in pugilism, straightened up and pushed the hair back from his forehead.

'Lord Ashwick!'

'Benson.' Adam's tone was menacing. 'I do not believe that your employer pays you to come to fisticuffs on the king's highway?'

Benson's glance turned to Annis. 'I beg your pardon, Lord Ashwick. I was attempting to defend Lady Wycherley.'

'Very commendable of you, Benson.' There was amusement now in Adam Ashwick's tone. 'You may safely leave Lady Wycherley's defence to me now.'

Annis felt his breath stir her hair. She tried to turn to look at him, but he was holding her too tight and too close, with one arm still about her waist and the other holding the reins, and effectively trapping her in front of him. His chest was hard against her back and Annis could feel the beat of his heart. She kept very still.

'Yes, my lord.' Benson sketched a bow to Annis and turned away to marshal his workmen, and Adam reined in the chestnut stallion, which was tossing its head skittishly at the crowd. He raised his voice again.

'Get back to work, all of you! Don't you have better things to do than stand around here causing trouble?'

'No, my lord!' someone shouted. 'This is as good as a play, and cheaper!'

There was a rumble of laughter. The tension was dissipating now and the crowd started to chatter and melt away. Annis felt Adam's arms relax a little about her, but he showed no signs of letting her go. He looked down at the hapless carter and his mate.

'As for you, Marchant, and you, Pierce, I should haul you before the magistrates for breach of the peace!'

The carter looked sheepish. 'No harm done, m'lord. Apologies, my lady. We never meant to hurt you.'

'Pay your toll and get going,' Adam said abruptly. He turned his head and spoke in Annis's ear.

'And now, Lady Wycherley, what the deuce are you doing here?'

Annis turned in his arms and found that his face was very close to hers. There was a frown between his brows and his gaze was very stern. At such close quarters Annis could see his features in perfect detail. His eyes, so cool and grey, were fringed by thick black lashes. There was a

crease down one cheek that deepened when he smiled. His
skin had a golden sheen and there was a trace of stubble
darkening his jaw and chin. It felt odd to be so close to
him. Odd in an entirely pleasurable way. Annis felt warm
and a little light-headed. Her body softened almost imper-
ceptibly against Adam's and, as his arms tightened about
her again, she saw a flash of desire mirrored in his eyes,
hot, sudden, shocking.

'What are you doing here?' Adam repeated, very softly.

Annis straightened up hastily.

'I was paying my toll, my lord,' she said acerbically.
'As one does.'

Adam's gaze went from her flushed face to the carriage,
and back again. 'You are here alone?'

Annis was starting to feel guilty as well as flustered. It
made her more annoyed. 'No. I am not alone. I have my
coachman and groom.'

'Lafoy's coachman—and Lafoy's coach.'

Annis sighed sharply. 'As you see, my lord. Would you
let me down, if you please? Whilst I appreciate your in-
tervention, I should like to continue to Starbeck now.'

Adam shook his head. 'Presently. I would like to speak
with you first, if you please.'

Annis opened her eyes wide. 'Here?'

'Why not?' Adam gave her a crooked smile. 'I find I
rather like…our current situation.'

Annis was not in a position to argue. Adam drew rein
alongside the coach and leaned across to address the
shaken coachman.

'Drive up to the first crossroads. It leads to Eynhallow
and you should have no trouble there. I shall bring Lady
Wycherley along in a moment.' He pulled the horse back
and raised his whip in salutation as the coach lurched
ahead of them, following the cart up the track. Then he

tossed a coin to the tollkeeper and swung down from the saddle, holding his arms out to help Annis dismount.

Annis was both disconcerted and annoyed that she had no other choice but to accept his aid. It was a long way down to the ground and she had no desire to turn her ankle by trying to jump. She placed her hands lightly on Adam's shoulders and slid down, feeling his arms close about her again to steady her. For a second his cheek brushed hers, his dark hair soft against her skin, then he stepped back and released her gently.

'You are importunate, my lord,' Annis snapped, thoroughly ruffled now, 'both in the way you...you picked me up and the way you set me down!'

Adam raised a quizzical brow. He looped the horse's reins over his arm. 'I beg your pardon if I disturbed you, Lady Wycherley.'

Annis turned slightly away and smoothed her skirts down in self-conscious fashion. Adam had disturbed her— very much—but she did not want to admit it. After a moment she was able to regain her composure and fall into step with him on the sun-baked road. The echo of the carriage wheels was dying away up the track and the builders had returned to their work on the tollhouse, and there was no sound but for the birds in the trees and the faint bleating of the sheep in the fields.

'You are not too shaken, I hope, Lady Wycherley,' Adam asked, casting her a look of concern. 'I doubt that they would have hurt you—you simply became caught in the crossfire.'

'I know.' Annis put her fingers to her cheek again. The bleeding had stopped, but it felt a little sore. 'I suppose I was ungracious just now, my lord, and I should thank you for your prompt action. It was kind of you to come to my rescue.'

Adam smiled. Annis's errant heart did a little flip at the sight of it. 'It was the first time that I have swept a lady off her feet,' he said slowly.

The air between them seemed to sizzle with the heat of the day—and something else.

'I doubt that,' Annis said, trying to remain practical, 'and, as a chaperon, I must object to being swept.'

Adam raised one dark brow. 'Why is that? Do chaperons never experience any adventure, my lady?'

'Certainly not. It goes against the grain.'

Adam stepped closer. 'I should imagine that the most useful experience for a chaperon would be to undergo all the things that might happen to one of your charges, in order to be able to advise them what to do in each circumstance.'

Annis choked on a laugh. 'An outrageous suggestion, my lord!'

Adam shrugged. 'Tell me if you change your mind, Lady Wycherley.'

Annis started to walk again, her fingers straying to her cheek where the cut was feeling hot and itchy in the sunshine. She saw Adam glance at her and then he took her arm.

'Come into the shade,' he said abruptly. 'I want to have a look at that scratch on your cheek.'

Annis tried to pull away, feeling panic stir in her again. 'It is nothing—'

'Nevertheless, I would like to make sure.'

Adam drew her into the shade of a spreading oak tree, dropped the horse's reins and left the stallion grazing docilely on the bank. He turned to Annis, taking her chin in one hand and tilting her face up to the light. His gaze was intent, his touch was gentle and impersonal, but Annis nevertheless felt as though it was branding her. She tried not to jump away. No one had touched her for a very long time. No one had *ever* touched her with such tenderness.

'Hold still…' Adam's voice was barely above a murmur, his fingers as light as the stroke of a feather. 'There is a graze on your cheek, but I do not think it will leave a scar.'

'It is nothing.' Annis said again. Her voice was shaky. 'Please, my lord—'

Adam dropped his hand. His gaze fell to her lips. Suddenly the air between them, hot and heavy already, seemed even more heated.

Annis found that she was shaking. 'I must rejoin my carriage, my lord,' she whispered. 'I am expected at Starbeck—'

There was a pause, then Adam stepped back. 'Of course. It is only a little further up the road.'

There was a stiff silence between them as they scrambled back down on to the track. When Adam offered her his hand to help her down, Annis hesitated before taking it. Finally, when they were once more walking up towards the crossroads, Annis spoke slowly.

'How is it, my lord, that it has become dangerous for me to travel alone in the countryside I have known all my life?'

Adam shrugged. 'These are unhappy times, my lady. Mr Ingram is tightening his grip on a populace already worn down by hunger and poverty. You saw the hostility to the imposition of the tolls just now. It is an even choice as to who is hated more here—Ingram for his greed and meanness or your cousin Charles Lafoy, who was one of them and has now become Ingram's creature.'

Annis's lips tightened. She felt indignation on Charles's behalf but she was afraid for him as well. She had had intimations of this in her letters from the Shepherd family at Starbeck, but this made it all much more real. And more serious.

'Is it truly so bad? I had not realised. I have read in the papers about the riot over the enclosure of Shawes Common and the arson attacks on Mr Ingram's property, but—' she frowned '—I had not imagined the hostility to be so strong.'

Adam cast her a look. 'Even in Harrogate it is sometimes easy to forget the feelings that run high out in the countryside. Perhaps your cousin does not yet realise how much he is disliked, or perhaps he feels that it is worth it for what Ingram must pay him.'

Annis flashed him a look of dislike. 'I do not believe you should make such an assumption, my lord! You can have no idea why Charles chooses to work for Mr Ingram.'

Adam gave her a cynical look. 'Do *you* know why he does? You are very loyal, Lady Wycherley, but perhaps that loyalty is misplaced. Unless I miss my guess, it will be put to the test all too soon.'

Annis stopped abruptly in the middle of the dusty road. 'Pray explain exactly what you mean by that, my lord!'

'With pleasure. I am speaking of Starbeck. It is common knowledge that Mr Ingram wants that property. Perhaps he has already made you an offer for it.' His searching gaze studied her indignant face. 'No? He will. He is waiting for Lafoy to do his dirty work for him.'

Annis raised her brows haughtily. 'And?'

'And Lafoy has already been preparing the ground. The reason that you have not had a permanent tenant at Starbeck for the past two years, Lady Wycherley, is that your cousin has deliberately avoided finding one. He wishes the house to fall down and for you to be unable to afford the repairs. That way Mr Ingram can step in—and make a lower offer.' Adam laughed. 'Did you not suspect any of this?'

'No!' Annis said hotly. She recovered herself. 'Nor do I believe you, sir. You are stirring up trouble because of your dislike for Mr Ingram.'

Adam shrugged easily. 'I cannot deny that I detest Ingram. That is beside the point, however. You will soon see that I am right.'

Annis glared at him from under the brim of her straw hat. 'You are an odious man, Lord Ashwick.'

'Why? Because I tell the truth?' Adam quirked a brow.

'No. You know what I mean. To set me against my cousin…'

Adam's expression became grimmer. 'I am sorry that you see it like that, Lady Wycherley.' He gestured to the carriage, drawn up ahead of them at the crossroads. 'Go to Starbeck! See for yourself.'

'I will!' Annis said. She was afraid that she sounded sulky, but could not quite help herself. She was very afraid that all the things Adam was saying might be true. He put his hand on her arm.

'But before you go, Lady Wycherley, just how odious do you think me?'

'I…oh…' Annis's gaze fell before his searching look. 'I beg your pardon, Lord Ashwick. I meant that what you said was odious, and not that you yourself…' She faltered. 'That is, I thought it unkind in you to speak as you did.'

'I see,' Adam said. He gave her a crooked smile. 'I suppose I should be grateful that you make a distinction.' He took her hand and pressed a kiss to the palm. 'Good day, Lady Wycherley.'

Aware that her face was now as red as a setting sun, Annis scrambled up into her carriage with absolutely no decorum. She tried to ignore Adam's hand outstretched to

help her, but he outmanoeuvred her by the simple expedient of taking her elbow to help her up. He stood back
and raised his hand in mocking farewell.

'Drive on!' Annis said crossly to the coachman, well
aware that even as the coach turned the corner and Adam
Ashwick was left behind, her palm still tingled with the
imprint of his kiss.

Annis's journey home that evening was uneventful,
which was fortunate as she had plenty to think about.
Whenever she tried to concentrate on the shocking dilap-
idation of Starbeck, she found herself thinking instead of
Adam Ashwick, and not of the Adam from whom she had
parted in a temper, but the one who had held her with such
heart-shaking tenderness. She was out of all patience with
herself by the time she reached Church Row and was glad
to partake of a solitary supper. She had just finished the
meal when there was a knock at the door.

'Your cousin is here,' Mrs Hardcastle announced, coming into the dining room and wiping her hands on her
apron. The housekeeper had been with the Lafoy family
for years and, when Annis had returned to England, had
gladly accepted a post in her household. Her husband, who
had died some ten years previously, had been the family's
coachman. These days Annis made do with a very small
staff, of which Mrs Hardcastle was the undisputed matri-
arch. She was a tiny woman with bright dark eyes and a
bosom encased in black that jutted like a shelf. It was
unfortunate, Annis thought, that the bosom was what always drew the eye first. Plenty of gentlemen had been
accused of 'sauce' for staring incredulously at Mrs Hardcastle's figure, when in fact it was difficult to look elsewhere.

'Powerful big bunch of flowers Mr Lafoy's got with

'im,' Mrs Hardcastle continued. She fixed Annis with a disapproving eye. 'He ain't come courting 'as he, Miss Annis?'

Annis put her book aside a little regretfully. She had been enjoying the peace. 'I doubt it, Hardy. Charles does not appear interested in the Misses Crossley and he has never shown any urge to marry me!'

Mrs Hardcastle sniffed. 'Well, I haven't seen a bouquet so large since Mrs Arbuthnot's funeral, Miss Annis. You bin reading books at the table again? T'ain't good for you, you know. You need a bit of company.'

'I like my own company,' Annis said, getting to her feet. 'Still, as Charles is here I suppose I had better see him. Please show him into the drawing-room, Hardy.'

When she went into the room, Charles was standing before the fireplace, a bunch of pink roses in one hand. He was fidgeting a little nervously with his neckcloth. When he saw Annis he looked simultaneously anxious and relieved, and came over to kiss her.

'Annis? You are well? Benson rode over this afternoon and told me what had happened at the tollhouse.'

'That was nice of him,' Annis said composedly. 'Are those flowers for me, Charles? How kind of you.'

'They are from Mr Ingram,' Charles said, holding the bouquet out to her a little awkwardly. 'He was most distressed to hear what had happened.'

'Please thank him from me.' Annis laid the flowers on the sideboard. 'It was an unpleasant experience, but I assure you I came to no harm.'

She sat down and, after a moment, Charles did the same, taking the chair opposite. He adopted such a concerned look that Annis was hard put to it not to laugh.

'Truly, Charles, I am very well. Lord Ashwick arrived

before too much harm was done. I fear your carriage has suffered a few dents, however.'

'Never mind the carriage.' Charles sat forward. 'Ellis said that Ashwick had turned up. I suppose I should be grateful to him for rescuing you.' He sounded both dubious and unwilling. 'The trouble is that every time I hear of Ashwick's involvement in one of these situations I am convinced he has stirred up the trouble in the first place!'

Annis raised her brows. 'I think you may acquit him of that, Charles. He was nowhere near the tollhouse when the altercation broke out. It was a carter called Marchant and his companion who started to goad the workmen.'

'Ellis told me,' Charles said glumly. 'Trouble is, Annis, there is more than one way of stirring rebellion. Ashwick's brother is the rector of Eynhallow, you know, and preaches fierily against exploitation.'

Annis sighed. 'If he is anything like Lord Ashwick, I imagine he is not subtle about it!'

Charles looked rather amused. 'I say, Annis, what has Ashwick done to upset you?'

'Oh, nothing,' Annis said quickly. She did not want to let her cousin know that it was Adam who had told her about Starbeck, for that did smack of making trouble. 'I find him somewhat brusque, that is all.'

Charles looked amused. 'I thought that you liked him.'

Annis gave him a straight stare. She was not about to admit to a partiality for Lord Ashwick, no matter that there was a grain of truth in Charles' words. 'Did you, Charles?'

Charles crossed his legs. 'Do not seek to gammon me, Annis! At the theatre the two of you looked more than cosy together.'

'As far as I am aware, Lord Ashwick is cosy with Miss Mardyn rather than anyone else.' Annis shifted a little. She knew that she was turning a little pink. 'Now, Charles, do not seek to distract me. I must speak with you about Starbeck.'

There was a knock and Mrs Hardcastle came in with a tray and two glasses of wine. She slapped it down on the sideboard.

'There you are, Mr Lafoy. Get that inside you. My nephew's best elderflower cordial, that is. Got yourself a wife yet, have you?'

She thrust a glass at Charles, who looked revolted for a second but manfully covered his lapse. 'Thank you, Hardy. No, I fear I have not yet found a lady willing to take me on.'

'You should ask your cousin to find you an heiress,' Mrs Hardcastle said, with a grim nod at Annis. 'Powerful good at settling these girls, Miss Annis is. Why, you should see her with these two little minxes we have now! As good as betrothed already, they are! Though why anyone would want to marry the elder girl—'

'Thank you, Hardy,' Annis said, a little desperately.

'Vulgar, vulgar, vulgar!' Mrs Hardcastle finished triumphantly. 'Excuse me, miss. I have to finish up in the scullery this evening. There's a mouse's nest in there. Quite a plague there was this last winter.'

'How on earth you cope with her I'll never know,' Charles said, as the door closed behind the housekeeper. 'I know she has been worked for the family for years, but surely it is time to pension her off?'

'Hardy would go into a decline if she were not busy all the time,' Annis said. 'She is like me in that respect, Charles. She would never forgive me if I told her we wanted to lose her services.'

'Have you asked her?' Charles enquired. 'She might be grateful to hang up her apron.' He took a sip of the wine and grimaced. 'Ugh! This is too sweet for me.'

'Pour it on the trailing ivy,' Annis instructed, waving towards the impressive collection of greenery that decorated a corner of the room. 'It thrives on the cordial! I have watered it often enough with mine.'

'So you wished to speak of Starbeck,' Charles said, when he had regained his seat. 'How did you find it, Annis?'

Annis looked him in the eye. 'It was shockingly bad, Charles. The roof leaks so much that one of the bedrooms has an impromptu indoor waterfall and the wood of the front door has swollen in the damp of the winter, then dried out in the summer and cracked across the frame. Several of the windows are broken and the place is infested with mice.' Annis made a hopeless gesture. 'And about it all is an air so tumbledown and neglected that I think it would take a fortune to put to rights. You know as well as I that I do not possess such a fortune.'

Charles was looking tired. He ran a hand through his fair hair. 'I have tried, Annis. The money you have sent me has all been passed to Tom Shepard to spend on the upkeep of the home farm. There is simply not enough to go round.'

'He told me.' Annis passed her cousin a glass of brandy from the decanter. 'He said that there were insufficient funds and that you had too little time to spend there.'

Charles flushed guiltily. 'It is true that I have been very busy of late. My work for Ingram...' He shrugged expressively.

'Tom was telling me that there has been a poor harvest these two years past and a bad winter this year. People are barely surviving, Charles.'

Charles shifted, leaning forward. 'Annis, I know you are opposed to selling, but for the sake of the estate you must consider it.'

Annis jumped to her feet. Her instinctive reaction was to refuse. 'No!' She swung around. 'Charles, one of the reasons that Starbeck is in such a parlous state is that there has been no permanent tenant for over two years.' She hesitated. 'Have you tried—truly tried—to find one for me?'

There was a moment when her cousin looked her in the eye and she was convinced he was going to tell her the truth. Adam's words rang in her ears: *The reason that you have not had a permanent tenant at Starbeck for the past two years, Lady Wycherley, is that your cousin has deliberately avoided finding one. He wishes the house to fall down and for you to be unable to afford the repairs. That way Mr Ingram can step in...*

Then Charles looked away and fidgeted with his empty brandy glass.

'Annis...' His tone was reasonable. 'Of course I tried...'

'I see.' Annis felt a chill. 'Yet you found no one.'

'It is not all bad news,' Charles said encouragingly. 'Mr Ingram would be interested in buying Starbeck from you, Annis.'

Annis glared at him. 'I am sure that he would, Charles.'

Charles got to his feet. 'I must go. Please think about Ingram's offer, Annis. It would solve your difficulties.' He came across to kiss her cheek and it was only by an effort of will that Annis did not pull away.

'Goodnight, Charles,' she said tightly.

After her cousin had gone, Annis sat by the window and looked out over the twilit garden. She could not bear to sell Starbeck. It would be like selling a part of her independence. As for Charles, for all his denials, she did not trust him. It had all happened just as Adam Ashwick had predicted.

Annis found that she was looking across to the houses

opposite, where the lights burned in the house Adam had taken. She wondered if he had returned to Harrogate that afternoon or whether he had stayed at Eynhallow. Then she wondered when she would see him again, and then wondered *why* she was wondering! Finally, in a burst of irritation, she twitched the curtains closed and went up to bed, to dream, blissfully, about being swept off her feet.

Chapter Four

Fanny and Lucy Crossley returned the following day, full of chatter and excitement about their stay with the Anstey family. There was a ball that night at the Granby, and on the following morning, Lucy vouchsafed that Lieutenant Norwood had suggested a carriage outing to the River Nidd at Howden.

'It is not very far and should prove a pleasant trip for a summer day,' she begged, when Annis expressed reservations about the plan. 'Oh, *please*, Lady Wycherley, do let us go!'

Annis was torn. On the one hand she had seen the growing regard between Lucy and Barnaby Norwood and wished to encourage it, Mr Norwood being a most eligible young man. On the other hand, Lieutenant Norwood's best friend was the dashing Lieutenant Greaves, and the last thing that Annis wanted was to throw Fanny and Greaves together. In the end, unable to resist the mixture of hope and pleading in Lucy's eyes, Annis agreed, consoling herself with the thought that she would be able to keep a close eye on Fanny and that Sir Everard Doble was also to be one of their party. The young baronet arrived for the outing with a volume of poetry clasped under one arm and a

boater with coloured ribbons adorning his head, and Lucy
and Fanny were hard put to it to conceal their mirth.

Mindful of the heat of the day, Annis had discarded her
evening blacks for a muslin gown in pale pink, with a
straw hat with matching ribbons and a pale pink parasol.
When she first appeared, Lucy's eyes lit up like stars.

'Why, Lady Wycherley, you look famously pretty!'

Fanny screwed up her hard little face. 'You look too
young to be our chaperon,' she said disagreeably, and Annis, smiling widely, reflected that that was as close to a
compliment as she was ever likely to get from Fanny.

It was a glorious day and the party was in high spirits
as they set off. Lieutenants Norwood and Greaves kept up
a flow of easy conversation with the girls, whilst Sir Everard sat reading his poetry and Annis looked out of the
carriage window at the view. Howden was an attractive
little village and there was a charming riverside path that
ran along the bank under the dappled shadow of the willow
trees. Fanny and Lucy chattered constantly, seemingly unimpressed by the natural beauty around them. Annis, having ensured that Fanny took Sir Everard's arm rather than
that of Lieutenant Greaves, was content to stroll along behind, enjoying the cool shade.

They reached a place where the bank opened out into a
wide meadow. Lieutenant Greaves started to recite some
poetry, in evident mockery of Sir Everard, who frowned
at such levity and walked off on his own. The girls giggled.
Annis turned away, irritated, and caught sight of a man
standing beneath the weeping willows, gazing out across
the water meadows to where the spire of a church cut the
heat haze. At the sound of voices he turned impatiently
and looked as though he was about to stride away. Then
he checked. Annis, with a mixture of surprise and hastily
repressed anticipation, recognised Adam Ashwick.

She hesitated. His stance was very much that of a person who wished to be left alone, but it seemed churlish to ignore him when it was obvious that they had recognised one another. After a moment she walked across to join him in the lee of the willows, and Adam sketched a slight bow.

'How do you do, Lady Wycherley?'

Annis could not tell from his tone whether he was pleasedu to see her but she thought that probably he was not. She suspected that he was annoyed that she had brought a group of chattering youngsters to spoil the peace.

She tilted her parasol to shadow her eyes. The reflection off the water was blinding.

'Good afternoon, Lord Ashwick. This is a beautiful spot.'

Adam Ashwick's lips twisted into a smile. 'It is indeed, Lady Wycherley. I often come her when I am looking for a little solitude.'

There was only one way to take that. Annis blushed and felt vexed, with him for his frankness and with herself for originally being pleased to see him when he so clearly wished to avoid company.

'Then I beg your pardon for spoiling your retreat, sir.'

She made to walk away, but Adam put a hand on her arm. 'Lady Wycherley. Forgive me, that was unconscionably clumsy of me. Will you not stay for a little?'

Annis hesitated. She had enough of an excuse to walk away if she wished, for Fanny and Lucy were now shrieking and running around in a most unladylike fashion. Lieutenant Greaves and Lieutenant Norwood were making impromptu boats from twigs and arranging a race down the river. Sir Everard stood a little apart, arms folded, looking disapproving. He had an unfortunate habit of looking down his nose, Annis thought. Even if he did not mean to appear superior, that was the effect it had. Within the light-hearted group he stood out like a sore thumb.

'Please,' Adam Ashwick said, persuasively, recalling her attention to him. 'If there is anyone I would care to share the view with, it is you, ma'am.'

The blood fizzed beneath Annis's skin as she blushed again under Adam's appreciative scrutiny. 'I am happy to rest a moment in the shade if I am not disturbing you, my lord,' she temporised. 'I may only be a moment, though.'

Adam gestured to a wooden seat set back a little from the water's edge. They sat down.

'I hope that you have recovered from your experience at the tollbooth the day before yesterday,' Adam said. 'I trust you took no lasting hurt?'

Annis laughed. 'I am in no danger of being overset by the experience, I thank you, my lord.'

A smile crept into Adam's eyes like sunlight on the water. 'I had not imagined that you would be, but it is conventional to ask. You do not strike me as a frail flower, Lady Wycherley.'

'Well, I should rather hope not. I could not make my own way in the world if I was forever wilting!'

Adam sat back a little and laid one arm along the back of the seat. Annis found she was strangely aware of his hand resting close to her shoulder. 'And you have made your own way for…how long, ma'am?'

'Since my husband died, my lord. Eight years, in fact.'

'You had no relatives to whom you might apply for help when you were widowed?'

'Oh, of course.' Annis made a slight gesture. 'Sibella and David offered me a home, as did Charles, but I did not wish to be a burden.' She smiled. 'Besides, I am a managing female, my lord. I could not bear to spend my time arranging flowers and taking tea when there are so many other things to do.'

'And you have Starbeck to support.'

'Indeed. I could not let Starbeck go.' Annis hesitated. 'It is my safe haven. Except—' she frowned '—it is not as sound as I would like it to be. It was quite a shock to see it two days ago.'

Adam nodded. 'I was afraid that you would find it so.' He looked at her very directly. 'I apologise if I offended you with my remarks about your cousin and Starbeck.'

Annis looked away. She felt hot and bothered, torn by several conflicting loyalties. 'Please do not apologise, my lord. I have already spoken to Charles.'

'And sorted matters out, I hope. It is a melancholy thing to be at odds with one's relatives when you are otherwise alone in the world.'

Annis felt a little pang inside her; for herself, for Charles, for the fact that Adam Ashwick understood how she felt even though she had never told him. 'It is indeed, sir. Sibella and Charles are all I have and I value them exceedingly.'

Adam nodded. For a moment they looked out across the river in silence.

'My late wife used to love this view,' Adam said abruptly. 'We would often walk along the river bank and stop here to rest. I had commissioned a painting of it for her, but she died before it was finished.'

A ripple of breeze ruffled the surface of the river and carried the shouts of the men and the excited calling of the girls to them. Annis could see Fanny hanging over the packhorse bridge to watch the progress of the race. Lieutenant Greaves was leaning over her shoulder, pointing and laughing. There was no sign of Sir Everard.

'I am sorry,' Annis said softly. 'I heard that you married young and were most attached to your wife.'

Adam gave her a lopsided smile. 'She was the light of my life for five years, Lady Wycherley,' he said softly.

There was a fierce ache in Annis's throat. 'I envy you, my lord.' She stood up abruptly. 'Please excuse me. I do not like to leave the young ladies for too long.'

Adam stood up too. He did not speak again, but Annis was very conscious of his gaze following her as she walked back across the meadow. There was a pain in her chest and she miserably acknowledged its cause. She was jealous; jealous that her own marriage had in no way lit up the world for anyone and, ignominiously, hotly envious of Adam's happy relationship with his wife. When she reached the bridge she looked back to where they had been sitting. She could not help herself. But Adam had gone.

Fanny and Lucy Crossley retired early that night, but Annis sat up with her book for a while, enjoying the solitude that only came to her after her charges had gone to bed. Finally, when she heard the clock strike a quarter past midnight, she put her book aside with a little sigh. She felt restless and knew that she was unlikely to sleep. Nevertheless her eyes were tired from peering at the print in the candlelight and the heat of the day was at last fading, and she knew she should go up to bed.

Annis blew out the candles, taking one with her into the hall, and went slowly up the stairs.

Fanny Crossley's bedroom door was ajar and a slight draught skittered along the landing, raising the corner of the rugs. Annis frowned. Fanny hated the cold and was always complaining that Harrogate was a miserable, chilly place, so it seemed odd that she should have her window open. Annis pushed the bedroom door a little wider and held the candle a little higher. The breeze from the window caught the flame and set it spluttering, sending dancing shadows across the bed. The empty bed.

During the previous month, Fanny had done plenty of things to try Annis's patience, but this was something else entirely. This was the worst thing that could happen to a chaperon. An empty bed, turned down for the night but pristine and unruffled. Open window, empty bed, missing débutante… The conclusion was inevitable. Fanny had either eloped or she had slipped out for some lovers' tryst.

Annis revised her first opinion. It was not as bad as it might be. After all, Lieutenant Greaves might have been *in* the room with Fanny, or even in the bed for that matter. Not that Annis had ever made such a shocking discovery, but she knew other chaperons that had. She checked the room again. The little minx had been so sure of herself that she had not even stuffed the bolster down the bed to make it look as though she was asleep. That was Fanny all over. Thoughtless, arrogant, risking all for a light flirtation…

Annis berated herself for allowing the Misses Crossley two days under Lady Anstey's lenient guardianship—two days which Fanny had no doubt turned to her advantage. She walked across to the open window, setting the candle down on the nightstand. There was no note, which rather suggested that Fanny had not eloped. Annis crossed to the closet and quickly checked through the dresses hanging there. All appeared to be present and there was no suggestion that Fanny had packed a travelling bag. Annis gave a little sigh of relief. There were girls who would run away taking almost nothing with them, believing that love would conquer all, but Fanny Crossley was not such a débutante—at least, not unless her importunate lover had a title.

Annis sighed and leaned out of the window to see how

Fanny might have escaped. There was no convenient ladder leaning against the wall and no drainpipe or clinging ivy to provide a foothold. Annis frowned in puzzlement. She had been in the drawing room all evening, but she had not heard Fanny slip downstairs. Yet it was evident that she had gone somewhere and Annis was convinced that Lieutenant Greaves was the key. Fanny wanted to make an advantageous marriage to a titled man, which was why she had fastened upon Everard Doble. But Sir Everard was dull and Fanny also wanted a little illicit excitement and a few stolen kisses. Hence the Lieutenant. Annis had always known that he would be trouble.

She latched the window. Fanny would probably be in the garden at the back of the house, clasped firmly in Lieutenant Greaves's strong arms beneath the summer moon. Annis closed the bedroom door behind her and slipped along the corridor to her own room to collect a cloak, hat and shoes. On the way she paused to peep around Lucy Crossley's bedroom door. Lucy's outline was a solid lump in the bed, her breathing deep and even. Annis pulled the door closed with a soft click and tiptoed to the top of the stairs, down into the hall and out through the garden door into the night.

In the house that backed on to Annis Wycherley's own, a light still burned in Adam Ashwick's study. Adam and his younger brother Edward were sharing a bottle of brandy and a game of cards. The brothers looked very alike, with dark, watchful faces and thick dark hair, though there was no grey in Edward's. He was stockier than Adam, with less of the sportsman's muscular physique, but he had a readier smile.

'So many invitations, Ash,' Edward said with a grin, nodding towards the mantelpiece, which was groaning beneath a pile of embossed cards. 'Mama, Della and I are never so popular when you are out of town!'

Adam grunted, unimpressed. 'Am I supposed to feel flattered?'

'Well, I would,' Edward said frankly. 'People throwing their wine cellars and their daughters open to you.'

'An unpleasant thought. I fear I shall not be accepting either offer, for I have too much business to attend to.' Adam tossed his cards down on the table. 'You win, little brother!'

'That makes a change.' Edward gathered the cards up and shuffled them. 'I was surprised that you came back from Eynhallow so soon, Ash. Can Miss Mardyn be the draw?'

'Hardly.' Adam flashed him the ghost of a grin. Edward was one of the few who knew that Margot Mardyn was not and never had been his mistress. The rest of Harrogate speculated at will. 'I am sure there are many other gentlemen only too happy to dance attendance on the diva.'

'It is usually the one who gets away that the lady wants,' Edward said sagely.

Adam laughed aloud at that. 'Wise words from a vicar, Ned!'

'I am sure that I see more of life here in Harrogate than you do in London,' Edward returned.

'Very probably. But I still maintain that Miss Mardyn will not miss my attentions. Why, when we last spoke she had been driving with a certain Lieutenant Greaves who is, I understand, a cousin to Lord Farmoor and in line for a pretty title of his own. She had also taken the spa waters with Sir Everard Doble and had her eye on Charles Lafoy. Quite enough for one woman to be going on with, even one so famously energetic as Miss Mardyn.'

Edward spluttered into his brandy. 'I say, Ash!'

'Did you not see one of her admirers spiriting Miss Mardyn away from the theatre the other night?' Adam asked. 'I'll say this for Margot—she works fast!'

'I believe the whole town thought that that was your carriage,' Edward said.

'They may think what they will.' Adam shrugged. He was notoriously impervious to public opinion. 'It was an interesting evening,' he added drily. 'I thought it civil of Della to speak to Charles Lafoy when he is Ingram's man of business.'

'I thought so too.' Edward hesitated. 'I sometimes wondered—' He stopped.

'What?'

'Oh…' Edward's ruddy face flushed redder. 'Nothing. I just wondered sometimes why Della has stayed in Harrogate after Humphrey died.'

Adam raised his brows. 'Surely because Eynhallow is her family home?'

'I suppose so.' Edward looked as though he was about to say something else, then thought better of it. 'She always enjoyed the bright lights of London when she was younger, but perhaps she don't care so much for that any more.'

'She has only been widowed twelve months,' Adam pointed out. 'Maybe when she is out of mourning she will choose to go back.'

Edward nodded. 'Poor Della. She was very young to be tied to a sickly wastrel.' He cast Adam a sideways glance. 'Much the same age as your Lady Wycherley, I suppose.'

'She is not *my* Lady Wycherley,' Adam said coolly, picking up his next hand of cards and studying them for a second. He found he was not concentrating. The idea of *his* Lady Wycherley seemed to have lodged in his brain with the tenacity of a burr. He looked up to find his brother's speculative grey gaze resting on him. 'Devil take it, Ned, what is it?'

'Nothing,' Edward said again. 'I thought that you seemed very cosy with Lady Wycherley at the theatre, that is all, and then you did mention that you rescued her from that mob at the tollhouse.'

Adam smiled. 'And I met her again today!'

'So?'

Adam sighed. 'So…what?'

'So, do you have an interest there, Ash? And must you be so deliberately obtuse?'

Adam grinned. 'I beg your pardon. I enjoy talking to Lady Wycherley and I do believe that it makes Lafoy nervous for his cousin to be speaking with the enemy. It is an excellent way to annoy him!'

Edward frowned. 'Are you using Lady Wycherley, Ash?'

Adam sobered. 'Certainly not. I like her.' He hesitated. 'In fact, I like her a great deal.'

Edward gave a low, soundless whistle. 'I see.'

'Hold fire, Ned! I am not suggesting that the banns should be read.' Adam sighed. 'Annis Wycherley has an aversion to marriage, so I understand. I formed the distinct impression that she holds her independence in high esteem. She is a most unusual female, to protect her liberty so zealously.'

'As she was married to Sir John Wycherley, I can understand her reluctance to remarry,' Edward said.

Adam raised a brow. 'Oh?'

'Wycherley was a dreadful old sea dog.' Edward shook his head. 'I don't believe he distinguished himself in any way in the navy, but he treated his wife like he treated his men, so I hear. With a rule of iron! I'm surprised the poor girl didn't mutiny!'

Adam pulled a face. If that was the case, it explained a great deal of Annis's aversion to the married state. He wondered why she had chosen to marry Sir John Wycherley in the first place. She had said that she had been widowed a long time, which meant that she must have married at a young age. Perhaps she had been seeking security. It was common enough…

'I thought that you said you went to Howden today,' Edward remarked. 'Was that where you met Lady Wycherley?'

'It was. I was walking down by the river where I used to go with Mary. Annis Wycherley arrived with those dreadful girls of hers, plus a couple of likely-looking young officers and that stick-in-the-mud Everard Doble.'

'I had heard that Doble was looking for a rich bride.' Edward looked cynical. 'Can he believe that Miss Crossley will grace Hansard Court?'

Adam laughed. 'Her fortune will certainly grace the place.' He took a swallow of his brandy, thinking back to the encounter with Annis Wycherley. There was something about her that drew him strongly and he had been thinking about her on and off for the rest of the day. Her candour and her innocence were both exceptionally attractive. They called forth an equal openness from him. He had been astounded to find himself speaking to her of his love for Mary, for he had seldom shared his feelings with anyone, least of all a mere acquaintance. Yet he had felt quite comfortable speaking to Annis.

Adam frowned. Innocence was not the first quality that one expected to find in a widowed chaperon, particularly a lady who had travelled as widely as Annis Wycherley and had also been her own mistress from a young age. If it came to that, innocence was not an attribute one came across very often at all, particularly not in the circles in

which he moved. It was not that Annis Wycherley was
naïve—far from it. There was simply some bright, open
quality about her that attracted him. When he had seen her
by the river in her pale pink muslin dress with the wind
ruffling the ribbons of her straw hat...

'Ash? Ash, your concentration is wandering,' Edward
chided. 'You have just discarded the Queen of diamonds,
which I'll wager you need, and you have ignored my repeated question into the bargain!'

Adam grinned. 'I am sorry, Ned. What was it you were
asking me?'

'Nothing of importance. I was merely enquiring whether
you would be returning to Eynhallow within the next few
days.' Edward picked up the brandy bottle and refilled
their glasses.

'I imagine so.' Adam sighed, his mind turning from Annis to less pleasant thoughts. 'I need hardly tell you, Ned,
that there is much work to be done there and, since paying
off Humphrey's debt to Ingram, I have had precious little
spare money to spend. Still, that does not excuse the
greater neglect. I am sorry I have been such an absentee
landlord these nine years past.'

Edward gave him a straight look. 'I understand your
reasons, Ash. Do you feel you have put enough distance
between yourself and the past now?'

Adam shifted uncomfortably. His life with Mary had
been bound up in the hills and the moors of Yorkshire,
and after she had died it had seemed that every view held
a painful memory. London, with its impersonal bustle, had
been a far easier place for him to live. He had neglected
Eynhallow for nine long years because he had not wanted
to be reminded of his wife. Yet today, when he had walked
beside the river, though he had still felt an ache of memory, the pain was gone.

'I believe I have,' he said slowly.

Edward smiled in wordless satisfaction and raised his glass in a toast. 'Here is to Eynhallow, then!'

They drank the toast.

'And to the future,' Edward added.

Adam smiled. He thought again of Annis Wycherley. When he had first met her he had thought casually that it would be interesting to know her better. Since then he had seen her a handful of times, yet already his feelings were stronger. Already he wanted more. That required some serious thought.

He got to his feet and drew back the curtain, unlatching the long doors that led on to the terrace. They swung open with a gust of summer breeze. 'I need some fresh air before I go to bed. I will see you in the morning.'

'Good night, Ash,' Edward said, draining his brandy glass.

Adam stepped over the threshold and went out into the dark.

It was a clear July night. The wind was blowing down from the moors again, chasing rags of cloud across the full moon. The trees that lined the gardens of the town houses tossed their branches and cast long shadows in the moonlight.

Annis had searched the whole garden by the light of the moon and had found no sign of the amorous couple. She was a little surprised, for the walled gardens of the town houses provided excellent cover for a pair of lovers. She could scarcely imagine Fanny being so lost to propriety that she would hold an assignation in the street. The thought troubled her, for it pointed to the likelihood of the girl having eloped after all. She was about to go back inside the house and raise the alarm, when a scrap of white on the grass caught her attention.

It was a handkerchief and it lay by the back gate. Annis picked it up. It was crisp white cambric and it held a faint trace of the lavender water that Fanny habitually wore. Annis sighed and unfastened the gate. It unlatched with a soft click that was lost in the soughing of the wind. Outside, in the lane that ran between the gardens, the shadows were deeper and the light of the moon barely penetrated between the high walls. Annis hesitated, not because she was nervous, but because, in spite of the evidence of the handkerchief, it seemed so unlikely that Fanny would be out here. She was a girl who liked all the comfort that money could buy, and a fumbled tryst in a dark alleyway seemed quite out of character in Annis's opinion. She took a few steps down the lane, peering into the darkness, then decided to go back. Fanny was not here, and Annis was becoming quite out of patience with the whole business. When she finally caught up with the girl she would give her a piece of her mind. She turned abruptly, took a step forward into the dark, and quite unexpectedly collided with someone who had been standing almost directly behind her.

'Ooof!' The air was knocked out of Annis's body. This was definitely not Fanny's diminutive figure, nor indeed did it appear to be Lieutenant Greaves, who was a willowy gentleman who looked as though a puff of wind might blow him over and disarrange his dandyish finery. This man—and Annis was quite aware that it was a man—was large and decidedly more unyielding. She tried to take a step back to free herself, but he had both arms about her and she could not put any space between their bodies. She could see nothing of him in the darkness, but she could hear his breathing above the thud of her own heart and feel the warmth of his hands through the thickness of her cloak. Despite the darkness and the suddenness of her ambush, his touch conveyed reassurance and she felt herself start to relax. The smell of him, the mingled scent of brandy and sandalwood and masculinity, wrapped up in the cold fresh night air, was insidiously attractive. He felt familiar, which gave her a wholly inappropriate sense of intimacy.

This was dangerous. Annis knew that she had to act, before her traitorous body failed her completely. Sharply, and completely against her instincts, she raised her knee and felt it make a satisfyingly accurate contact with his groin.

Adam felt sick and cold and breathless. The whole encounter, so unexpected and so startling, had lasted only a few seconds. One minute he had been holding a woman in his arms—a woman he had already mysteriously managed to identify as Annis Wycherley—and the next moment she had released herself in the most efficient way imaginable. He wondered vaguely who on earth had taught her that trick.

'Lord Ashwick? Lord Ashwick! Are you injured at all?' Her urgent tones cut through his pain. Adam leaned one hand against the garden wall and tried to regain his breath. The wave of nausea was receding a little now but he still felt damnably uncomfortable. He raised his head.

'Of course I'm damn well injured, Lady Wycherley! I thought that was your intention?'

There was a silence.

'I am most dreadfully sorry,' Annis said. Adam grudgingly allowed that she did sound genuinely remorseful. 'I did not realise that it was you, Lord Ashwick. Had I done so, I would not have hurt you.'

There was a pause whilst Adam's better nature slowly asserted itself. 'You did the right thing,' he said, still grudging. He straightened up slowly. 'Why wait to be sure? By then it might be too late.'

'That is exactly what my papa used to say.' Annis sounded relieved. 'He told me not to hesitate.'

'You evidently took his advice to heart.' Adam still felt bruised and bad-tempered. 'You were precisely on target.'

'I am grateful that you have taken the matter so well, my lord.' Annis was briskly practical now. 'Of course you really should not have grabbed me so roughly in the first place, and then it would never have happened. It was entirely your own fault.'

Adam gritted his teeth. He knew that there was an element of truth in what she said, but he had been taken by surprise as much as she. 'Thank you. I shall remember not to grab you should the occasion arise again.' He took a deep breath. 'I apologise, Lady Wycherley. I believe I swore at you.'

'Your apology is accepted.' Now she sounded almost prim. 'After all, I suppose I dealt you quite an injury.'

'You did.'

There was silence but for the wind in the trees. A night coach rattled past on the cobbles of the street, then there was a deep quiet.

'How did you know that it was me? It is too dark here to see clearly.' There was an odd tone in Annis's voice, as though she was asking against her will. She sounded intrigued but also wary, as though she did not really want to know the answer. Adam thought that he knew why. Whatever she had claimed, she *had* recognised him in the dark, just as he had known her. She did not understand why and it troubled her, but even so she could not resist asking…

Adam hesitated. The truth was that it had been one part deduction and nine parts intuition. When he had first caught hold of her his senses had been swamped with information, despite the darkness. A strand of her hair had brushed his face and it was soft and smelled faintly of honey. Her breathing had been light and quick, feathering his cheek. Her body had felt soft and yielding beneath the velvet slipperiness of the cloak. All these thoughts had gone through his head in a split second and his senses had stirred in response to her nearness. Then her knee had made contact with his groin and any stirrings had died a swift death.

Until now. Now he felt stirred all over again, disturbed by her proximity, thrown off balance by her presence there in the dark with him. It was unexpected. And exciting.

'I recognised you as soon as I touched you, Lady Wycherley.' Adam smiled a little as he heard the quick, indrawn breath Annis could not hide. 'Having once held you in my arms, I was bound to recognise you again. You have a most deliciously curved shape—'

'Lord Ashwick!'

Adam laughed. 'Surely all chaperons are aware that men are all the same, Lady Wycherley?'

He heard Annis smother a laugh. 'Oh! I should be angry with you, but... Anyhow, I *have* warned my charges many a time about men like you!'

'Well, then...' Adam's voice dropped '...no doubt you know exactly how to deal with me, ma'am.'

'I doubt it.' Annis sounded a little breathless and Adam smiled to himself. 'I have no personal experience of fending off rakes, my lord.'

'No? Well, I am not a rake.'

'Indeed?' She sounded doubtful. Adam was charmed. The Annis Wycherley he had met before had been in control. Now she sounded younger and less sure of herself. It intrigued him that the proper chaperon should have a softer edge.

'I confess I had seen no evidence of your rakishness in the daylight, sir, but—'

'But?'

'One cannot be too careful. I do not know you well.'

'I assure you that I am utterly harmless.' Adam took her hand in his. His fingers, long and strong, interlocked with hers. 'You may remember that when we met at Eynhallow I suggested that all chaperons should have the relevant experience to advise their charges. Tell me, Lady Wycherley...' he spoke very softly '...if you were advising one of your young ladies on how to deal with this situation, what would you suggest?'

He heard Annis take a deep breath. 'Firstly I would tell her that she should step into the light, sir. The darkness is altogether too intimate.'

'Ah. It is indeed.'

'Then...' her voice faltered a little '...I would tell her to bid you a brisk goodnight.'

'That is eminently sensible advice.' Adam smiled. The longer they talked, the more acutely conscious he became of her physical proximity and he was certain that she felt the same way, in spite of her wariness. Something was holding her there in the darkness, talking to him. He was determined to prolong the encounter.

'Perhaps you might also have taught her the elements of self-defence? Nothing is so ruinous to the intentions of a potential rake than the blow you dealt me just now.'

'Oh...' He heard a breath of a laugh as Annis answered him. 'It is a useful if extreme strategy, my lord. It was all I could think of at the time. If I had had my pistol I might have shot you, of course.'

'That might also be a useful deterrent, I suppose. Except that you do not have it with you now.'

'Fortunately for you.'

Adam sighed. 'I am only sorry that you felt you needed to defend yourself against me in the first place. If you had already recognised me, you must have known that I would not have harmed you.'

There was an odd pause. The darkness was indeed creating an atmosphere of intimacy between them and Adam felt instinctively that Annis would be honest with him.

'I did not know it was you, Lord Ashwick. I thought perhaps it might be, although how I knew…' She sounded confused. 'I did not feel that I was in danger, but one cannot always trust to intuition.'

Adam took her hand and drew out of the shadows and into the moonlight by the garden gate. The pale silver light fell on her face. She looked absurdly young to him, despite her composure. All her features were as neat and precise as she was herself, except for her mouth, which was the most unconsciously sensual thing that he had ever seen. He found it was all he could do to stop himself kissing her. His pulse quickened. He brought his hand up to touch her hair, a fleeting touch, there one moment, gone the next. It felt soft and silky beneath his fingers. He wanted to tangle his hands in it and tilt her face up to his. Her eyes were dark and wide in the moonlight.

From their first meeting at the inn there had been something between them, some affinity. He remembered that encounter now—that moment when their eyes had met and she had looked hastily away. And whenever he met her there was the same pull of awareness, though he knew she had tried very hard to repress it. This sensation, though…this was something else entirely. Now he felt an attraction stronger than anything he had ever experienced.

Perhaps it was the fact that they had bumped into each other in the dark and he had therefore had no preconceptions about chaperons, or frumpish dresses or her being Charles Lafoy's cousin. Perhaps it was her perfume, honey and cinnamon, teasing his senses. It brought to mind soft skin and tumbled sheets. He thought of the matchmaking matrons in *ton* society. Never in his life had he responded to a chaperon in the way he was reacting to Annis Wycherley now. He wanted to catch hold of her and crush her to him.

'You did not tell me why you were out here in the first place.' Adam spoke a little abruptly. He knew that he was going to have to let her go soon, but he did not want to do so. He saw something in her face change, as though she had suddenly remembered something very important. She pressed a hand to her mouth.

'Oh! I had forgot! I am out here because I am looking for someone.'

Adam raised his brows. 'One of your charges?'

'Yes…' Annis whisked through the garden gate, clearly recalled to a sense of duty. 'Please excuse me, my lord. I must go.'

Still she hesitated, standing under the spreading branches of the apple trees whilst the moonlight, filtering through the dancing leaves, patterned her in black and white. It was as though she could not quite tear herself away.

Adam put out a hand.

'Wait!'

She paused. 'My lord?'

'May I call upon you tomorrow?'

He saw her frown. 'I think not.' She hesitated, on the edge of flight. 'You are aware that I am a chaperon.'

'Yes. So?' It seemed irrelevant to him.

'So it would cause conjecture if you were to visit. People would judge me to be flighty, entertaining gentlemen callers. It is simply not appropriate.'

Adam was not inclined to give up so easily. 'I cannot see why it should be unsuitable for me to call,' he said. 'Surely you must have some time to yourself?'

Annis gave him a faint smile. 'Unfortunately not. A chaperon always needs to be vigilant. Which is why I am out here in the first place. Now, please excuse me. I really must go.'

'Wait.' This time Adam spoke in a murmur. One of her hands was resting on the top of the gate and now he put his hand over hers. Before she could divine his intention he leaned forward, drew her closer and kissed her very lightly on the mouth.

She felt sweet and soft, and, as soon as his lips touched hers, Adam wanted to pull her into his arms and kiss her until she was breathless. She seemed frozen with surprise, as though she had never been kissed before. Without pausing to think or, more importantly, to allow her to do so, he slid an arm about her waist, drawing her hard against the wooden panels of the gate, and kissed her again.

This kiss was deliberate and skilful. His lips teased hers, coaxing them apart, moving with persuasive insistence. He felt her yield and drew her closer still, cursing the cold solidity of the gate between them. This was far, far more intoxicating than he had ever imagined. As he felt her tentative response to him, desire exploded within him. He ran one hand into her hair and held her head still, plundering her mouth with his. Then he felt a shudder go through her and she stepped back from him, her hands against his chest, warding him off.

'No, please…' Her face was bemused in the moonlight, her breathing ragged. 'I cannot do this.'

He sought to recapture her hands. 'Why not?'

'Because…' her expression showed her uncertainty '…I do not do things like that.'

'You just did. And I dare swear that you enjoyed it.'

'I… Yes… No. That is nothing to the purpose.' She was regaining control. He wanted to kiss her until she lost it again.

'Why did you kiss me?' She sounded genuinely puzzled.

'Because I wanted to.' Adam shifted a little, releasing her. He felt bereft without the touch of her hand. 'And also because I was afraid that if I asked you first, you would say that it was inappropriate for a chaperon to be kissed.'

She laughed a little disbelievingly. 'Why, so it is, sir. I cannot quite believe that you did it.'

'Believe it. And that I would like to do it again.'

'Oh, no.' Now she took several decided steps back. 'I am no easy entertainment for a rake.'

'I hardly thought you so and I have told you I am no rake. I do not make a habit of kissing chaperons. In the main they are too old and unattractive.'

She laughed again. 'You are absurd, my lord. And unpardonably rude as well.'

'I know. Open the gate.'

'Certainly not.'

'Open the gate. Please, Annis.'

She hesitated visibly. A flash of sheer masculine triumph went through him as he saw the struggle she had with her own feelings and desires. He waited.

'No, I shall not.' Determination gave strength to her tone. 'I have a position to maintain, my lord, and I shall not compromise it further.'

It would be easy enough for him to open the gate himself—or to vault over it. She could not prevent him. They both knew it. The breeze whispered in the branches above them whilst they waited, her gaze holding his. His desire for her was simmering now, but Adam knew it could be rekindled at a second's notice. Yet something held him back. Passion, he was accustomed to, although perhaps not as intense a desire as this. Respect was something else. He admired Annis's strength of will and her determination to do the right thing, even as he thought of overriding her and taking what he wanted. Her resolve was part of her attraction. Passion…and respect. It was a powerful combination. He found he had to honour it.

'Goodnight then, my lady,' he said reluctantly. 'I shall look forward to seeing you again.'

'Goodnight, my lord.' Her tone had eased. Relief? Reluctance? Both, perhaps. 'I see you spoke the truth. You are not such a rake after all.' There was no challenge in her voice, only amusement.

He laughed ruefully. 'I told you I was no such thing. But…I would still like to see you again.'

He saw the shadow of her smile. 'I am persuaded that you will change your mind, my lord. Everything always looks different in the daylight. Goodnight.'

She disappeared up the path to the house and her footsteps died away. Adam was left to make his way back up his own garden and on to the terrace in thoughtful silence.

His wife, Mary, had died when he was only twenty-three and for a while, after the initial grief had dulled a little, he had briefly indulged in all the superficial hellraising of a rake on the town. His efforts to forget Mary had been hopeless. His liaisons had seemed tawdry and supremely unfulfilling, and every time, the cool, sweet memory of her had reasserted itself easily, reminding him that he had not buried his grief at all. Eventually he had joined the army, gone abroad, and fought his battles against the French rather than struggling against his demons at home.

He had been so young when he had fallen in love with Mary that he had never cultivated the hard, dismissive attitude to women that he saw reflected in so many of his contemporaries. To him it had been impossible to see his wife merely as an ornament to grace his home, the mother of his heirs. He had wanted her to be both of those things but they had also been intimately attuned, madly in love. Adam recognised now that it had been a first and very special love that he had had for Mary, but there was no reason to suppose that, had she lived, it would not have matured into something deeper and wiser.

Alas that it had not been meant to be. After he had returned from the Peninsula, he had hardly eschewed all women, but he had never met anyone that he wanted to marry. He had never even considered it. But in the nine years of his widowerhood he had never been moved to passion the way that Annis Wycherley had moved him tonight. He thought ruefully that he must have been without a woman for too long, to want someone so irrationally and so immediately. The only other person that he had ever been drawn to so quickly was Mary.

Annis Wycherley. Fair and sweet, not an innocent young girl and yet strangely untouched. He remembered once again her hesitancy, the way her lips had softened beneath his, warming in response. Such unpractised sweetness could not be feigned and just the memory of it made his body tighten in response.

She had taken a step back from him in more ways than one that night, distancing herself from the disconcerting affinity that had bound them together in the darkness. As a chaperon, he could understand her reserve, but it did not discourage him. He wanted Annis Wycherley and he knew that she was also attracted to him. He was determined to know her better.

* * *

Annis closed the garden door and locked it behind her. Just for a moment, out in the darkness, she had forgotten all about Fanny and the urgent need to find her, and that was unforgivable. Just for a moment, when Adam Ashwick had kissed her, she had forgotten that she was a chaperon.

She shivered slightly. She met plenty of eligible men in her work, but almost all of them were looking through her to see her charges and the fortunes that they brought with them. Annis could not blame them. In public she dressed with deliberate, self-effacing dullness and behaved with stultifying propriety. It would have been impossible for her to do anything else, for surely no one would employ a flighty duenna. Yet Adam Ashwick had not looked through her. He had seen her, even in the dark. Seen her, pursued her, almost caught her. She could barely believe that she had let him kiss her. Or that she had kissed him back.

'I do not do things like that.'

'You just did. And I dare swear that I enjoyed it.'

She had, too. No one had ever kissed her like that. In fact, no one had really kissed her at all. Not with passion and intensity and a sweetness that had melted all her resistance. It had taken her completely by surprise.

'I cannot quite believe that you did it.'

'Believe it. And that I would like to do it again.'

She did not doubt him. No false modesty, nor convention, nor reserve could deny the fact. He had wanted to kiss her and she had wanted him to do so, wanted it with an ache that she could still feel deep within her.

Annis drew a deep breath. Such a situation was not part of her plans at all. She had married young, for security. There had been nothing of love about it. She certainly did not wish to be ambushed by romance now, at the advanced age of seven and twenty, when she had a living to make and an estate to support and no intention of falling for a man who could turn her untried emotions inside out.

She frowned a little. She had known that she was drawn to Adam Ashwick, but she had severely underestimated the extent of that attraction. The direct, complex and perplexing man that she had met in the daylight had given no hint of this other deep and passionate side to his nature. Annis shivered convulsively. These were dark and uncharted waters and she would do better to avoid them.

Except that she had already encouraged him. She knew she had, seduced a little by the moonlight and the romance and more than a little by Adam himself. He had surprised in her a depth of passion she had not known existed. Now that she was alone again it felt like folly, but at the time it had been very sweet.

She hurried along the garden corridor. She had told Adam not to call and no doubt he would not put himself to the trouble of contradicting her. Which was just as well, for she was not at all sure what she could say to him if she were to see him again. It would be awkward. It might be embarrassing. Matters always looked different in the cold light of day, and this was one incident that was best left to moonlight and memory.

And now, she had to find Fanny.

A sliver of light from beneath the door of the servants' quarters caught Annis's eye as she went down the corridor to the hall. In these small town houses the servants' quarters were small, consisting only of a tiny office for the butler, the kitchen and a small dining room. Annis did not employ a butler, and had only four indoor servants—five if one included the maid who waited on Fanny and Lucy. All of them should have been abed by now.

Annis opened the door and went down the stairs. There was a furtive rustling sound, as though a large mouse was running wild in the kitchen. Flickering candlelight betrayed the litter of a large feast: breadcrumbs, chunks of cheese, slivers of ham. At the end of the table sat Fanny, her cheeks bulging, crumbs scattered down her nightdress. For the first time in the acquaintance, Annis thought that Fanny looked discommoded.

'Oh! Lady Wycherley! I was a little hungry…'

'So I see,' Annis said. She felt simultaneously vastly relieved and slightly irritated. 'Tidy up after yourself, Fanny, and go up to bed. You are like to have nightmares with all that cheese.'

'Yes, ma'am,' Fanny murmured submissively. Her sharp eyes took in Annis's outdoor clothes. 'Have you been out, ma'am?' she asked innocently.

'Only into the garden,' Annis said. 'I thought that I heard an intruder and went out to check that everything was secure.'

'How brave of you, ma'am!' Fanny said, eyes huge. 'That is just what I would expect of you. I would never venture out in the dark alone, of course, for my aunt, Lady Mary Crewe, says that it is not at all the done thing.' She stuffed the remaining piece of cheese into her mouth, adding as an afterthought, 'Was anyone out there?'

'No,' Annis said, turning away. 'There was no one at all.'

Chapter Five

Annis was accustomed to keeping her own counsel, but she was surprised to find how strong was the urge to confide when she had luncheon with Sibella the following day. Her cousin had a nose for gossip and an insatiable interest in all things romantic or matrimonial; indeed, Annis often thought that when Sibella was on a scent she was more tenacious than a terrier. It was with this in mind that she told her only the bare outline of her encounter with Adam Ashwick, leaving out all the bits that Sibella would be interested in. What would Sibella say if her notoriously down to earth cousin confessed to kissing a man who was almost a stranger and further, admitted that she had found him shockingly attractive? She would scent a romance and would be forever trying to throw Annis in Adam Ashwick's path, which would be both embarrassing and unhelpful. Annis loved Sibella, for she was warm and comfortable company, but she was not subtle.

'So,' Sibella said, when Annis had finished the tale, 'did you ask Lord Ashwick what he was doing lurking in the lane in the middle of the night?' She stirred another spoonful of sugar into her cup of chocolate. 'It seems a strange time to be taking the air. Do you think that he was waiting for Fanny or Lucy Crossley? Perhaps whilst Fanny was attending to her midnight feast, Lucy was intending to creep out?'

'I think it most unlikely, Sib.' Annis helped herself the last half scone. 'Lucy Crossley has a *tendre* for Barnaby Norwood, as you know, and unlike her sister she is unlikely to do anything foolish to put a potential match at risk. Barney is young and handsome, as well as being the younger son of Lord Norwood, and Lucy is head over ears in love with him.'

'Well, Lord Ashwick is young and handsome, if it comes to that.'

'I do not consider a man of two and thirty to be young,' Annis said. 'Nor is Lord Ashwick precisely handsome.'

Her cousin arched her perfectly plucked brows. 'Lord, you are very exacting! Where does youth end for you, Annis, and middle age begin?'

Annis laughed. She had had this discussion many times before with her cousin, who stubbornly refused to acknowledge that they were growing older. 'Oh, at six and twenty, I think. And you and I, my dear, are both on the shady side of that!'

Sibella looked down at her comfortably spreading figure, clothed today in a gown of blue-and-white striped sarcenet. 'Then I *like* being middle-aged!' She asserted. 'I have three delightful children, a doting husband and a comfortable home.'

'And all before you reach the age of thirty.'

'Hush!' Sibella shuddered. 'I will not have that word spoken in this house.'

'Why not?' Annis smiled maliciously. 'David is already thirty and looks very well upon it and Charles will be thirty in December and I myself will be thirty—'

'Stop!' Sibella held up her hand. 'You will not be thirty for at least two and a half years.'

'You look very well preserved for your age,' Annis said commiseratingly, a twinkle in her eye. 'No one would believe you a day over five and twenty, Sib!'

'Thank you.' Her cousin patted her blonde curls. 'Unlike you, Annis. Where did you get that atrocious dress? It puts years on you! I fear I shall not be going out in public with you if you affect such frightful fashions!'

'Fortunate that no one saw me arriving at your door, then,' Annis said, 'or you would lose your position as Harrogate's most fashionable hostess once and for all. You know that I almost always wear bombazine and a turban, Sib! What self-respecting chaperon would not?'

'Well, you look like a ape-leader! Surely you did not purchase that at Mr Frankland's shop?'

'I did.' Annis stroked the grey bombazine dress lovingly. 'He bought it in especially for me, you know. Apparently everyone else is wearing silk and muslin this summer.'

'Of course they are. It is cooler, for one thing.' Sibella put her head on one side and viewed her cousin with a jaundiced air. 'You know, Annis, you could be quite good looking if only you tried harder. You are lovely and slender—'

'I am considered too tall for a woman.'

'But you have a most elegant figure. If only you did not disguise your curves under those drab clothes—' Sibella broke off as Annis blushed bright red. 'Oh! Whatever have I said?'

'Nothing,' Annis said hastily, putting her plate down with a clatter. She remembered Adam's words: *'You have a most deliciously curved shape'* and she almost ended up spilling her tea as well, her hand shook so much.

Sibella was looking at her strangely. 'What is the matter, Annis? You look very red.'

'The heat!' Annis said hastily, fanning herself vigorously. 'I feel a little warm.'

'Well, I did warn you about the bombazine.' Sibella frowned. 'Where was I? Oh, yes, I was suggesting improvements to your appearance.'

'May we please change the subject, Sib?' Annis asked desperately.

'In a minute. Do you not wish for the benefit of my advice? Your hair is a very pretty blonde colour if only you would let it show—'

'It is unfashionably without curl,' Annis snapped. She pushed away the memory of Adam touching her hair in the moonlight, running his hands through it as he tilted her head up to kiss her. The whole encounter seemed extraordinary. She still could not quite believe it. Adam Ashwick had kissed her. She, Annis Wycherley, a widowed chaperon of seven and twenty, who did not have a romantic bone in her body. She drained her teacup and reached for the pot again. Tea was always efficacious in soothing ruffled sensibilities, so Mrs Hardcastle said.

'You have a beautiful complexion,' Sibella was saying, determined to continue with her appraisal.

Annis sighed. 'And freckles! That, as you know, is death to any pretensions to beauty. Now, may we end this litany?'

Sibella, an accredited beauty since her girlhood, sighed as well. 'All I am saying is that if you did not dress as a dowd it would be a start.'

Annis had herself back in hand by now. 'If I did not dress as a dowd, as you put it, no one would send their wards and daughters to me to chaperon. Remember the fuss that time I went as a governess and did not have the sense to cover up my hair! One would have thought that a glimpse of blonde hair was enough to send a man into a love-struck daze!'

'Oh, it is,' Sibella said, smiling a little self-satisfied smile. 'I have always found it so.'

'Well, I have not—' Annis broke off, realising that this was not entirely true. Adam certainly seemed to have liked her hair. She wriggled a little uncomfortably on the sofa, wishing that she had never raised the subject of Fanny's jaunt the previous evening. It had also raised some other memories that had kept her awake long into the night.

Sibella was still looking at her oddly. 'Are you sure you are quite well, Annis? You seem strangely distracted today and not at all like your usual self. Perhaps your meeting with Lord Ashwick has disturbed you more than you make out.'

'It has nothing to do with Lord Ashwick,' Annis said quickly.

'I see. All the same, it must have been splendidly romantic to meet him out in the garden—in the dark.'

Annis swallowed hard. She had a strong urge to change the subject, but she knew that Sibella would view that as deeply suspicious. Her best option was to affect a cool and casual air, but she was not sure she could carry that off. Whatever else she felt, cool and casual was not it.

'Umm. I would not say that it was romantic. I was looking for Fanny, of course, and Lord Ashwick... Well...' Annis fidgeted slightly as she tried to think of something to say without giving herself away '...he was very pleasant...'

'Pleasant! Annis!' Sibella rolled her eyes. 'Half the ladies in Harrogate would have given their diamonds to be in your shoes last night and the only word you can come up with is pleasant!'

Annis looked defensive. 'What would you have me say? I suppose there are those who would reckon Lord Ashwick charming.'

'How half-hearted you sound!' Sibella's big blue eyes opened wide. 'The *York Herald* was far more fulsome in its comments.'

'Of course. Its publisher wishes to sell many papers and to have all the ladies swooning over Lord Ashwick must surely increase its circulation.'

'Lud, what a cynic you are, Annis!'

'I fear so.' Annis smiled. 'Experience breeds cynicism.'

Sibella tutted. 'What nonsense. I am sure Lord Ashwick is well worth swooning over.'

'If one is the swooning kind one could do worse, I suppose.'

'He has quite a reputation.'

Annis smiled. 'These London gentlemen always do. Some women find those sort of dark good looks unbearably attractive.'

'But not you?' Sibella gave Annis an arch look. 'At least you could have some sympathy with his situation. He has a tragic past.'

'Yes...' Annis thought of the time by the river when Adam had told her of his love for his wife. She felt a little low. The encounter in the garden had been romantic and passionate, but it seemed trivial in comparison to the devotion Adam had felt for Mary.

'I imagine Lord Ashwick's past will encourage many a young lady to think that she will be the one to help him love again!' she said, with deliberate flippancy. 'And how odiously mawkish would that be?'

'You do not have any finer feelings, do you, Annis?' Sibella was looking very irritated now. 'You are handed an opportunity that most right-thinking women would clamour for and what do you do—precisely nothing! I despair of you.'

'Next time that I meet Lord Ashwick in the dark I shall be sure to take your advice,' Annis said, getting to her feet. 'You are a blessing to any indigent chaperon in search of a lord!'

She tried to duck the cushion that her cousin threw with surprising energy and accuracy. 'Ouch! Sib, I did not deserve that.'

'You did,' her cousin asserted. She put out a hand and rang the bell for the maid. 'When do the Misses Crossley return? I could scarce believe my luck when you arrived unaccompanied today!'

'They are back tonight, after a visit to the theatre with the Ansteys. Miss Mardyn is not dancing tonight, I am glad to say. It is *The Forest of Hermanstadt*, which I understand to be a melodrama, so it should suit Fanny very well. Poor Clara Anstey, I doubt she will enjoy the company for all her mother pretends she does. Fanny makes her cry.'

'I am not surprised.' Sibella yawned. 'That child will be one of society's most spiteful, cattish creatures in a few years, Annis. Do you know, she told me that she thought I had quite good taste for a cit's wife! The little madam.'

Annis smothered a smile. 'Oh, dear, she is a dreadful girl. Although I do think that comment merely lacked polish, Sib. Fanny needs more practice before she is truly malicious!'

Sibella sniffed. 'She is quite impertinent enough for me. Besides, David is not a cit! He is a gentleman.'

'How lucky you are. Many of us have to earn money to survive.'

Sibella shuddered. 'Oh, do not be so blunt about it, Annis!'

'Oh, Sib, do not be such a snob!' Annis laughed. 'Money makes the world go round, they say.'

'No, I am sure that that is love!' Sibella frowned.

Annis, quick to avoid a return to Sibella's favourite subject, made for the door. 'If you will excuse me, I shall have to run. Days without Fanny and Lucy are so precious and I am trying to squeeze so much into today.'

Sibella brightened. 'Do you go to the shops?'

'I do. To Gilbertson and Holmes for some new fabric to make an evening gown, and to Wilson's Library, of course.'

Sibella struggled to her feet. 'If you will but allow me fifteen minutes, I shall join you.' She saw the look on her cousin's face and said pleadingly, 'No, Annis, it will not take me an hour to get ready, I swear! Besides, we may take the carriage, which will be quicker. You will not be wasting any of your precious time.'

Annis sighed and gave in. 'Oh, very well. But I know you. You will be wanting to go to Robey's to buy that china ornament of the girl with the apple basket that we saw last week, and once you are in there you will spy something else to your taste…'

Sibella smiled happily. 'Oh, I do hope so. After all, Annis, I need to purchase some trifle to compensate me for being seen with you in that hideous bombazine!'

'You are such a good influence on me, Sib, that I feel I may end up buying poplin instead,' Annis said, as her cousin hurried out of the drawing room, calling for her maid as she went.

'Poplin?' Sibella said over her shoulder. 'For an evening gown? Dearest Annis, I shall not rest until you are arrayed in silk!'

'Did anyone call whilst I was out, Hardy?'

Annis, laden with a roll of muslin, three books from the

circulating library and two week-old copies of the Leeds Mercury, which Hargrave's bookshop always let her have for free, entered the hall of her town house in Church Row and put her parcels down with a sigh of relief. Mrs Hardcastle promptly picked them up again, putting the books on a side table, the material at the bottom of the stairs and the papers under her arm to be taken into the drawing room.

'Mind what you do with those parcels. You know I cannot abide mess, Miss Annis.'

'I am sorry,' Annis said. She tried to sound casual. 'So, did anybody call, Hardy?'

''Appen they might've done.' Mrs Hardcastle put her hands on her hips and watched as Annis drew off her spencer, gloves and bonnet. She took the spencer and laid it gently over the back of the hall chair. 'Were you expecting someone, Miss Annis?'

'No, not really,' Annis said. It would have been both troubling and pleasing of Adam Ashwick to pay his compliments in the daylight, but perhaps on balance she should prefer to forget the whole incident. 'I thought that Mrs Bartle might call,' she said hastily, seeing that Mrs Hardcastle's suspicious gaze was still upon her. 'She said something about a trip to the theatre next week.'

'Aye, well, she didn't pay a visit.'

'Oh. Well, never mind—'

'Lady Copthorne called,' Mrs Hardcastle said. 'She said that you had done a right good job on Miss Fanny and she wondered whether you would consider taking her Eustacia to London for the Little Season.' Mrs Hardcastle sniffed. 'I said as I'd ask you. Between you and me, Miss Annis, you'd do better to refuse.'

'Would I?' Annis looked intrigued. 'I would have expected you to encourage me to accept gainful employment for the autumn, Hardy.'

'Aye, well, if you thought Miss Fanny was bad, Miss Copthorne is worse,' Mrs Hardcastle said darkly. 'Don't say as I didn't warn you, Miss Annis!'

'I shall remember that,' Annis said meekly, thinking that it was a shame she could not always be choosy in her employment. Much of the money she had earned from chaperoning the Crossley girls was already earmarked, intended for improvements to Starbeck.

'A gentleman called,' Mrs Hardcastle added, as Annis started up the stairs. Annis paused, feeling a tickle of anticipation.

'Indeed? Which gentleman was that?'

'Mr Flitwick,' the housekeeper said. There was a twinkle in her berry black eyes. 'Said he needed to measure your foot again for those new winter boots you ordered.' She made it sound as though the cordwainer had suggested some unspeakable perversion. 'To my mind, Mr Flitwick is a bit too anxious to take your measurements, Miss Annis. 'Tis my belief he sees you as a most suitable wife for a prosperous merchant.'

Annis grimaced. 'Oh, dear. Hardy, surely you are teasing me? Mr Flitwick cannot wish to marry me!'

Mrs Hardcastle looked triumphant. 'He doesn't wish to now. I told 'im as you were too good for the likes of him!'

'Oh, Hardy, you didn't!' Annis looked horrified. 'The poor man! He was probably not interested in the first place and now he will be hopelessly embarrassed.' Another thought struck her. 'And I will never get my boots, for he will not speak to me again!'

'Gimson's make boots as well,' the housekeeper pointed out, 'and what's more, Mr Gimson is very happily married already.'

Annis sighed. Mrs Hardcastle had always protected her with the enthusiasm of a mother bear looking after a single cub, but sometimes that enthusiasm went a bit far.

'Thank you, Hardy,' she said. 'I shall bear that in mind when I choose my purchases in future.'

Mrs Hardcastle beamed. Annis ascended another three steps.

'A *second* gentleman called,' Mrs Hardcastle said. This time her tone suggested that Annis was a hussy to have so many gentlemen on a string.

Annis raised her brows. 'And was he good enough for me, Hardy?'

'Don't know about that.' Mrs Hardcastle frowned. 'Mebbe. Francis Ashwick's boy—mind those books, Miss Annis!'

The library books tumbled from Annis's hand and bounced down the stairs to land at Mrs Hardcastle's feet.

'Mess!' that lady mourned, bending creakily to pick them up. Then, 'Thank you, Miss Annis,' as Annis ran back down the steps and put a hand under her elbow to help the housekeeper straighten up.

'This gentleman,' Annis persisted. 'Lord Ashwick, you said—'

'Aye?'

'What did he say when he heard that I was out?'

'Said that you'd told him not to call.'

Annis felt a little deflated. 'Yes, I did.'

'So I asked him,' Mrs Hardcastle said triumphantly, 'why he had bothered to call if you'd told him not.'

'And he said?'

'That it had been a pleasure to meet you in the moonlight and he wanted to pay his respects in the daylight.'

'Very pretty of him.' Annis smiled a little. 'One cannot fault his turn of phrase.'

'Handsome is as handsome does in my book,' Mrs Hardcastle sniffed. 'T'would be a very unusual gentleman who would be good enough for you, Miss Annis.'

Annis's shoulders slumped a little. 'I do not look to marry again, Hardy, truly I do not.'

Mrs Hardcastle patted her hand and passed the books over again. 'Don't blame you after that Sir John, love. Shockin' martinet, that man was. But not all men are like that.'

'I know.' Annis hesitated, a hand on the banister. 'It is just that I could not bear it again, Hardy—accounting for my every move, being allowed no liberty to read, or walk out on my own, or do any of the simple things that give me such pleasure—' She broke off. 'Excuse me. I think I shall go up and rest for a little.'

'What you need is a nice glass of elderflower cordial to refresh you,' Mrs Hardcastle said comfortingly. 'I'll bring it up for you. And don't worry about that Lord Ashwick, love. He'll be back. I'd stake my life on it.'

Annis looked at her and Mrs Hardcastle thought that she looked very young. Young and bewildered.

'Will he?' Annis said. 'But the trouble is, Hardy, I do not know if I want him to. I do not know what I want at all.'

The following day was hot and cloudless. Annis and her charges spent the morning shopping in High Harrogate, where Fanny purchased a bonnet and Lucy, rather sweetly, bought a gift of Whitehead's Essence of Mustard Pills for their uncle. Annis then suggested a walk on The Stray, which was not popular. Fanny hated to exert herself and was inclined to sulk.

'Must we do so, Lady Wycherley? The poor people graze their sheep there and it is uncommonly dirty!'

At that moment, Lucy espied a group of gentlemen riding towards them. 'Oh, look, Fanny! It is Captain Hammond, Lieutenant Greaves and…' she blushed '…Lieutenant Norwood. Lady Wycherley—' she turned a flushed, eager face towards Annis '—may we walk a little way with them? Just across to the livery stables at the Granby?'

'Of course, Lucy,' Annis said gravely, amused at how attractive a walk had suddenly become. She was certain that Lieutenant Norwood was going to declare himself soon and so was making sure that he and Lucy had every opportunity to be together.

The gentlemen dismounted and there was a flurry of greeting. Lucy took Barnaby Norwood's arm and Annis watched in secret entertainment as Fanny tried to decide whether to walk with Captain Hammond or Lieutenant Greaves. Captain Hammond had the rank, of course, but the Lieutenant was decidedly more dashing. And whichever one she rejects, Annis thought, will end up having to escort me! Her lips curved into a little smile at the thought of the young man having to hide his disappointment.

'Good morning, Lady Wycherley.'

Annis jumped and spun round. She recognised Adam Ashwick's voice, although his tall figure was little more that a silhouette against the sun. Annis suddenly wished that she were carrying a parasol like the girls. Not only did she feel decidedly too hot in her grey bombazine, she also felt strangely vulnerable. She raised a gloved hand to shade her eyes.

'Good morning, Lord Ashwick.'

Adam smiled at her. 'May I offer you my arm across The Stray, ma'am? It looks as though your party is headed that way.'

At the same moment, Fanny made her choice in Lieutenant Greaves's favour and turned back to Annis.

'You may have Captain Hammond, ma'am, which is only appropriate as he is senior and so are you—oh!'

Her gaze fell on Ashwick and narrowed slightly. 'Lord…Ashwick, is it not? I believe we saw you at the theatre, sir.'

Adam bowed very slightly. 'Miss Crossley.'

Fanny fluttered, transparently intent on monopolising him. She dropped Lieutenant Greaves's arm and bustled forward, placing herself between Annis and Adam. 'Well, this is famous, sir! We met in London earlier in the Season.'

'I recollect.' There was something in Adam's tone that suggested his memory of her was not a particularly outstanding one. 'I hope that you are well, Miss Crossley. Miss Lucy…'

He bowed and Lucy Crossley blushed, as well she might.

'Are you settled in Harrogate for a space, my lord?' Fanny was gushing now and Annis watched, torn between amusement and embarrassment on the girl's behalf. She had a dreadful feeling that Adam was about to deliver a crushing set-down.

'For a while,' Adam said, a slight hardness entering his voice. 'At the moment, however, I am here to escort Lady Wycherley wherever she wishes to go.'

Fanny turned to Annis and her gaze sharpened. 'Lady Wycherley? But…did you know that she is our chaperon, my lord? I was not aware that you even knew her.'

Adam looked at Annis. There was a smile lurking deep in his eyes.

'Well,' he said, 'I do.' He held out his arm to her. 'Shall we proceed, ma'am?'

There was an edge of authority to his voice that no one cared to gainsay. Fanny turned back to the spurned Lieutenant and in short order she had taken his arm, Lucy had fallen in with Lieutenant Norwood again and the luckless Captain Hammond had taken charge of the three horses and was leading them back to the livery stable.

'Oh, dear,' Annis said ruefully, as she and Adam fell into step behind the other four, ' I was so afraid that you were about to give Miss Crossley a most tremendous set-down, my lord. I must thank you for your forbearance.'

'It is more than the silly little chit deserves,' Adam said. There was a flash of anger in his eyes. 'Did I know that you were their chaperon, indeed! She should be grateful for that privilege instead of being intolerably snobbish about it! You have all the qualities she needs to learn and yet she has the impertinence—' He broke off, scowling blackly.

Annis glanced at him, a little shaken by the vehemence of his tone. His grim gaze was fixed on the back of Fanny Crossley's head and there was a frown between his brows. When he saw Annis looking at him, however, his expression lightened and he smiled.

'I beg your pardon, ma'am. I should not have said that.'

Annis smiled back. 'Do not apologise, my lord. I know that some of my charges think themselves better bred than I—'

'And some, knowing they are not, are even more ill behaved, I'll warrant!' Adam laughed grimly.

Annis made a slight gesture. 'Whatever the case, it does not upset me. I take their money and I do my work.'

There was a small silence between them.

'I am glad that I have caught up with you at last, ma'am,' Adam said in an undertone, as they fell back a little from the main group. 'I called to see you yesterday, but found only your housekeeper at home.'

Annis nodded. 'Mrs Hardcastle. Yes, I understand that she quizzed you shamelessly about your visit.'

'I remember that her mother was much the same,' Adam said, ruefully. 'Did you know that her family worked for my father at Eynhallow? They are true Yorkshire stock, calling a spade a spade.'

'At least one knows where one stands with such blunt honesty,' Annis said.

'Indeed. I believe that you are also Yorkshire born and bred, Lady Wycherley? There is about you the same sort of frankness. It is refreshing and unusual to find in *ton* society.'

Annis smiled slightly. 'I hope that I am not so forthright as Hardy! But I am certainly Yorkshire born, my lord, if not bred. My father being in the navy, we travelled about a great deal.'

'Of course. I had not forgot.' Adam's gaze was warm as it rested on her and Annis felt herself blush a little. She had been fearful that when they met again Adam might approach her with some familiarity, which would be embarrassing, particularly in public. Now she realised that she need not have feared this. Though there was a shadow of a smile about his mouth as he watched her, she could not fault him for his manner to her. He was as respectful as ever she could have demanded. She felt herself relax a little.

'What of your own antecedents, my lord?' she queried lightly. 'Can you claim a true Yorkshire pedigree?'

'Certainly, for both my parents are from the county. Further back the bloodline is more mixed.' Adam squared his shoulders. 'I do believe there have even been some instances of Ashwick and Lafoy alliances, Lady Wycherley. Our two families go back a long way.'

'I cannot believe that, for we have always been of yeoman stock,' Annis said, laughing, 'and far too far beneath the notice of the Ashwick lords! Mrs Hardcastle says that your family has grown mighty high in the instep, my lord!'

Adam looked amused. 'I see that people have been talking.'

Annis looked at him from under her lashes. 'People do talk about you. It is only natural when you are one of the most...' she hesitated '...one of the most prominent landowners in the locality.'

Adam sighed. 'I accept that but I think it unfair that you should set me so high when you are the granddaughter of a Marquis and connected to half the noble families in England!'

Annis laughed. 'If you have heard that, you must also have heard that my mother's family do not acknowledge me. When one's mother runs away with a sea captain I fear it is inevitable.' She made a slight gesture. 'It is perfectly understandable that people should discuss *you*, my lord, but I cannot believe that anyone has been talking about *me*!'

Adam stopped and took her gloved hand in his. 'I have been asking about you,' he said softly.

There was something in his tone that brought the blood up into Annis's cheeks. She knew that this was the moment she had to make certain things clear between them.

'Then pray do not ask about me in future, sir.' There was a note of entreaty in her voice. She freed herself and walked on. 'I have a job of work to do, and it does not allow for an idle flirtation with the local lord of the manor.'

It was Adam's turn to laugh. 'How charmingly medieval you make that sound, as though I go around taking my pleasure with the local populace! I do assure you, ma'am, that is hardly my intention.'

'No…' Annis looked troubled '…but when we met two nights ago…'

'Yes?'

'I feel that I must tell you… Oh, how difficult this is!' Annis raised her eyes to his face. 'I fear that you must have received a certain impression of me which is quite false, my lord. I do not generally go around embracing strange gentlemen in the garden—' She broke off in acute embarrassment.

Adam gave her a brief smile. 'You need not tell me that, Lady Wycherley. I never imagined that you did.'

Annis gave him a glance that was half-ashamed, half-grateful. 'Thank you, my lord. So we are agreed that it should never have happened.'

Adam straightened slightly. 'I certainly did not say that. That is a different matter entirely.'

Annis shot him a pleading look. 'But surely—'

'I am not going to pretend that I did not enjoy it.' Adam met her gaze very directly. 'You would want the truth from me, I know, and the truth is that, given the opportunity, I would do exactly the same thing again.'

Annis's face flamed. He was not making this easy for her. In a town the size of Harrogate it would be well nigh impossible to avoid him and her chaperon's duties meant that she was obliged to enter into society. She could not escape Adam, but she had already resolved that the two of them should behave as though the moonlight encounter had never occurred. Now Adam was telling her he did not want to forget it.

'Please understand that I have a living to earn, sir,' she said urgently. 'Whatever it is that you want, whatever game you are playing at my expense—'

Adam stopped abruptly and turned to her. His face was stern. 'I play no games, Lady Wycherley. What I want is to know you better. There, it is said and now you cannot misunderstand me. Yet if you do not desire the same thing, tell me now and I shall not trouble you again.'

There was a silence whilst Annis struggled with her feelings. She could not deny that she found his company enjoyable, but the demands of her profession were strong and stronger still was her fear of losing her independence for a second time.

'You left it too long,' Adam said quietly.

Annis looked at him. There was a spark in his gaze that lit something within her, something that made her shiver.

She frowned. 'You are very direct, my lord. You compel me to answer.'

'I am renowned for my frankness,' Adam said. He smiled. 'What is your answer?'

Annis gave him a very straight look. 'My circumstances do not allow for me to pursue your acquaintance, my lord. Regardless of my feelings, as a chaperon I cannot afford to give rise to gossip and conjecture through my behaviour. That is all there is to it. Please say that you understand.'

Adam sighed. 'I understand your reasoning. I even admire your resolve. I simply do not agree with you.'

'It does not need for you to agree, my lord,' Annis said, a shade acerbically, 'only accept.'

Adam shrugged. 'Then I respect your position, ma'am.' His expression eased a little. 'However, I hope you will at least accept my escort across The Stray?'

'Of course. Thank you.' Annis tried to smile, but her heart felt leaden. This had been her choice and yet now she felt quite miserable to have given him his *congé*. She had seldom felt such a conflict between her feelings and her inclination and she did not care for it.

She became aware of Fanny's inquisitive face peering at her. The girl was almost tripping over as she tried to see what Annis and Adam could be talking about together. Annis gave herself a little shake and rearranged her face into the blandest of expressions. She raised her voice slightly.

'Do you find it strange to be no longer in the military, Lord Ashwick? I understand that you sold out a few years ago?'

Adam saw the direction of her gaze and took his cue from her. 'In some ways I find it odd, Lady Wycherley. It gives a structure to life that can be lacking otherwise. But I have Eynhallow, and an unconscionable amount of work to do to get the estate back into shape.'

He smiled at her. 'And what do you do with your time, ma'am? I find myself intrigued to know of the entertainments available to young ladies—and their chaperon!'

Annis smiled self-deprecatingly. 'I am sure that you do not, my lord. I can think of little that would interest you less.'

Adam quirked a brow. 'I assure you that I am very interested to know how you spend the day, ma'am. You are always so busy.'

'Well…' Annis made a slight gesture '…there are plenty of activities for the young ladies to indulge in. We might visit Wilson's Circulating Library, or the shops, or go for a small walk, as you see.'

'And in the evenings I suppose there are always the dances at the Granby or the Crown or the Dragon.'

'Every evening is accounted for by some social outing,' Annis agreed. 'The Theatre Royal has a show on alternate nights to the balls, and then there are the private parties, of course. Sometimes we even venture out of Harrogate to visit the surrounding countryside.' She laughed. 'Fountains Abbey was a great hit with the Misses Crossley, you know, and Knaresborough even more so. The castle ruins could have been taken straight from one of Mrs Radcliffe's books, complete with clanking chains and resident ghost!'

Adam smiled at her. 'Did they like the Dropping Well?'

'Miss Lucy did. Miss Crossley found it a little slow and said she was afraid she would be turned to stone herself with the boredom of it all!'

They laughed together. And stopped together. And looked at each other in a silence fraught with possibilities. Then Adam sighed.

'You are not making this easy, Lady Wycherley. You are delightful company, you know, and I would not deliberately deny myself that pleasure.'

Annis looked away. 'Thank you for the compliment, my lord.'

'I find it astonishing that you have not married again, particularly as you must meet plenty of gentlemen in your line of work. Can there be a rational explanation?'

Annis laughed unwillingly. 'There is a simple one. I always try to divert the attention of the gentlemen towards my charges. *They* are the ones requiring to make an advantageous match, not myself.'

'My dear Lady Wycherley…' Adam drew her slightly closer '…you could not divert my attention to them if you tried!'

Annis bit back an answering smile. It was the devil's own job to resist that charm. The warmth, the dangerous intimacy, was still there between them despite her refusal to acknowledge it and her determination to avoid him.

'I am happy to say that the Misses Crossley are both already spoken for, my lord, so you would be too late, anyway,' she said primly.

'And yourself?'

Annis allowed a tinge of coldness to creep into her tone. 'As you are aware, sir, I have already been married and have no inclination to repeat the exercise.' She tilted the brim of her bonnet slightly to block his view of her face.

'You must have married very young.' Adam's tone had softened.

'I did. I was seventeen.' There was a lump in Annis's throat and she had no notion where it had come from. She turned to look at him and the sun dazzled her momentarily. With relief she realised that they had reached the far side of The Stray and were almost at the Granby.

'Thank you for your company, my lord,' she said formally. 'I believe our ways part here.'

'And you are certain that I am not to see you again? I cannot convince you to change your mind?' He was dangerously persuasive. Annis steeled herself against that charm.

'In a town the size of Harrogate I imagine it will be inevitable.'

'That was not precisely what I meant.'

'I did not think that it was.' Their gazes locked. Annis took a deep breath. 'The answer to your question, my lord, is no. I explained why earlier.'

Adam gave a sharp sigh. Annis could see the annoyance in his eyes. 'I cannot agree—' He broke off, running a hand through his hair. 'Confound it! This is not what I had wanted. I cannot believe that I have agreed to your strictures.'

Annis gave him an appealing look. 'Please, my lord! We did agree…'

Adam sighed again. 'I know. I am regretting my promise deeply.'

Fanny and Lucy were busy disentangling themselves from their escorts with much chatter and giggling. Annis gave Adam her hand.

'Thank you, Lord Ashwick.' She was not speaking of his escort and they both knew it. 'I am indebted to you.'

Adam gave her a faint, rueful smile and bowed. 'Good day, Lady Wycherley.'

He walked away. Fanny and Lucy stared after him, mouths inelegantly agape.

'He is very handsome,' Lucy ventured.

'No, he is not!' Fanny snapped. 'He is too plainly dressed. And his manners lack polish.'

Annis's lips twitched. Fanny had evidently taken offence that Adam Ashwick had not shown more of an interest in her.

'Come along, girls! Let us take a little luncheon here and rest in the shade before we take a carriage back home. We need to have plenty of time to prepare for the ball tonight.'

Lucy brightened but Fanny was still staring after Adam's departing figure, her lower lip stuck out.

'Did you know that Lord Ashwick ran off with the vicar's daughter, Lady Wycherley? How frightfully vulgar is that?'

'I should have thought it was of all things romantic,' Lucy said bravely.

Fanny gave her sister a scornful glance. 'He has a shocking reputation,' she said. 'Why, they say that after his wife died, he became the greatest libertine in London! He is not at all suitable company for a chaperon and I am surprised that you allowed him to approach us at all!'

'Thank you, Fanny,' Annis said tranquilly, mentally counting the number of days until Sir Robert Crossley came to take his nieces away. 'It is thoughtful of you to warn me. I do not believe that any of us were in imminent danger and, anyway, I never listen to spiteful gossip.'

She turned and shepherded her charges into the inn, and

the door swung closed behind them, hiding Adam Ashwick's tall figure and taking away the temptation for her to watch him into the distance. She had sent him away, and stopped something before it had really started. It had been the only thing to do, yet she could not help wondering what would have happened if she had given in to her instincts and agreed to meet him again. Now she would never know.

Chapter Six

'Had you thought about dosing yourself up with the spa waters, Ash?' Edward Ashwick enquired over dinner one evening a week later. 'They say that it is sovereign for ill humours and you have been like a bear with a sore head this week past.' He shot his brother a grin. 'I do not scruple to mention it because the whole family is aware of your bad temper.'

'The whole house is aware...' Adam's sister Della murmured.

'Probably the whole town,' the Dowager Lady Ashwick finished.

Adam allowed his gaze to move around the table from one to the next. Both his siblings and his mother were watching him with identical expressions of sympathy in their grey eyes. The Dowager Lady Ashwick, a diminutive brunette who had been married from the schoolroom and was still extremely well preserved, even though she was on the very shady side of forty, gave him a fond maternal smile.

'We thought that it might be difficult for you returning to Harrogate after so long, darling,' she murmured. 'We *do* so sympathise...'

'Of course,' Della echoed compassionately. 'Pray be as unpleasant to us as you wish, Adam. We shall not take offence.'

A reluctant smile pierced Adam's gloom. 'I beg your pardon. I had no idea that I was being so ill humoured.'

'Surly,' Edward confirmed.

'Testy,' Della agreed.

'Grumpy,' the Dowager said sadly. 'I suppose it is all to do with Lady Wycherley.'

Adam put down his knife and fork and gave his brother a hard stare. 'What have you been saying, Ned?'

'I? Nothing, I swear.' Edward looked the epitome of virtue. 'Della happened to comment to me that she had seen you walking on The Stray with Lady Wycherley last week—'

'The devil she did!'

'And I observed that you had spent some time in that lady's company and that you seemed to admire her.'

'Which we already knew, Adam,' The Dowager said. 'Ned was breaking no confidences, I assure you. We all saw you at the theatre that night. You looked positively *épris*! We were so happy for you, darling.' A tiny frown marred her brow. 'Except that you do not seem so cheerful now. Whatever can have gone wrong?'

Adam frowned ferociously. He could scarcely be indelicate enough to tell his mother that he ached for a woman he could not have, but that was the nature of the problem. He had not seen Annis Wycherley for seven days now and she haunted his thoughts and his dreams. He had even found himself walking past the house in Church Row hoping to catch sight of her. It was juvenile and sentimental, but he did not seem able to help himself. He had fallen hard and no one was more surprised than he.

'Lady Wycherley and I are mere acquaintances,' he said

shortly. 'She has indicated that she does not wish to take our association any further.'

'Ah,' Edward said significantly. 'That explains everything, of course.'

'Has she misunderstood about Miss Mardyn's position?' Della enquired innocently. 'That might account for a reluctance to pursue the acquaintance. If so, perhaps I could explain to her—'

Adam scowled. 'Pray do not even think of doing so, Della.'

The Dowager was looking puzzled. 'I do not entirely understand, Adam. Lady Wycherley indicated that she did not wish to see you and you…agreed?'

Adam's scowl deepened. 'I did, Mama. One cannot force one's attentions on an unwilling lady.'

Della smiled. 'Very noble of you, Adam. Yet Lady Wycherley seemed to be enjoying your company when I saw the two of you together. Whatever can you have done to give her a dislike of you?'

Adam threw down his napkin and got up from the table. He was sorely tempted to tell his interfering family to mind their own business, but he knew that they had his best interests at heart. Besides, he owed them an apology for his bad moods. He found himself providing a reluctant explanation.

'It cannot have escaped your notice that Lady Wycherley is a chaperon.'

'A very proper one.' The Dowager nodded.

'Indeed. Thank you, Mama. That is exactly it.' Adam swallowed his glass of wine and walked over to the window with an impatient step. 'A proper chaperon cannot entertain gentleman callers without losing her reputation. Lady Wycherley drew this fact to my attention and I was forced to agree with her. It is as simple as that.'

'I can understand her point of view,' Della agreed. 'People can be so gossipy and cattish. Yet if your intentions are honourable, Adam... At least, I take it that you *do* have honourable intentions?'

Catching Edward's amused eye, Adam reflected on the difficulties of even attempting to engage in a courtship under his family's eye.

'I would have if I was given the chance!'

'Then we may help you,' Della said.

'Yes, indeed,' Lady Ashwick said. 'If you have honourable intentions, Adam, I pledge my support as well. I should like it above all things to see you wed again.'

Adam felt slightly bemused. His family seemed to be working even faster than he was. 'Thank you. Would you vouchsafe to me exactly what you intend to do?'

The Dowager waved an airy hand. 'There is no great difficulty. Della and I shall contrive for Lady Wycherley to speak with you again.' She gave her firstborn a fond smile. 'After that, it is entirely up to you, Adam, and if you do not take your opportunity you will not deserve her anyway!'

'And if you would take the spa water in the meantime, Ash, it will be the better for all of us,' Edward added.

The sound of the bell broke into their laughter. The butler's footsteps approached.

'Mr Ingram has called, my lord,' Tranter said expressionlessly. 'I have put him in the study. He asks for a moment of your time.'

Some of the warmth and laughter seemed to drain from the room. Della had turned pale and now she rose to her feet, steadying herself against the edge of the table.

'Mama, I believe that I shall retire. No, pray do not concern yourself. I am quite well. I simply do not wish to meet Mr Ingram.'

The Dowager nodded. She took her daughter's arm.
'Neither do I. Come, let us go upstairs and decide on our
gowns for the next ball. Adam, Edward…you will excuse
us? I trust that that man will not take up too much of your
time.'

'Do you wish me to leave you to see Ingram alone,
Ash?' Edward asked, as he and Adam went out into the
hall. 'Whatever your preference.'

Adam shook his head. 'I would rather that you were
with me, Ned. The man is a slippery customer and I would
rather have a witness—and some moral support.'

Edward nodded and they went into the study together.
Ingram was standing before the fireplace, examining the
invitations that adorned the mantel. He turned to look at
them. Neither Adam nor Edward spoke.

'Good evening to you, gentlemen both. Ashwick…
Reverend… I apologise for calling in the evening but when
a man is busy at work during the day…' Ingram's greeting
was breezy but his eyes were shrewd as they moved from
one brother to the other.

Edward inclined his head slightly. A faint, cold smile
touched his lips for a fleeting moment before he moved
away and took up his station by the fire, one booted foot
resting casually on the marble step, his arm along the mantel. As a means of making Ingram move away, it was admirable. Adam remained just inside the door, his stance
wary, his expression closed.

'Good evening, Ingram.' Adam's voice was smooth but
not at all welcoming. He did not offer Ingram his hand.
'What can I do for you?'

'I'm come to ask a favour of you, my lord,' Ingram said.
He had a cultured voice, but where Adam's tones held a
careless patrician drawl Ingram's were a little too carefully

cultivated. Very occasionally, when under stress, he would waver back to the flatter vowels of his childhood.

'How intriguing,' Adam said politely. He could feel Edward's gaze on them, full of suspicion—and warning. Ned knew that he had a hot temper buried deep under the easy exterior and if anyone could provoke it, this man would. 'I was under the impression that our business was concluded, sir. The debt is paid.'

Ingram nodded. He removed his gloves and came forward to the fire, dry-rubbing his hands before the blaze. 'I know I'm not welcome in this house. The matter of your brother-in-law's debts was unfortunate, but business is business, my lord.'

'It is certainly unfortunate that the one business that you and Lord Tilney ventured into together did not prosper,' Adam agreed, with an edge to his voice. He hated this fencing, this polite fiction, when they both knew that this man had brought the Ashwick family close to ruin. The debt, thirty thousand pounds, had been huge and the Ashwicks had never been rich.

'Aye, the debt is settled, right enough,' Ingram said now, his tone friendly but his gaze piercing. 'There was another matter, however, which I believe that both you gentlemen may help me with.'

'And that is?' Edward spoke for the first time. He took a draught of brandy, but his gaze never left Ingram's face.

'Property, influence…' Ingram thrust his hands into his jacket pocket and rocked back on his heels, turning towards Adam again. 'You have a very pretty parcel of land that abuts my estate at Linforth, my lord. I hear that the farm there is not so profitable for you, but I could make it turn in a tidy income. With some of my improvements it would soon be on its feet again.'

'I hear that people do not like your improvements, Ingram,' Edward said coolly. 'There is discontent in the villages—'

Ingram barely flicked him a glance. 'They'll learn to live with it.' He looked at Adam. 'If you could see your way clear to selling the farm to me, my lord—at a reduced rate, of course, seeing as how it's in poor shape...'

'I cannot do that.' Adam felt the anger rising in him and forced himself to crush it down. He kept his tone even. 'I have a tenant in that farm, Ingram, and even if I did not I have no wish to sell.'

There was a taut silence in the room.

'Ah, well,' Ingram said, after a moment, 'you might wish to reconsider in a moment, my lord. But first I had a favour to ask, like. On behalf of my wife.'

Adam raised his eyebrows. Ingram shifted a little.

'Venetia—my wife—has taken it into her head to enter society. And as you are so influential in those circles, my lord, we thought you might smooth our way, sithee. You and your brother...' he gave Edward a mocking bow '...have the entrée to so many events that we, alas, do not.'

Adam turned away. He knew it was Ingram, not his wife, who had overweening social ambitions and he was damned if he was going to assist him. 'You are already prominent in local society, Ingram. I do not see how I may help you.'

'There's society and society, is there not, my lord?' Ingram said. His tone matched Adam's for blankness. 'Now I may be welcome to attend the town assemblies on account of my money, but there are some drawing rooms where I cannot enter—' He broke off as he caught the ghost of a smile that passed between Adam and Edward. 'I see you understand me, my lord. Society is a mighty tricky thing for a self-made man. So much snobbery...'

'Disgraceful as it is,' Adam said coolly, 'I do not believe that I can change that for you, Ingram.'

A faint flush came to Ingram's cheek. 'Like I said, my lord, you may wish to reconsider. It would be embarrassing if I were to make public the details of your brother-in-law's debt…'

Adam's head came up sharply. 'I understood that we had a gentleman's agreement that the details would never be published, Ingram.'

Ingram spread his hands in a helpless gesture. 'Not being a gentleman, my lord, I would not understand the principle of such a thing. However, I could learn very quickly if you were prepared to host a dinner for Venetia and myself, just as a start, like…'

Adam took a deep breath. This was blackmail, no more, no less. He had agreed to settle the debt and had thought that he had got off fairly lightly with the settlement that Lafoy had negotiated. Now he saw that that had just been the beginning. First there was the property. Ingram had chosen to strike when he knew that the Ashwicks were weak through payment of Tilney's debt. He would whittle away at the Eynhallow lands to expand his own estate, making life a misery for the tenants and villagers should Adam choose to cut his losses and sell. Then there was the more intangible issue of influence. There was no doubt that Adam could, if he chose, bring Samuel Ingram and his wife into fashion. He had the social power to do so for, in a small society like Harrogate, plenty would follow his lead. He felt revolted at the thought. To have to compromise his own principles and toady to Ingram simply because his brother-in-law had made a bad business decision… It was intolerable. It was not just pride or snobbery talking, Adam thought furiously. He hated to be coerced by any man.

'I am sorry but I cannot help you, Ingram,' he said, very firmly. 'I do not choose to enter Harrogate society myself and therefore cannot undertake to sponsor anyone else.'

Ingram shrugged. 'No hasty decisions, lad. I am sure that you would not wish Lord Tilney's poor judgement to become a matter for common tittle-tattle.'

Adam felt his temper slipping. 'If you understood more about being a gentleman, Ingram, you would know why I say tell everyone and be damned!' he said, through his teeth. 'Although I would deplore your behaviour, I would not lower myself to comment upon it in public!'

Ingram's mouth thinned to a tight line. 'Well, well, my lord, there's plain speaking! You might be so hardy, but what would your dear sister say? Such a charming lady, but not strong since her husband's death…not strong at all.'

Once again there was a tense silence. Adam caught Edward's look of mingled warning and disquiet. He knew his brother well and he knew that look. Ned was telling him to play for time, to give them a little breathing space. Adam made a final attempt to clamp down on his anger. An expression that was colder still hardened his lean, masculine features.

'Very well, then, Ingram. I will give consideration to your proposals, but you must give me a little time.'

Ingram relaxed. 'That is very sensible of you, lad. I'll call again in a day or two. My Venetia is not a patient woman, you see, and would like an answer soon as maybe.' His eyes narrowed to slits. 'See to it, laddie.'

Adam gave him a stony look. 'I hear you, Ingram.'

Edward moved across to the door and held it open. Ingram, showing the first signs of hesitation he had displayed all evening, paused for a moment before he marched through.

'Good night, my lord. Good night, Reverend.'

He appeared to expect some response, but when none was forthcoming his expression hardened and he stomped out, his footsteps echoing across the stone flags of the floor.

There was an ominous calm in the study until the sound of Ingram's footsteps had faded away and then the front door closed. Edward was the first to break the silence.

'As well that Della had already retired for the night,' he observed. 'She can scarcely bring herself to be civil to Ingram if she has the misfortune of bumping into him. She ain't *weak*, though! Ingram is barking up the wrong tree there!'

Adam's face was a mask that splintered suddenly into vivid anger. 'God *damn* the man! I feel like a fish wriggling on the end of his line!'

Edward took his brandy glass from his hand, moved over to the oak sideboard and poured more brandy for both of them.

'Your metaphor is not apt,' he said slowly. 'I was watching you and a wolf at bay springs more easily to mind. Ingram should have a care not to push you too far.'

Adam took the proffered glass and stalked across to the fire, kicking a log deeper into the glowing embers. There was a hiss of flame.

'Steady,' Edward observed. 'Hoby will never forgive you if you set fire to those boots, Ash. Besides, imagine the figure you would cut, hopping around on one leg as you try to remove them without the help of your valet! Not worth it, old fellow.'

Adam's dark expression lightened with a glimmer of a smile, but he did not pause in his restless pacing. 'If only there had been one iota of evidence to suggest that the business with the *Northern Prince* was not above board.'

'Wishful thinking, old chap.' Edward swallowed his brandy in one gulp. 'The ship went down right enough. It was just our bad luck.'

'Then if not that, how did Ingram persuade Humphrey to invest in the first place? Perhaps he was blackmailing him.'

Edward shook his head. 'Ash, Humphrey may have shown bad judgement in borrowing heavily at a time of economic uncertainty, but sadly that was in character.'

Adam was silent. He knew that this was true.

He threw himself down in his armchair. 'If I could find any suggestion that Ingram's business dealings are illegal—'

'Others have tried that. The man is too clever to be caught. Besides, just because Ingram is ruthless in business does not make his dealings illegal.'

Adam brought his fist down hard on the arm of his chair in impotent anger.

'Damn it, Ned, the man is provably a blackmailer! What was he trying to do this evening?'

Edward shrugged. 'I concede that, but his methods are cunning. He would say that all he has asked of you is a favour...'

'And if I do not comply, he will drag Humphrey's name through the mud.' Adam swallowed a mouthful of brandy, frowning hard at the flames in the grate. 'Well, devil take it, he will have to make good his threats. I will not become Ingram's pet poodle and entertain him and his wife, and I am sure that Della will understand my reasons!'

'You may find that Ingram has greater matters on his mind soon,' Edward observed. 'I hear he has offered the tenant farm at Shawes for an exorbitant rent. The villagers already hate him for enclosing Shawes Common, and if we have a poor summer and wages are low, that hatred will erupt.'

There was a silence, but for the sigh of the wind in the trees outside.

'There was already trouble at one of the new tollhouses this week and it is only half-built.' Adam frowned. 'Do you think that matters will get worse, Ned?' He knew that Edward, as Rector of Eynhallow, had far closer an understanding of what went on in Harrogate's surrounding villages than any of the landowners could hope for.

'We have all the ingredients.' Edward looked grim. 'If there is a food shortage and a poor harvest, there will be crime and unrest. We've seen it happen before, Ash. And Ingram is turning the screw on a populace already sunk in poverty. I have a bad feeling…'

'It's an interesting prospect, albeit it a damned unpleasant one.' Adam shifted a little in his chair. 'There's already been the fire at Shawes.'

'Arson,' Edward said, nodding. 'It was meant as a warning, but Ingram is so thick-skinned it would take more than that.'

'What can we do?'

'Keep an ear to the ground. If there is trouble in the villages, there may be a way to take advantage…'

Adam raised his brows. 'Devil take it, little brother! Is that really a man of the cloth speaking?'

'God helps those who help themselves,' Edward said righteously.

'Does he? I don't believe I've ever read that bit of the Bible! Would it be next to the passage about men of God stirring up trouble from the pulpit?'

Edward looked positively angelic. 'I am sure you overestimate my influence, Ash.'

'I am sure that I do not.' Adam gave him a straight look, which Edward met with one of his own.

'Of course,' he said reflectively, 'we should dwell on the one matter that requires our gratitude…'

Adam raised his brows enquiringly.

'That Ingram at least has no daughters of marriageable age!' Edward said, with a grin. 'Or we should both be leg-shackled before you could say thirty thousand pounds in debt!'

'It gives a whole new meaning to the phrase parson's mousetrap,' Adam agreed gravely.

The weather broke the following night and it rained for the whole of the next day, putting Fanny and Lucy in a fretful mood and echoing Annis's own feelings of gloom. She sat on the window seat in the drawing room, watching the rain streak the glass and the passers-by hurry along the pavements, head into the wind, umbrellas held before them like bayonets. Fanny and Lucy picked at their needlework and chattered. Annis sat quietly, wishing that Adam would call and reminding herself that he would not since she had specifically asked him not to. Nevertheless, she missed him.

In the evening they were invited to dinner at Hansard Court, Sir Everard Doble's home just outside Harrogate. It was both an opportunity for Fanny to inspect the house and for the widowed Lady Doble to inspect her prospective daughter-in-law, and everyone was on tenterhooks. The dinner was poor and the house dark and dismal, but Fanny's desire for a title outweighed all else and she sparkled, making Annis wince with only a few ill-mannered remarks. After dinner, whilst Fanny entertained them on

the pianoforte, Lady Doble plumped herself down next to
Annis on the sofa.

'The chit will do well enough, I suppose.' Lady Doble
did not trouble to lower her voice, and Annis reflected that
her future mother-in-law might almost outdo Fanny in vul-
garity. 'How much money will she be bringing?'

'Forty thousand pounds,' Annis said, lowering her
voice.

'Forty thousand, eh?' Lady Doble bellowed. 'Perfect!'

After that it was only a matter of form for Sir Everard
to whisk Fanny off to the conservatory to propose and to
be accepted. Annis left Hansard Court feeling deeply relieved for a great many reasons, and wrote to Sir Robert
Crossley that very night.

It was Miss Lucy Crossley's turn to receive a declaration
the following week, when Barnaby Norwood came up to
scratch and delivered himself of a romantic proposal in the
drawing room. Annis congratulated Lucy wholeheartedly,
wrote a second letter to Sir Robert, and felt almost eu-
phoric with relief. Even Fanny, whose pride was satisfied
to be marrying a baronet rather than a mere Honourable,
was gracious to her little sister.

The Monday night ball the following week took place
at the Dragon and both Crossley sisters were boasting
about their engagements. It was another humid night. Annis sat amongst the chaperons, fanning herself ineffectually
and wishing that she had not chosen turkey red for her
gown that evening. With the current heat it was likely to
be a close match for her face. The combination of a
crowded ballroom, a hundred candles and a hot summer
night was not a happy one. Even the feather in her turban
was wilting.

She turned her head slowly to scan the dance floor. Lucy was dancing the quadrille with a half-pay officer, but was behaving with the perfect decorum of a girl whose future was already assured. Barnaby Norwood was watching indulgently and chatting to a group of fellow officers. Annis smiled to herself. Lucy was a sweet girl and deserved her happiness. Fanny was dancing with Sir Everard and looking very pleased with herself. Annis's smile became a little cynical. Fanny knew that all eyes were upon her, envying her the good luck and forty thousand pounds that had secured Sir Everard's title.

The door to the ballroom opened and a number of late-comers pressed their way into the throng. The Master of Ceremonies was bowing and scraping, and Annis's smile turned wry as she recognised the new arrivals. Samuel Ingram and his youthful wife Venetia were always warmly welcomed to the town's social events. It mattered little that Ingram was the son of a lighthouse keeper and the beautiful Venetia was a first-rate shrew. Their money, like Sir Robert Crossley's, cast a golden glow.

There were those who disapproved, of course. Annis's position amongst the chaperons gave her the perfect opportunity to witness the tight-lipped displeasure of some of the town's high sticklers. Old Lady Cardew and Lady Emily Trumpton were whispering malignantly like a pair of witches. Annis caught the phrases 'appalling drop in standards' and 'any old riff-raff at these events'. There were some circles in which the Ingrams would never be welcome. The Cardews and Trumptons would never invite them to grace their drawing rooms.

Following Mr and Mrs Ingram through the door were Charles, Sibella and David. Annis felt a mixture of strong affection and annoyance. She could not bear the way in which Charles in particular was in Ingram's pocket, and at times like this it stuck in her throat to see her family in Ingram's retinue. She was guiltily aware that she had been avoiding Charles since the issue of the sale of Starbeck had arisen. She had pleaded her work as an excuse and had been glad to put him off. Now she rather suspected Charles would press his case. What was worse was that she would be obliged to do the pretty to the Ingrams tonight for Charles's sake. Samuel Ingram always treated her with courtesy and Annis had a suspicion that he did so because of her title and because he was not sure of her exact social position. She had to work for a living, but the fact that she was a Marquis's granddaughter and the widow of a knight certainly confused the issue in his eyes.

The country dance ended and Annis watched as Sir Everard offered Fanny his arm and guided her over to an alcove where they could converse together. Fanny was behaving very pleasantly that evening, but Annis knew better than to take her gaze off her. Out of the corner of her eye, she saw that Lucy was now dancing with Lieutenant Norwood, and a very pretty pair they made. Annis relaxed slightly. From that point of view the evening was going well.

She stifled a yawn. Nothing particularly exciting ever happened at the Harrogate assemblies. In the summer the residents of the town were joined by the fashionable throngs who came north to take the spa waters, but the place still had a genteel quality, which she was sure the raffish London crowd found rather quaint.

Sibella waved at her across the ballroom and gestured that she would be coming over in a moment. Annis waved back and smiled. Some very late arrivals were just entering the ballroom. The Master of Ceremonies was bowing so low he had almost doubled himself up. Someone of more consequence than Mr and Mrs Ingram, then. Annis raised her brows.

Adam Ashwick walked in, accompanied by his brother and the Dowager Lady Ashwick. Annis's heart jumped once in recognition, then settled to a steady beat. She deliberately looked away, hoping that her colour had not betrayed her brief moment of confusion. She doubted they had noticed. Generally speaking, no one ever looked at chaperons very closely. Annis fidgeted on her rout chair. She felt confused and strangely out of countenance to see Adam again, regardless of the fact that he would probably not approach her. She had missed him and something had felt out of kilter ever since she had dismissed him. Nevertheless, she knew that she could not weaken now.

There was no doubt that the Ashwick party was working its way towards her quarter of the room. The Dowager Lady Ashwick and her younger son were both well known in Harrogate society and were stopping to speak to their many acquaintances. Since the new Lord Ashwick had spent much of the previous nine years either abroad or in London, he was being introduced to new arrivals and reacquainting himself with old friends. Annis took a deep breath to steady her nerves.

She allowed her gaze to rest on Adam's face for a moment, making sure that he did not catch her watching him. He looked very elegant in pale fawn inexpressibles and a black swallowtail coat and his neck cloth was tied in intricate folds that only a London valet could achieve. He was smiling as he answered some question from Lady Cardew and he looked charming, distinguished, everything that Annis might ever have wanted. She felt a pang of mingled regret and longing.

Annis forced her gaze away and looked at Della Tilney, elegant in the lavender of half-mourning, and from there

to the Dowager and to Edward Ashwick. Unlike his elder
brother, Edward did not have the figure to carry off evening dress well. His was a more rotund and rather comfortable figure and though his features were very similar
to Adam's, his face was much more open, with a pleasing
warmth of expression. Annis found herself warming to his
easiness of manners as she watched him greet Lady Cardew and Lady Emily Trumpton. He soon had the old tab-
bies eating out of his hand.

Adam Ashwick looked across at her and caught her
gaze, and Annis felt a wave of heat wash over her from
the top of her head to the tips of her toes. She stood up
and started to edge away from the crowd milling about the
Ashwicks. She had reckoned without Della Tilney and the
Dowager, however, who now excused themselves from
Lady Cardew and cut off her retreat without appearing to
do so. It was neatly and seamlessly done.

'Lady Wycherley, how charming to see you again. How
do you do?' The Dowager was only a small woman, but
somehow she appeared to be blocking Annis's path and
Annis knew that she could scarcely dodge around her.
Della Tilney was approaching on the left now in a clever
flanking manoeuvre that Annis could have sworn was deliberate. She drew to a reluctant halt.

'Good evening, Lady Ashwick, Lady Tilney…'

'I believe that you are already acquainted with my elder
son, Lord Ashwick,' the Dowager said. For a second Annis
was certain that she saw a spark of mischief in her eyes.

She cast Adam a brief glance. 'Good evening, my lord.'

'It is a pleasure to meet you again, Lady Wycherley.'

Adam Ashwick's voice was smooth and amused. He
took her hand in his. Annis risked another look at his face.
His cool grey eyes were smiling into hers and in that moment she read all his suppressed amusement at the sight

of her in her matronly red dress and matching turban. A vision came into her mind of herself as she had been the night they had met in the garden: the black cloak, her hair free about her shoulders, abandoned and wild. She felt herself blush like a débutante at her first ball and looked away hastily.

The Dowager had excused herself, taken her daughter's arm and moved on, leaving Annis and Adam together. It had been very neatly done.

'I wondered if you would care to dance, Lady Wycherley,' Adam continued. The pressure of his fingers on hers increased slightly until Annis was obliged to look up again. She met his gaze with a straight look of her own.

'I thank you, my lord, but chaperons do not dance.'

Adam raised his dark brows arrogantly. 'Why not? Is there some law against it?'

Annis frowned faintly. 'Not exactly—'

'Then you need to consult nothing but your inclination, Lady Wycherley. Besides, I did not ask whether chaperons danced. I asked if you would care to dance with me, which is a vastly different question.'

Their gazes locked. Annis bit back a smile.

'I see that you are as forthright as ever, my lord. You put me in an impossible position! How am I to refuse without giving offence?'

Adam grinned. 'You cannot. Give in to your fate.'

'Then I suppose that it would be quite pleasant to dance with you.'

His hand was warm on her arm as he steered her on to the floor.

'Only quite pleasant? You are severe, ma'am.'

It was a quadrille. They drew together, clasped hands and drew apart again.

'It is delightful to see you again,' Adam said, in an

undertone. 'You observe how good I have been in obeying your strictures and staying away from you.'

Annis gave him a cool look. 'I imagined that you had been busy at Eynhallow, my lord.'

'Did you? I assure you that I would have abandoned all my plans to spend some time with you. Still, it is pleasant to know that you have been giving my circumstances some thought. I have missed seeing you, Lady Wycherley. Did you miss me too?'

Annis gave him a speaking look and he laughed. 'So you did. How encouraging.'

'I have been far too busy,' Annis said primly.

'To good effect, I understand. I hear that you are to be rid of your charges in a few weeks, and that they are likely to depart in a blaze of glory. An engagement to Sir Everard Doble for one, I understand, and the younger Norwood son for the other. I congratulate you.'

Annis smiled. 'Thank you. I hope that congratulations will be in order, my lord, but I am making no assumptions.'

'Once the Misses Crossley have left you will no longer be a chaperon, will you?' Adam continued, with limpid innocence. 'How do you plan to pass your time then, ma'am?'

Annis gave him a sharp look. 'I shall then be a chaperon on holiday, my lord,' she said sweetly. 'I intend to spend some time at Starbeck before going to London for the Little Season.'

'Do you accompany another young lady to London?'

'Of course. It is my job. I shall be chaperoning Miss Eustacia Copthorne.'

Adam gave a soundless whistle. 'You must enjoy a difficult challenge, ma'am. I declare your choices become more testing each time! You would do better to give it all up and spend some time with me.'

'Would that be less challenging, Lord Ashwick?'

Adam smiled. 'Maybe not, but it would be more enjoyable. For both of us.'

They parted, turned, crossed hands and drew together again. Annis took the opportunity to check that Fanny and Lucy were both well in view. They were—and they were gawping at her, along with half the population of the ballroom. As Annis had said, chaperons simply did not dance. It was as though most people assumed they were either incapable of dancing or somehow exempt from the normal entertainments of society.

The dance was ending and Adam offered her his arm for the customary circuit of the floor.

'That was not so bad, was it?' he enquired lightly. 'Perhaps you might give me permission to call on you at Starbeck, ma'am—before you become a chaperon again?'

Before Annis could reply, Charles was at her elbow, pointedly proprietorial.

'Good evening, coz. Your servant, Ashwick…'

The men exchanged polite bows. Once again there was an air of constraint between them, then Charles said, a little awkwardly, 'Mr Ingram asks if you would care to escort my cousin over to join his party, my lord.'

Annis hesitated and felt Adam stiffen as well. It felt suspiciously like some sort of trap. Charles had delivered the invitation with the unmistakable ring of a royal command and Annis could see that Ingram was watching them across the room with something approaching a gloating pleasure. Evidently he did not expect a refusal.

She saw the angry colour come into Adam's face, saw him hesitate as though he was searching for the appropriate words, and with a flash of insight wondered what hold

Ingram had over him. Whatever it was, it seemed dangerous. Adam looked as though he would happily throttle the
man.

After what seemed an age, Adam turned to her and
bowed with scrupulous courtesy. 'You must excuse me,
Lady Wycherley. I have no wish to offend you, but I fear
I cannot accept Mr Ingram's invitation.'

He kissed her hand, turned sharply on his heel and
strode away.

'Well!' Charles said, as he and Annis turned as one to
watch Adam go. 'Of all the dashed poor manners—'

'Can you truly blame Lord Ashwick for declining Mr
Ingram's invitation?' Annis demanded. 'It seems to me
quite natural that he should want nothing to do with him,
and rather insensitive of Mr Ingram to push himself on
Lord Ashwick's acquaintance!'

Charles looked defensive. 'Yes, but the old man asked
me specially to make sure of Ashwick—'

'Oh, I see! You are worried for yourself and fear that
you will be in bad odour with your employer because you
failed to bring in the prize catch!' Annis looked at him in
exasperation. 'Really, Charles, are you a man or a mouse?
There must be plenty of other business in Harrogate and
around even were you to forfeit Ingram's favour—'

She knew that she was beating her head against a wall
even as she spoke. There was a stubborn, closed expression
on her cousin's face and after a second Annis sighed and
took his arm. 'Both you and Mr Ingram will just have to
make do with me, Charles, and I only do it as a favour to
you because you are my cousin. I don't like the man either!'

Chapter Seven

Fifteen minutes later, Annis had said all that was polite
to Samuel Ingram, exchanged a few words with Sibella
and David, and was looking round a little anxiously to try
to locate Lucy and Fanny. She was conscious that she had
allowed them rather too much latitude that evening. What
with the unexpected invitation to dance with Adam Ashwick and the unwelcome summons to join the Ingrams'
party, her chaperon's duties had come a poor third. Naturally there was a price to pay, and that price was that
Fanny had disappeared.

As Annis reached the edge of the dance floor, Lucy
Crossley, pretty in a pale blue dress that matched her eyes,
came up and caught her arm.

'Lady Wycherley, I am a little worried about Fanny…'

'Yes?' Annis kept her voice discreetly low, looking
round covertly to make sure that their conversation was
not attracting any attention.

'She said that she was going to the ladies' withdrawing
room, but I am afraid…' Lucy hesitated and Annis saw
concern warring with a surreptitious glee in her face
'…that is, I know she has a *tendre* for Lieutenant Greaves
and I wondered if they had gone out into the gardens.'

'I see,' Annis said.

'I am not trying to get Fanny into trouble...' Lucy had a look of limpid innocence that contradicted her words.

'Well,' Annis said, clamping down on her irritation, which was only made worse by the gleam of hopeful spite in Lucy's eye, 'I hope that Fanny may remember that she is affianced to Sir Everard Doble, and the Lieutenant may remember that he is a gentleman.'

Lucy giggled. 'Lord, I don't think so, Lady Wycherley! Barnaby says that Lieutenant Greaves is the worst flirt in Harrogate!'

'Yes, very well, Lucy!' Annis frowned. 'I will go to find Fanny, though I am sure this is all a hum. Now, please stay with Lieutenant Norwood until I come back with Fanny, and if Sir Everard Doble comes over, pray tell him that we shall come out to the carriage in a moment.' She fixed Lucy with a severe look. 'I trust that you, at least, will behave with discretion!'

'Oh, yes, Lady Wycherley.' Lucy assumed her most angelic look.

'Good. I am sure that there is no call for concern. I shall see you directly.'

Annis sighed. She liked Lucy a great deal more than Fanny, but she supposed it was no surprise that the girl was relishing her elder sister's apparent fall from grace. Fanny had seldom treated Lucy with kindness and now Lucy was having a small revenge. Annis had absolutely no faith that Lucy would hold her tongue. She was a sad rattle and Annis knew she would tell Barnaby Norwood what was going on and then the story would be round Harrogate in no time. Fanny would be branded a flirt, Sir Everard might cut up rough, and all before Sir Robert Crossley had come up with Annis's payment.

A search of the ladies' withdrawing room confirmed

what Annis had already suspected; Fanny was nowhere to be found and the attendant had not seen her. Annis retraced her steps to the passage and paused for thought. There were no gardens at the Dragon and the possibilities for private conversation were therefore very limited. Could Fanny and Lieutenant Greaves have gone into one of the public rooms, hoping to grasp a few moments on their own? If so, Annis thought they were taking an enormous risk of discovery, but perhaps that might add to the excitement.

First though, before she panicked, Annis thought that she should try the supper room. Given Fanny's penchant for food, it was entirely possible that she might be found tidying up the crumbs left over from supper. Annis had noticed that Fanny had been particularly partial to the pigeon pie that evening…

Fanny was not in the supper room and the servants who were clearing the food away had not seen her. Annis went out into the Dragon's impressive entrance hall and opened a door at random. It was the library and it was quite deserted at this time of night. The fire was lit and one candle burned, but the room was empty. Next door was the writing room, and as Annis opened the door she heard voices.

'I 'eard as you were looking for information about Mr Ingram, my lord. I've got something that might interest you, but it'll cost you…'

'How much, Woodhouse?'

Annis recognised Adam Ashwick's incisive tones and paused, her hand still on the doorknob. Neither man appeared to have heard the door open for they were standing at the far end of the room in the window embrasure. The long windows were, in fact, slightly ajar. Woodhouse had his back to the door and Adam was half-turned away from it. Annis heard the clink of guineas. She could also smell the strong scent of ale. Every time Woodhouse moved another wave of it filled the room.

'For two hundred I could guarantee to point you in the right direction, m'lord.'

'I will pay you three hundred, you old scoundrel.' Distaste and amusement warred in Adam's voice, 'Here is half that on account and the rest will be on delivery, but for that I expect the best quality information. And proof, Woodhouse. Otherwise Ingram will tell me to go hang!'

Annis drew a sharp breath. She knew that she should withdraw, for Fanny Crossley was certainly not here and whatever Adam was discussing with Woodhouse was none of her business. She had known that he was no friend to Ingram and if he sought information to bring the man down, then that was his affair. She was about to tiptoe back the way she had come, when she heard Woodhouse mention Charles's name. She paused.

'A little tip, my lord...' Woodhouse gave a cackle of laughter. 'You should look into Mr Lafoy's activities. There's a gentleman that could do with watching. Ingram's right-hand man, so he is.' He hiccupped loudly. 'What you're after is treasure, my lord. Buried treasure. Or sunken treasure perhaps. Look to the skies and into the depths. That's my advice!'

Adam sounded impatient. 'What the devil are you talking about, man? You're so drunk you're not making sense—'

A draught from the open window tugged the knob out of Annis's hand and the door swung to behind her, closing with a soft, stealthy click. Both men spun around. Woodhouse swore and dived for the open terrace door and Adam came quickly across the room towards her.

Annis experienced a moment of pure panic when she wanted to run away. This would be ridiculous, however, and within a second she realised that she would have to brazen it out. She put her hands behind her back, resting her palms against the door panels, and waited for Adam to join her. His greeting was typically blunt.

'What the devil are you doing there, Lady Wycherley? Eavesdropping?'

Annis blushed a furious red. 'No, of course not, Lord Ashwick! I have lost Miss Fanny Crossley and thought that she might be in here. I can see that she is not, however, so I shall leave you.'

She turned towards the door. Adam was quicker than she. He leaned one hand against it and held it closed.

'Just a moment, Lady Wycherley. Do not be so hasty.'

Annis gave him a haughty look 'My lord?'

Adam grinned. 'Pray do not turn starchy with me, ma'am.'

Annis glared. 'Then do not prevent my egress from the room, sir.'

Adam stood back with exaggerated courtesy. 'You are, of course, free to go. I should be grateful if you would grant me a moment, however.'

Annis sighed sharply. 'Very well, my lord. You have a minute only. I must find Miss Crossley.'

'Of course. There was something I wished to ask you. Did you hear my conversation with Woodhouse?'

Annis met his gaze. 'I heard some of it.'

'I see. Were you deliberately listening?'

'No, indeed! Why should I? I have not been *spying* on you, Lord Ashwick!'

Adam's lips twitched. 'I beg your pardon. I was not suggesting that you were dogging my footsteps! I merely thought that if you had heard something of interest, you might have stopped to listen.'

Since this was precisely what Annis had done she felt a little awkward. 'I…heard a little. Not all.'

'So you know that Woodhouse has offered to furnish me some information about Mr Ingram's business dealings?'

'I know that you are paying him to do so,' Annis said coldly. 'I fear that you are wasting your money, my lord. Woodhouse is three parts disguised for most of the time. I doubt that he has any useful information to sell you at all.'

'We shall see,' Adam said imperturbably. 'What concerns me more now is what you intend to do about my activities, Lady Wycherley. Will you tell Lafoy?'

There was a silence. Annis had not thought that far but now that she did, she realised she had no idea what she would do. She said, with no hint of challenge, more out of simple curiosity, 'How would you stop me?'

To her surprise, Adam laughed. 'My dear Lady Wycherley, I could not begin to try! I can only tell you that whilst it is true I might be interested in information to discredit Ingram, I have no direct quarrel with your cousin, and I beg you to keep quiet.'

Annis hesitated. 'If you bring down Ingram, you will inevitably hurt Charles in the process.'

Adam's gaze was very direct. 'That might be true.'

'I cannot agree to that.'

Adam sighed. He drove his hands into his pockets. 'I suppose I would not expect anything else of you, ma'am. May I suggest a compromise? I will tell you what I discover—if you will keep my secret.'

Annis sought his gaze. 'You will tell me before you take any action?'

'I shall. I give you my word.'

'Then I agree to your terms, my lord. I will keep the secret.'

There was a pause. 'As easy as that?' Adam said, in an odd tone.

'Of course. What did you expect—that I would extract some kind of payment?' Annis put her head on one side. 'Now I come to think of it, that would be useful. I am always so lamentably hard up—'

Adam laughed again. 'What I meant, as you well know, is that you are a woman of principle. As such I could not imagine you condoning my behaviour. I should be interested to hear your reasoning, ma'am.'

Annis shrugged. 'It is simple. I do not approve of Mr Ingram's methods. As long as you do not hurt Charles—'

'I shall not, I promise you.' He took her hand and kissed it. 'Thank you, ma'am. Against all the odds I think you must trust me.'

His voice was a little husky. Looking up, Annis saw the flash of expression in his eyes, the desire, sensual and disturbing. She tried to pull her hand away. He held her fast. For a second they stood quite still, whilst Annis' heart started to hammer.

'My lord—' she began, but he covered her mouth with his before she could say another word. The room shifted and spun and Annis brought her hands up to clutch at Adam's jacket to steady herself. He kissed her with languorous slowness, teasing a response from her, repressing his own urgency beneath a gentleness that seduced her. Annis slid her hands over his shoulders and tangled them in his hair, pulling him closer.

Adam needed no urging. His kiss claimed her lips again and this time it was insistent, hot and wild with need. Annis made a little sound of surrender deep in her throat. She was conscious of nothing except the sensation of pleasure he aroused in her, and a deep longing to be closer still.

A door closed quietly down the corridor and Annis jumped, pulling away as though she had been stung. Adam caught her elbow to steady her. She felt shocked and light-headed. Her hands were shaking and her voice was shaking too.

'This is scandalous behaviour for a chaperon! I am supposed to be preventing Miss Crossley from behaving in just such a fashion rather than indulging in a flirtation of my own in the library! I cannot think what I was doing... I cannot believe...'

'Is that what you think this is, Lady Wycherley? A light flirtation?' Adam sounded almost as breathless as she. He also sounded angry. 'Devil take it—'

Annis looked at him. Adrift with a mixture of disbelief and condemnation for herself, she had not thought how Adam might feel. She took a steadying breath. 'I beg your pardon. I did not intend to make it sound—'

'Demeaning?'

Now she was sure that he was angry. She stopped and looked at him, her hazel eyes wide.

'Of course I did not intend to make it sound demeaning! Nor light and frivolous, for that matter. I only meant that I should not be indulging in such behaviour—'

'Should you not?' Before Annis could guess his intention, Adam moved so that he had his back against the door. He put out a hand and pulled her negligently back into his arms. 'I am not sure what I should do with you, Lady Wycherley. Kiss you until you admit this is not merely a meaningless flirtation?'

His lips were an inch from hers. Annis could feel his anger and his desire, latent in the lines of his body. She met the blazing grey eyes.

'Very well, I confess it is no mere flirtation,' she whispered.

Adam kissed her hard, then let her go. 'I feel sure we shall talk of this again, but for now we had better find your charge. But first…' He scrutinised her and shook his head, the smile back in his eyes. 'Oh, dear, Lady Wycherley. For once it *does* look as though it is the chaperon who has been kissed in the conservatory.' He held the door of the writing room open for her. 'That is exactly where I should look for Miss Crossley, if I was you.'

Annis was trying desperately to gather her shattered composure. Later, she told herself fiercely. Later you may think about this and decide what you are going to do. For now you must find Fanny and fulfil your chaperon's duties. She stole a look at Adam's face. Being a chaperon had never been quite so difficult as it appeared to be at the moment.

'The conservatory…' Annis tried to concentrate. 'I had not remembered that there was one.' She looked at Adam suspiciously. 'Did you see Miss Crossley go in there, my lord? You should have told me earlier.'

'No, I did not. It is merely a guess.' Adam hesitated. 'I am a little acquainted with Miss Fanny Crossley—or at least with her behaviour.'

Annis narrowed her eyes. 'You have said nothing before.'

'Certainly not. I was aware that I could ruin her prospects if I chose and then you, Lady Wycherley—' Adam sketched her a mocking bow '—would not receive your fee!'

'Oh!' Annis felt cross and curious in equal measure, but curiosity won. 'Well, I do think it most underhand of you not to tell me, my lord, but you may make up for it now.'

Adam smiled. 'Very well. You are aware that Miss Crossley was in London for the Season?'

'Of course.'

'She managed to attract the notice of the younger brother of a friend of mine.' Adam sighed. 'We all thought that John was making a frightful ass of himself over her, but he is young and Miss Crossley can be quite charming when she tries. Alas, when she discovered that he was not the heir to the Canvey title as she had supposed, she threw him over and tried to seduce Lord Burley instead. In the conservatory!'

Annis shot him an appalled look. 'Good God!' She quickened her pace. 'Does Miss Crossley know that you are aware of her history?'

'I doubt it. I said nothing, but you know how people talk, Lady Wycherley.' Adam shot her a look. 'I believe that was the reason why Miss Crossley failed to catch a husband in London. There were plenty interested in her fortune but her reputation was not so sweet.'

'I *knew* there must be a reason—' Annis broke off. 'Sir Robert insisted that there was nothing wrong, but I suspected there was a reason why his nieces had not taken.'

They reached the door of the conservatory and Annis pushed it open. She heard Fanny's voice at once, impassioned, and very much in the style of Mrs Siddons.

'Ever since we met in London I have been hopelessly in love with you.'

'Oh, lord,' Annis said, under her breath. 'If only I had been quicker I could have averted this! I fear Miss Crossley is quite carried away with her own eloquence!'

Lieutenant Greaves's fluting tones interrupted Fanny, sounding amused. 'Lud, Miss Crossley, it was only a bit of fun! If I'd thought you were after anything other than a flirtation—'

'Oh, but you did! You knew I cared for you!'

The two protagonists were standing behind a rank of huge potted palms and were therefore most taken aback when Annis and Adam Ashwick materialised suddenly beside them. Lieutenant Greaves paled and dropped his weary man-of-the-world stance at once, looking suddenly far more like the young and painfully inadequate youth that he was. Fanny burst into tears.

'Conduct both ungallant and unbecoming to a gentleman in the Light Dragoons,' Adam said pleasantly, as the luckless Lieutenant Greaves tried to flatten himself against the glass window. 'I should think twice before toying with a lady's affections again, lad.'

'Sir, yes, sir!' The Lieutenant shot Fanny an agonised glance. 'All a misunderstanding, sir…'

'I am glad to hear it,' Adam said, turning to Annis. 'Lady Wycherley, are you agreed that this is all an unfortunate mix-up?'

'Yes,' Annis said.

'No!' Fanny said. Her face was as red as Lieutenant Greaves's was pale. It was clear she did not wish him to get away with it—or away from her.

'I think,' Annis said, iron in her tone, 'that you will agree it is all a misunderstanding, Fanny, when you have had time to think about it.'

Adam gave the Lieutenant an ironic bow. 'Run along, Greaves!'

'Sir!' The Lieutenant drew himself up ramrod straight, almost saluted, and practically ran out of the conservatory.

'Silly young fool,' Adam said. 'I hope that will teach him to be more circumspect in future.' He turned to Annis. 'I will leave you to deal with this, Lady Wycherley.' His gaze softened. 'I have not forgotten that I am in your debt. At your service, Miss Crossley…'

He strode out of the room. Fanny started to sob.

'Now, come along, Fanny,' Annis said briskly, 'I am sure that you do not wish Lucy and the others to think that you have been crying. Nor Sir Everard, for that matter.'

Fanny muttered something unintelligible.

'After all,' Annis continued, shepherding her charge out into the corridor, 'it would not do for people to think that there was anything wrong. Sir Everard might think that you did not wish to marry him.'

'I do not!'

'Nor wish for a title or the pleasure of dancing at your sister's wedding as the new Lady Doble!' Annis finished, playing several of her trump cards in one hand.

There was a small silence. Annis could tell that Fanny, a practical girl at heart, still found it difficult to abandon her dream, no matter how foolish.

'I want to marry James Greaves,' the girl said mutinously. 'You could have made him marry me, Lady Wycherley, if you had kicked up a fuss!'

'I do not think so, Fanny,' Annis said coolly. 'Men like Lieutenant Greaves are not interested in settling down. Besides, it was very bad of you to try and entrap him, you know. It grieves me to say so, but you could have ended up as a laughing-stock and with a ruined reputation into the bargain!'

There was another silence whilst Fanny digested this. Annis took the opportunity to collect their cloaks and to send a maid into the ballroom to fetch Lucy. Eventually, when she thought that Fanny had reached the self-pitying stage, she added mendaciously, 'Of course, Fanny, you do realise that Lieutenant Greaves is not good enough for you, don't you?'

Fanny sniffed, wiping her nose on the edge of her cloak.

'He is heir to Lord Farmoor. I have only just discovered it.'

Which explained a good deal, Annis thought. Fanny's discovery about the handsome Lieutenant had turned him from a flirtation into a marriage prospect, and knowing that she had not very long, Fanny had acted quickly.

'I fear your intelligence is only partially correct, Fanny dear,' she said. 'As I understand it, Lieutenant Greaves is Lord Farmoor's heir at the moment, but his lordship has just married a young bride. It would be a tremendous risk, and just when you have secured a baronet as well.'

'Oh!' Fanny looked thoughtful.

Annis sighed. 'I know it must be very painful for you now, but you will soon see that I am in the right of it to discourage the match. Look at the Lieutenant's behaviour tonight! It was scarcely that of a gentleman. Oh, no, Fanny dear, it is better this way. Now look—Lucy is coming and Sir Everard. We shall just behave as though none of this has happened, and the day after tomorrow your uncle will be sending the news of your betrothal to the *Gazette*.'

Fanny gulped and nodded, rubbing away the evidence of tears. 'Very well, Lady Wycherley. I can see that your advice is sound. After all…' she brightened '…I may marry a lord next time, may I not?'

'Indeed you may, Fanny,' Annis said, realising that Fanny already had her widowhood planned before the knot was tied. *That is if you can find one to take you!* she added silently.

Later, in the privacy of her bedchamber, Annis removed her turban, unpinned her hair, took off the turkey-red dress and poured herself a generous glass of madeira.

She felt that she deserved a strong drink for saving both Fanny and herself from disaster. The foolish chit had come within an ace of ruining her own betrothal and Annis's future into the bargain, but all could now run smoothly. Sir Robert Crossley would be making the journey to Yorkshire the following week to take his nieces back to London for the purchase of their trousseaux. Then Annis would be free to go to Starbeck for a space and take a well-deserved rest.

She brushed her hair slowly. The long, lustrous strands fell about her face and down to her waist. She knew that the sensible course of action would be to have it all cut off since she spent so much time hiding it, but some spark of vanity prompted her to keep it long.

Annis paused, hairbrush in hand. Not even the business with Fanny could make her forget what else had happened that evening. She started to think about Adam kissing her, then deliberately forced her mind away and made herself concentrate on the curious scene Adam had had with Woodhouse in the hotel writing-room. Could the man really know something to the discredit of Samuel Ingram—and of Charles? Would Adam keep his word and tell her if he discovered any evidence? Annis shook her head thoughtfully. She was not entirely sure what impulse had prompted her to promise to keep Adam's dealings a secret. Certainly she deplored Ingram's behaviour, but anything he did touched Charles too, and she would do nothing to harm her cousin. Annis wriggled uncomfortably. It was odd, but she did trust Adam Ashwick and she did not know why. The same impulse that had prompted her to trust him the night they met in the dark was at work now. And impulses could be so very dangerous…

Annis finished undressing, climbed into bed and reached for her novel, but she did not read it and soon set it aside, staring instead at the candle flame. It had been blissful to be held in Adam's arms. His kisses had set her senses ablaze. She could not deny it. And it was not just a light flirtation. She knew it had angered him to have their actions cheapened thus. So now she was being honest. She had never wanted a man as she wanted Adam Ashwick. Truth to tell, she had never really wanted—needed—a man at all. She had thought that she never would. She had been naïve.

Annis sighed. As far as she could see, there were three courses of action for a woman in a position like hers. She could continue to work for a living, she could become a shady widow living off the generosity of men in return for her favours, or she could marry respectably again. A small smile curved Annis's lips. She had never previously considered becoming a courtesan, but now the idea held distinct possibilities. If she were to be the mistress of such a man as Adam Ashwick… Her smile vanished. She knew enough of the world to know that such arrangements seldom lasted. Was she to become like a parcel, passed from hand to hand, slightly tatty about the edges? That was not so appealing an idea. Besides, she had the strong belief that Adam would not countenance such an arrangement. He wanted her—she knew that he did. Yet she was also certain that he was a man of honour and would propose marriage. She might seduce him, but he would still insist on marrying her. And his will was as strong as hers.

Marriage. Annis's gaze narrowed. Most women would not think twice. Most women would be delighted. She was not most women. She shuddered to remember the horror of her marriage to John Wycherley and the way he had tried to control even the smallest aspect of her life. Preserving her independence was the only answer and she would do well to remember that.

She picked up her book again. Before long, her eyelids were drooping and the book fell from her hand to rest on the coverlet. It was left to Mrs Hardcastle, tapping at the door because she could see that there was still a light burning, to blow out the candle on the nightstand and leave Annis to sleep.

'There's a letter for you this morning, Miss Annis.' Mrs Hardcastle, pin neat in black bombazine, held the missive out to Annis as though it was in somewhat questionable taste. 'Tom Shepard brought it. Tom the younger, that is. Apparently his father is laid up with the lumbago.'

'Dear me.' Annis unfolded the letter. As though there were not enough difficulties to deal with at Starbeck, without Tom Shepard falling ill. 'Did Tom the younger not wish to come in?'

Mrs Hardcastle looked shocked. 'He came into the kitchen, ma'am! He certainly would not come in *here*.' Mrs Hardcastle gave the drawing-room a disapproving look. 'Why, he might have met one of your young ladies!'

'I am sure that they would have been delighted to meet him,' Annis said drily. Tom Shepard the younger was exceptionally good looking and as a farmer's son would have a certain rustic appeal to the Misses Crossley.

'Him's too bashful,' Mrs Hardcastle said, shaking her head. 'I was hoping he'd make a match with my youngest niece, Cicely, but he was too shy and now she's been snapped up by Jim Durkin, over Saltaire way.'

'It would have been quite safe for Tom to come in,' Annis said. 'Fanny and Lucy are gone to visit the Promenade Rooms with Sibella this morning, for I have an appointment in town and Sib promised to escort them on my behalf.'

Mrs Hardcastle wiped an invisible speck of dust from the table with the corner of her apron.

'It's you that young Tom is sweet on, Miss Annis, not

the girls! I heard him tell that you rode like an angel and were the most gracious lady he'd ever met. Then there's Ellis Benson, over at Linforth. They say he was a holding a torch for you for ever so many years.' Mrs Hardcastle looked disapproving. 'You never see what's under your nose, Miss Annis.'

Annis looked up in the liveliest astonishment. 'Ellis Benson? Tom Shepard? Really, Hardy, you make me sound like…like a female Casanova!'

Mrs Hardcastle pursed her lips. 'Well, there's talk, Miss Annis. Mostly about you and that fancy Lord—'

'Lord Ashwick?' Annis started to open the letter. 'I do not want to hear any gossip, Hardy.'

'No? All right, then.'

Annis unfolded the paper. 'What are they saying?'

'Knew you wanted to know,' Mrs Hardcastle said with satisfaction. 'Only that he means to marry you—'

'What?' It was such a sudden and unexpected confirmation of her thoughts the previous night that Annis dropped the letter on the floor.

'Everyone has noticed 'im courting you.'

'There is nothing to notice!' Annis stood up in agitation and walked over to the window. 'Lord Ashwick is not courting me, Hardy. I am a chaperon. I make matches for other people.'

Mrs Hardcastle sniffed. 'Can't see what's in front of your face if you ask me, Miss Annis. Too busy arranging marriages to see when someone wants you instead of your girls!'

'I assure you that you are completely mistaken!'

'Well, we'll see,' Mrs Hardcastle said, massively unconvinced. 'Another pot of tea, ma'am?'

'Thank you. That would be nice.' Annis raised her

brows. 'What will you be doing today, Hardy? Waging war on the mice again?'

'No time for that when I have the young ladies' rooms to clean out,' Mrs Hardcastle said. 'Tomorrow, mebbe. There is another mouse nest up in the attic.'

'I am aware of it,' Annis said. 'Last night the little creatures were scampering across the ceiling at all hours. It sounded like an army marching through!'

After Mrs Hardcastle had gone, Annis poured herself a second cup, lay back in her chair in a most hoydenish fashion, and gave a huge sigh. Mrs Hardcastle's representation of her as Harrogate's *femme fatale* seemed quite unreasonable, particularly as Miss Mardyn was visiting the town and was surely more worthy of gossip. With another sigh she turned her attention to the letter.

'Dear Lady Wycherley,' it read, in careful print, 'Mr Ingram's agent has called again, telling us that you intend to sell the farm and that the rents will go up. You know that we could not abide to be Ingram's tenants, nor could we afford it. We cannot believe that you would sell to him, madam. Please tell us what is happening as we do not know what to believe. Some of the sheep have been taken again and we are in dire straits. Respectfully yrs, Tom Shepard.'

Annis crumpled the letter up in her hand. A huge, hot fury took her as she thought of Tom and Eliza Shepard out at Starbeck, trying to scrape a living from a farm that barely brought in enough income to support one person, never mind a family, and being bullied by Ingram's agent into the bargain. Their elder son, John, had left to find work in the nearby town of Leeds in the last year, defeated in his attempts to wrest a living from the poor soil and the few sheep that grazed the upper pastures. Annis had promised to look after Tom, Eliza and their remaining family, just as her father had always done, but now that Ingram was sniffing around the farm and the estate, she felt frighteningly vulnerable. This was the second time that Tom had written asking for advice, and in a way it was timely, for she had an appointment to see Samuel Ingram that very morning. She had decided to tell him once and for all that she was not interested in his offer for Starbeck.

Annis stood up, tension making her fidgety, and walked across to the window. She would have liked to ask Charles for advice, but as Ingram's lawyer it was hopeless to expect him to be impartial. Annis knew that he would tell her that the Shepards should sell—and so should she. In some ways to sell Starbeck would be a huge relief, but in others it was quite out of the question. She had inherited the welfare of the villagers along with the house and she was not prepared to shirk that responsibility. Besides, she hated Ingram's bullying tactics and was determined not to give in. He would be the worst landlord she could ever wish upon her tenants.

She thrust the letter into her reticule and went to don her pelisse, bonnet and half-boots. There had been a thunderstorm the previous night and it had left the air fresh and pleasantly crisp, making it a nice morning for a walk. Ingram's chambers were only just around the corner. As she turned into Park Row she saw a smartly dressed couple just disappearing around the corner in front of her. The lady was Miss Mardyn, resplendent in a chic gown of striped brown satin and nodding ostrich plumes. Annis could only see the back of the gentleman's head, but he was tall and dark. Adam Ashwick, perhaps. The thought made her feel even more bad-tempered.

In her anxiety, she was early and found herself obliged to wait in a small antechamber, where a supercilious clerk shuffled paper and watched her out of the corner of his eye. Annis tried not to fidget. After fifteen minutes she was certain that Ingram was deliberately keeping her waiting and as time ticked by she became more and more angry. Eventually the door of Ingram's inner sanctum opened and Annis's heart sank as her cousin Charles came to escort her in. Behind him she could see Ingram himself—and Woodhouse, whom she had last seen only the previous night, talking to Adam Ashwick. The clerk gave her a look like a startled rabbit and ducked his head, as though trying to melt into the furniture. Annis had no intention of breaking her word to Adam, but the sight of the clerk made her feel even more uncomfortable to be there.

Ingram came forward to bow over Annis's hand, his manner odiously smooth and yet somehow managing to convey that his time was precious and he could only spare her three minutes of it.

'Lady Wycherley. What may I do for you, ma'am?'

'Thank you for seeing me, Mr Ingram,' Annis said coldly. She took the chair that he indicated, and then wished that she had not when he remained standing. 'I am sure this will not take long. It concerns the proposed sale of Starbeck, the estate and the farm.'

'Ah!' Ingram gazed vaguely out of the window and across the street, as though the view was far more interesting than Annis. 'Yes. I hope that you have seen the sense in selling, Lady Wycherley.' He laughed mirthlessly. 'Although I fear that Mr and Mrs Shepard seem disinclined to become my tenants!'

'Mr and Mrs Shepard are tired of being harried by your agent!' Annis said. 'They have empowered me to tell you so, Mr Ingram. They would appreciate it if you called your man off and did not press the matter any further. And whilst we are on the subject, so should I. I do not wish to sell the Starbeck estate—'

'Estate!' Ingram gave a short laugh. 'You set yourself high, ma'am, to call it thus! A ruined house and few acres of land!'

Annis kept a grip on her temper. 'A few acres that you evidently value highly, Mr Ingram! Your agent has been most pressing!'

Ingram shrugged. 'Benson will continue to press until you all see sense, Lady Wycherley.'

'By taking our sheep and making matters even more difficult?' Annis was incensed. She cast a glance at Charles, but he did not meet her eye. He was looking flushed and unhappy.

'Surely you do not think that there was any connection between the sheep disappearing and Benson's visit?' Ingram seemed amused. He hooked his thumbs into the pockets of his shiny black waistcoat. 'Tut, tut, what an imagination you do have, ma'am!'

'Annis,' Charles said suddenly, 'please try to see reason—'

Annis swung round on him. 'All I can see, Charles, is that you appear to have misplaced your family loyalty!'

'Your cousin is in a difficult position, Lady Wycherley,' Ingram said. 'He can appreciate the value of my plans. Now, he is the head of the family, so do you not think you should be guided by him? He has your best interests at heart, you know. And those of your tenants.'

Annis, who had been waving the Shepards' letter about in the air, stuffed it in her bag and stalked towards the door.

'Our ideas of what is in the best interests of Starbeck are clearly divergent,' she said coldly. 'I will bid you good day. Both of you,' she added sharply, as Charles moved to escort her out.

'A moment, Lady Wycherley—' Ingram said quickly. Annis turned.

'I am persuaded that you may come around to my point of view, ma'am,' Ingram said. 'There are usually ways to help people see that it is in their own interests…'

Annis knew that the colour had left her face. She felt a little sick and the bright room suddenly seemed darker. She felt frighteningly vulnerable.

'Are you threatening me, Mr Ingram?'

'Good gracious me, no, ma'am!' Ingram gave a puffy laugh. 'But you know how difficult it is to eke a living from Starbeck and its surrounding farms. You have mentioned yourself that the sheep go missing. If there were to be a fire, for instance, and the livestock killed or the buildings damaged, that would make life even more difficult for you and your tenants. Or there is your own line of work…' His voice changed subtly, became even more silky. 'A word dropped here or there about your suitability as a chaperon… One has to be so very careful of a reputation, and there are those who say that you have been consorting with Lord Ashwick…'

Annis's eyes flashed. 'There are those who say that you consort with the devil, Mr Ingram! One must not believe every foolish rumour that one hears. Good day to you. Pray do not trouble to show me out, Charles.'

When she reached the bottom, white-painted step outside, Annis hesitated for a moment, a hand on the railings, drawing a lungful of fresh air to try and calm herself. There was a step behind her and Charles's voice:

'Annis—'

'Charles,' Annis said with dangerous calm, 'do not speak to me, I beg.'

'Annis…' Charles ran a hand through his fair hair '…in a little while I may be able to help you.'

Annis waved his excuses away. 'All you have to do,' she said dully, 'is to show a little family feeling, Charles. I used to rely upon you.' The sunlight was making her eyes sting. She hoped that she was not going to cry. 'I do not want to talk about it. I do not even want to think about it! Go away!'

She left him standing on the steps and set off down the street. She was not certain whether it was busy or not. The figures of the passers-by blurred before her eyes and she scrubbed her face sharply. If Ingram should start to drop hints that she was unreliable or that there was something scandalous in her behaviour... Her financial survival was tenuous enough as it was, and no one would employ her if they suspected that her reputation was damaged. She was to all intents and purposes alone in the world and gossip was so harmful, even when it was untrue.

Then there was Starbeck. Her father had bought the estate as a place to retire; although he had died before he had returned to England, Annis had been happy to take on the house and its obligations. That had been before the sheep stealing had become rife and the villages began to seethe with hatred towards Ingram, a hatred which she felt so strongly herself now. She detested bullies.

Annis tried to think about her options, but her mind was a scramble of images. Sibella's household could not afford to support her as a pensioner and the last person she would accept help from was Charles. He had paid for her little town house in Church Row, so if they became estranged she would have to leave... Perhaps she would have to leave Harrogate altogether and go and live at Starbeck herself and become a farmer...except that she knew nothing about farming and she had little money and Starbeck was barely inhabitable...

She swiped at some nearby railings in helpless and hopeless anger. 'Hell and damnation!'

'Lady Wycherley?'

Annis swung round. Adam Ashwick was standing a bare few yards away, having evidently witnessed her unladylike attack on the railings. He was looking at her with amusement and speculation in his grey eyes. Annis inclined her head with haughty composure, trying to hide that fact that her thoughts were all mixed up. Along with images of herself locked in Adam's arms the previous night were thoughts that at least she was not wearing her turban this morning, followed by the unwelcome idea that Adam had probably come straight from his mistress. She blushed.

'Good morning, Lord Ashwick.'

'It is a very pleasant morning in fact, Lady Wycherley,' Adam said politely. 'However, you do not appear to be finding it so. I trust that you have not damaged your umbrella?'

Annis looked down at the umbrella a little self-consciously. 'I do not believe so. I am afraid that I was venting my dissatisfaction.'

Adam raised his brows. 'I see.' He smiled at her. 'I hope that the problem is not insurmountable. May I be of service to you in any way?'

Annis hesitated. It was tempting to pour out her difficulties about Starbeck as she needed an ally and she already knew that Adam was in dispute with Ingram. Yet there was still Charles to consider, for even if he had apparently forgotten family loyalty, she had not…

'I thank you, but no, my lord. And I must apologise for my ill manners. A trifling business transaction is going a little awry. I am persuaded that all will be well soon.'

'I see,' Adam said again, slowly. His thoughtful gaze

moved from her to the door of Ingram's offices and back
again.

'May I escort you back to Church Row, ma'am?'

'Thank you, but I have some shopping to do first.'

'Then perhaps I might walk with you to Park Street? I
too have a few errands to run.'

It was difficult to refuse. Annis rested her hand lightly
on Adam's proffered arm as they strolled along the pave-
ment.

'I hope that your difficulty with Miss Crossley last night
was successfully resolved,' Adam said. 'Is the betrothal to
Sir Everard still current?'

Annis smiled a little. 'It is, I thank you.'

'Then that cannot be the source of your displeasure.'
Adam frowned. 'Let me guess. That means it must be Starbeck, I suppose.'

'You are partially correct, my lord.' Annis laughed.
'There are two causes for vexation and one of those is
indeed Starbeck. My cousin—' She stopped, feeling guilty.
'It seems that everyone feels I should sell, but I do not
wish to do so.'

She felt Adam stiffen. 'Am I to understand that Mr Ingram has made you an offer for the estate?'

Annis cast him a swift sideways look. He was frowning
abstractedly. 'Yes, he has,' she said. 'You may be easy
however, my lord. I have refused it.'

Adam shot her a look from under lowered brows. 'That
cannot have made you popular. I infer that you are under
a deal of pressure from Lafoy as well as Ingram?'

Annis nodded unhappily.

'And can you afford to run the estate yourself?'

Annis shook her head. 'No. I can stave off ruin for a
little, but I have only a small annuity. That and what I
earn—' She stopped, aware that she was vouchsafing a

great deal of personal information to him. He seemed all too easy to confide in.

It appeared, however, that Adam was prepared to be equally frank in return.

'I cannot abide the thought of Ingram owning the land, but you know my parlous financial state. I cannot afford to buy Starbeck from you myself or I would surely do it.'

Annis gave a little, dispirited shrug. 'I am sure that I shall think of a solution, sir.'

'You mentioned two problems,' Adam said. 'If Starbeck is the first, what is the second?'

Annis glanced at him under her lashes. 'The second is more personal, my lord. I do not think… That is, it would not be right for me to tell you.'

Adam looked amused. 'Good God, why not? Is Ingram blackmailing you, Lady Wycherley?'

Annis looked at him. 'No. At least, not exactly. He exerts pressure where he knows it will have the greatest effect.' She remembered the scene in the ballroom and Adam's hesitation to do Ingram's bidding. 'Is he blackmailing *you*, my lord?'

Adam looked startled. He stopped walking and spun round towards her. 'Why would you think that?'

Annis smiled. 'I believe that is the first time you have not given me a straight answer to a straight question, my lord. It leads me to suspect that I am correct.'

Adam sighed. 'Like you, ma'am, I am under pressure. You are aware that my brother-in-law was in debt to Ingram. He is using the threat of releasing the detail of that debt as a lever.'

'To gain what? Surely not Eynhallow?'

Adam looked grim. 'No, he has yet to go that far. Influence is what he wants from me, Lady Wycherley. Social recognition…acceptance… He may whistle for it!'

'Oh!' Light dawned on Annis. 'Last night at the ball, when Charles invited you to join Ingram's party, was that a part of his plan to gain acceptance?'

'I imagine so. I think he believed that I would give him countenance, but I was not prepared to accede to his wishes. The man is nothing but a contemptible bully.'

Annis stifled an unexpected giggle. 'Oh, dear, he must have been so vexed with you! I know that I should not laugh, but it is pleasant sometimes to see Mr Ingram gainsaid. And Lady Emily Trumpton and Lady Cardew were muttering last night about what a jumped-up nobody he was and how they would never accept him. It is fortunate that you did not agree to sponsor him, my lord, or they would have thought you had taken leave of your senses!'

Adam laughed. 'I would rather not offend Lady Cardew if I can help it for she is a fearsome old battleaxe. But you have not told me what Mr Ingram's hold is over you, Lady Wycherley. What could you possibly have done to give him the means to blackmail you?'

Annis's laughter faded. 'It is nothing as desperate as that, I assure you, my lord, just some nasty threats—'

'About what?'

Annis sighed. 'I have explained to you before that a chaperon's reputation is a vulnerable thing, my lord. Mr Ingram has also noticed that fact.'

'He seeks to threaten you with gossip?' Adam said slowly. 'About what?'

'About you, my lord,' Annis said candidly. She saw him frown and added hastily, 'Oh, have no fear—if it were not that I am sure that he would find something else. You said yourself that the man is adept at finding a lever.'

'The man crawls in the gutter,' Adam said, and there was such anger in his tone that Annis was taken aback.

'Please…I am sorry that I mentioned it to you.'

'I am not.' Adam gave her a very straight look. 'I was not aware, however, that there had been any conjecture about us.'

Annis remembered what Mrs Hardcastle had said and hastily disregarded it. 'I am persuaded that there has not. It is all manufactured.'

Adam was frowning. 'What if that was not the case, Lady Wycherley?'

'I beg your pardon?'

'What if the gossip was true and I was paying court to you? You know that from the first my sole interest has been in you. We could make the gossip true and then there would be no scandal.'

Annis stared at him. She had been grappling with the difficulties of Ingram's blackmail and this latest idea took her quite by surprise.

'I...but...' Annis pulled herself together. 'We have spoken of this, my lord. You know that I would have to discourage your attentions. It is clearly impossible.'

'How so?' Adam closed the gap between them.

Annis's gaze fell. 'Because... Because I...I have already explained to you that my situation as a chaperon does not allow it.'

'That situation will end when the Misses Crossley leave, will it not?'

'For the time being. But it is my profession. I am to go to London for the Little Season. It is all arranged.' Annis gestured distractedly with her hands. Adam caught them both in his.

'So that is your first objection. What else?'

Annis had the desperate feeling that she was fighting a losing battle. 'There are many. I prefer to be independent.'

'I could change your mind.'

Annis frowned. For the first time, a tiny corner of her

mind whispered that he might be right. 'That is very arrogant, my lord.'

'Very well. We shall see. What else?'

'There is your mistress. I saw you with her earlier.'

Adam laughed. 'I collect that you mean Miss Mardyn?'

'Who else?' Annis looked at him severely. 'Unless you have more than one mistress in keeping?'

'I have none, I assure you. I have no interest in Miss Mardyn. Whoever you saw with her, it was not I.'

'Well, never mind.' Annis had belatedly realised that she might sound jealous. It was true, of course, but she did not wish Adam to know that. Nor did she wish to give credence to the idea that she was actually considering his suggestion seriously. She freed her hands.

'This is ridiculous. You cannot wish to pay court to me. Such things simply do not happen to me.'

Adam smiled. 'I hesitate to contradict a lady, but it just has done. Do you truly find it so surprising that I might wish to pay my addresses to you?'

Annis frowned. 'I suppose I must believe you, but...' Her troubled gaze searched his face and she burst out, 'This is foolish, my lord. We have only recently met—'

'That is true. It does not mean that we need to remain strangers, however.' Adam smiled. 'I thought that you liked me a little.'

Annis sighed. 'You know that I am attracted to you, my lord.'

She saw the flash of all-male satisfaction in his eyes. 'Then give me a chance.'

Annis hesitated. The pull was very strong. But so was the pull of memory and she knew that marriage was not for her. She would never forget that stifling feeling of being trapped. She shook her head. 'I am sorry, my lord. I cannot do that. I must bid you good day.'

As she walked off she knew that he was still watching her and as she turned the corner she could not resist a look over her shoulder. Sure enough, he was standing where she had left him and there was a rueful smile still on his lips. When he saw her turn to look at him he inclined his head, very deliberately, as though reminding her that she might have held her resolve this time, but that he was determined too, and he knew she was weakening.

Chapter Eight

Sir Robert Crossley came to collect his nieces the following afternoon. There were many false professions of affection from Fanny, some genuine ones from Lucy and sincere gratitude and a fat purse of money from Sir Robert himself. After the carriage had drawn away, Annis went back into the drawing room, kicked off her satin pumps, plumped herself down on the sofa, and tossed her turban in the air.

Sibella called at three o'clock and she had a treat for Annis up her sleeve.

'I have had such a good idea,' she began, as they descended from her carriage outside the Crown Hotel. 'I thought that you deserved a reward, Annis, for refraining from strangling that odious Miss Crossley, so I have arranged for us to bathe. Far better to take a hot spa bath than to drink the waters! Mr Thackwray is very busy this afternoon, but he has squeezed us in.'

'Oh good,' Annis said glumly. It was kind of Sibella to have thought to offer her a treat, but it was many years since Annis had taken the bath cure and she knew there must be a reason for that. Probably it was because the water was disgustingly malodorous. She could smell it already as they followed Mr Thackwray up the Crown's imposing mahogany staircase. The place was thronging with guests.

'I forget how popular Harrogate has become in the high summer,' Sibella commented. 'Why, it seems more crowded every year!'

Mr Thackwray beamed. 'The sulphur cure is remarkably efficacious, ladies, and, if I may say so, Harrogate has a certain quality that is lacking in other spa towns. Some of the southern spas have become decidedly *déclassé*, I fear…'

'At least the Bath Spa has a Pump Room,' Sibella whispered to Annis when their host's broad back was turned. 'Here we have to make do with a well with a canopy over! I heard one London lady say that she expected no better from the North, although she supposed that the lack of refinement added to Harrogate's rustic charm!'

Annis laughed. 'Surely the town is rich enough these days to build a Pump Room? Although it would not surprise me if Mr Thackwray opposed any such development. Why, he must make a fortune by offering medicinal baths here in his hotel!'

Sibella, who swore by the sulphur cure, frowned. 'You must own that rheumaticky patients are far more comfortable here than having to dip themselves in the sulphur well, Annis! I think Mr Thackwray offers a fine service.'

Mr Thackwray's suite of rooms was indeed comprehensive. Stretching along the whole of the first floor of the hotel were a series of small bedchambers with bathrooms in between, all interconnected to offer the opportunity for guests and visitors alike to sample the pleasures of the spa bath. The hotelier now stood aside to usher them into a small room in which two wooden baths stood side by side.

The air was thick with steam and the smell of rotten eggs. An aproned attendant was emptying a copper pan into one of the baths and smilingly offered to help them off with their outdoor clothes. Mr Thackwray, bowing, beat a discreet retreat.

'Ugh!' Annis said, hanging back as her cousin went behind a screen and divested herself of her clothing, 'why, it smells to high heaven in here and looks hot enough to broil a lobster! Why do you do this to yourself, Sib?'

Sibella discarded her dressing robe and slipped into the water. She lay back, closed her eyes and smiled beatifically at her cousin.

'It is splendidly enjoyable, Annis, once you get used to it. I can only have the waters warm at the moment because of my condition, but I find it very soothing. What is more, it is a sovereign cure for all sorts of maladies from the rheumaticks to the smallpox. It helps to cure the lesions, you know.'

Annis stared hard into the water. The thought of what might be lurking in there was deeply unappealing. 'You do not have the lesions, Sib. They do change the water for each customer, do they not?'

'Of course!' Sibella turned her head and opened her eyes. Her short blonde hair was already sticking up in damp spikes. 'Now be a good girl and get in. You will soon see how thoroughly pleasant the experience can be!'

The attendant helped Annis to unbutton her dress, then left the two ladies to bathe, informing them that she would be back in an hour's time to help them dress. Annis dipped one toe in the water and grimaced.

'Ouch! That is very hot!'

'That,' Sibella said patiently, 'is the point, Annis.'

'It is all very well for you, sitting there is a warm tub! I am broiling here!'

Annis lowered herself gingerly into the bath. The sides were steep and the tub bore an unfortunate resemblance to a coffin. The water came up to her chin and it was extremely hot. The smell of sulphur rose from it like a cloud. Annis wrinkled up her nose and tried not to sneeze. The idea of a coffin seemed most apt—if the scalding water did not cause a heart attack and carry you off, the smell surely would. That was if the rheumaticks had not got you first, of course.

'Ugh!' Annis tried not to inhale. 'I have seldom felt the need to take the waters before. Now I know why!'

'You must breathe, Annis,' Sibella said, turning her head in her cousin's direction. 'Otherwise you will not have the benefit of the efficacious vapours. They are renowned for clearing the head.'

'That I can well believe.' Annis found the smell of sulphur was so intense that it felt as though it was splitting her skull in two. Not for nothing was Harrogate's spa also known as the 'Stinking Spaw'. Visitors might travel from miles around to take the waters and townsfolk like Sibella might claim it to be healthful, but Annis suspected that it was all some huge jest at their expense. No doubt Mr Thackwray was even now rubbing his hands at the thought of the gullible parting with their money for the fashionable cure.

'It is very good of you to introduce me to the pleasures of the spa,' she said, 'but a little shopping would have sufficed!'

'We can do that as well,' Sibella said sleepily. 'Oh, Annis, it is good to have some time with you. You seldom have the chance to chat when you are chaperoning those wretched girls and I know you are off to Starbeck in a few days. For all that it is only four-and-twenty miles away, it sometimes feels like hundreds!'

'On those roads it certainly does,' Annis said feelingly. Travellers on the Skipton and Starbeck roads often had the bruises to prove it for days afterwards. Starbeck was set high on the Yorkshire moors and many of the roads were poor and badly kept. Annis thought it unlikely that Ingram's tollbooths would improve matters. Doubtless the money would go directly into his pockets.

She sighed and lay back in the water, following Sibella's lead and closing her eyes. Now that she was becoming more accustomed to it, the spa water was actually very relaxing. She was starting to feel sleepy and content, a world away from Ingram and his veiled threats and the problems at Starbeck and the provocative dilemma of Adam Ashwick. She really should not have entertained his proposals of courtship for a second, but he was strangely difficult to resist—and devilishly attractive…

Sibella yawned. 'Are you glad to be rid of your charges, Annis?'

'Oh, prodigiously! Though Sir Robert Crossley paid well, it was nowhere near enough to compensate for the wilfulness of his odious niece! If Fanny Crossley does not run away before the wedding, I shall be most surprised!'

'The other girl was a sweet child,' Sibella said, 'and perhaps Miss Crossley was unhappy, Annis. Unhappiness can make people very bad-tempered. I remember Mama was a martyr to the gout and it made her very cross indeed.'

'You always look for the best in everyone, Sib,' Annis said affectionately. 'I do believe you might even excuse Mr Ingram if you tried!'

'That reminds me—I saw Charles at luncheon,' Sibella said. Her tone had changed and Annis knew her well enough to guess what was coming. 'He told me that you and he are at daggers' drawn. Oh, Annis, I do so hate it when you are at odds!'

Annis hated it as well. She was fiercely fond of her cousins, particularly as they had made her welcome when her husband had died and she had returned home to Yorkshire. The Lafoys had held land in the Yorkshire Dales for centuries, but their estate had dwindled to nothing in the previous generation. Charles and Sibella's father had been the spendthrift squire who had lost their small patrimony, necessitating Charles to learn a profession and Sibella to marry. Annis's father was the younger son, a sea captain who had bought the small estate of Starbeck for when he retired from his travels—except that he had died before this had happened. Annis, the only child, had vague memories of flying visits to Starbeck during his time ashore, but the rest of the time was a blur of lodgings in Southampton and Plymouth, school in Bath, a passage to India and the final brief, blazing summer in Bermuda. Annis's mother had died there, shortly after her father had been lost at sea.

'I am sorry, Sib,' Annis said sincerely. 'I know that you feel it keenly when Charles and I quarrel and I hate it too. I know that he has a living to make, but I cannot stomach him working for Samuel Ingram. The man is nothing more than a ruthless bully!'

Sibella's pretty face crinkled up with distress. Annis seldom criticised Charles to his sister for she knew it was not fair. In Harrogate Sibella was protected from the rumbling discontent that dominated village life and so was unaware that the name of Ingram was fast becoming a curse in the hamlets that surrounded Starbeck.

'I am sure Mr Ingram cannot be all bad,' Sibella said unhappily. 'I hear dreadful things about him, but surely they are exaggerated. I know that he wishes to buy Starbeck, Annis, but he is offering a good price—'

'Oh, let us not speak of that!' Annis said hastily. 'It will only put me out of humour and I did so want to enjoy this afternoon. I deserve it!'

Sibella was still frowning. 'Yes, but speaking of Mr Ingram, Charles told me at luncheon that there has been more trouble at Linforth. Apparently there was a riot in the village last night, and one of Mr Ingram's barns was looted and burned. Charles was very angry, but I always think that the villagers must be so poor they cannot help themselves.'

Annis sighed ruefully. 'Dearest Sib, you know as well as I that rioting is a capital offence and cannot be condoned.'

'I know.' Sibella sighed. 'But when one is so poor, Annis…'

'Yes,' Annis said. 'I know. I believe it must be intensely difficult. And it is not as though they do not have provocation. I heard that Ingram evicted some of the villagers last week because he wanted a higher rent for their cottages. They had nowhere else to go and one woman went into labour prematurely and lost her baby as a result…' Annis winced. 'No, I cannot blame anyone who rebels against him.'

'Charles also said that he thought some of the local gentry might be stirring up trouble,' Sibella said. 'Apparently the leader of the rioters spoke like a gentleman and rode a bay horse. Ingram has offered a reward for information.' She turned her head to look at Annis. 'Who do you think it could be, Annis? Is it not intriguing?'

'Fascinating,' Annis said. She was disconcerted to find herself remembering that Adam Ashwick had a bay horse in his stables. 'There are not many men who fit the bill.'

'No.' Sibella looked thoughtful. 'There is Sir Everard Doble—'

'A ridiculous idea!' Annis laughed. 'As well suspect a tailor's dummy!'

'Well, then, how about Tom Shepard?'

'Perhaps…' Annis frowned. There had been a bay stallion in the stable at Starbeck as well. 'There is Mr Benson…'

'But he works for Ingram!'

'So does Charles, so I suppose they are both out of the running.' Annis sighed. 'I always believe that it is the most unlikely candidate in these cases.'

'Lord Ashwick?'

'Close. I suspect his brother. You mark my words, Sib, the Honourable Mr Edward Ashwick will prove the culprit!'

Sibella gave a gurgle of laughter. 'Oh, Annis, you are dreadful, blaming the rector! He is such a nice man as well.'

'So? I do not see why that disqualifies him. Indeed, I admire anyone who has the audacity to stand up to Ingram, capital offence or no!'

'Oh, well…' Sibella smiled '…we shall see, for I am afraid he is bound to be caught. Why, someone will turn him in for a reward of one hundred pounds.'

'Do not be so sure,' Annis said. She was remembering the scene at the tollhouse. 'Whoever is leading the rebels, the villagers will see him as one of their own. They will not turn coat, Sib.'

'Oh, well,' Sibella said again, 'let us speak of something more cheerful, Annis. Let us talk about you! Why do you not marry again and settle down?'

Annis laughed. 'You never give up trying, do you, Sib!'

'I should think not. I am very happy…' Sibella smiled blissfully '…and I think that you could be too!'

Annis shook her head. 'I cannot imagine it,' she said. 'You were fortunate in your choice, Sib, but I could not consent to remarry simply to secure my future. That was how I made such a disastrous mistake in the first place! No, give me my independence any day.'

Annis could see that Sibella was looking distressed again, as she did when anything did not quite fit with her own, ordered view of life. Sibella would no more wish to be independent than she would walk naked down Park Street, and she was not comfortable with those whose way of life was less conventional than her own. Annis reflected that her cousin had been lucky. Though she had been penniless, her beauty and sweet nature had attracted a gentleman of modest means who truly loved her.

Annis's life had not been so smooth. Her peripatetic childhood had been most stimulating, but it had ended in a dreadful fashion when her father was lost at sea and her mother died soon after, leaving Annis's whole world crashing about her when she was only seventeen. She had grasped the marriage to John Wycherley without thinking, needing only a little certainty at a terrible time. It was later that she had discovered that her security was bought at a heavy price.

'One day you may meet a man who pleases you,' Sibella said hopefully, her face clearing. 'Perhaps we shall even find you a husband in Harrogate this summer! There are plenty of the fashionable crowd up from London.'

I have met a man who pleases me, Annis thought involuntarily, the image of Adam Ashwick rising unbidden in her mind, *but I have no intention of risking everything because of it!*

She did not express her thoughts and gave her cousin a

smile instead, knowing that Sibella was happy now as she contemplated a conventional match for her. Her cousin had tried to marry her off plenty of times before. Unfortunately her judgement was not always sound. The last potential husband, an army colonel on furlough, had later been cashiered for stealing supplies and selling them on.

'I fear you would find it a tall order catching a husband for me,' she said, stretching out in the bath. 'Not only do I have no fortune, but I am not even passably good looking. Though I can scarce complain, I suppose, having made myself look an old frump for the past five years! No, Sibella, I am well and truly at my last prayers now and I am content for it to be so.'

Her damp hair was clinging to her cheeks now with a mixture of condensation and perspiration, but it did not feel too unpleasant. The warmth of the water had seeped into her bones, making her body feel soft and pliant.

Sibella snorted. 'That was not what I had heard. I heard a certain rumour that Lord Ashwick was most attentive to you, Annis. Indeed, it must be so, for did he not dance with you at the ball at the Dragon? I hear he never dances.'

'If it comes to that,' Annis said, 'neither do I.'

'Well, then!' Sibella's blue eyes sparkled. 'Do you like him?'

Annis considered the option of escaping Sibella's questions by submerging herself under the spa waters and rejected it ruefully. She would surely die of the smell.

'Yes... I suppose I do.'

'I knew it!' Sibella clapped her hands and set up a tidal wave. 'You must like him very much to admit to even a small partiality. So...' She paused invitingly.

Annis grimaced. 'Do not ask me, Sib. You know that it only makes you unhappy when I do not agree with you that marriage is the universal panacea.'

For once, Sibella did not argue. 'You mean…because of John? But, Annis, not all men are so domineering—'

'I know!' Annis said hastily. 'I am sure David is a paragon of male perfection. It is simply that I cannot risk such a thing again, Sib. Oh…' she threw her cousin an appealing look '…if you knew how repressive it was, not to be allowed out of the house except when John decreed, to be told how to dress, what to read, who to see! Having gained my freedom, how may I ever trust myself to a man again? I think I would run mad if I married again only to find myself so constrained!' She put her hands up to her face briefly. 'I swear, Sib, that I thought my head would burst with the misery and frustration of it all. I actually prayed for John to die and free me, and how dreadful and desperate is that?'

Sibella's face was sad. 'I do understand, Annis. I know you were ill with the wretchedness of it all. Yet that does not mean that all men are the same. I am persuaded that when you fall in love you will trust the man enough to take that risk. One day you will surprise yourself.'

'And surprise you, I'll warrant!'

'No.' Sibella shook her head. 'I shall not be surprised in the least.'

Annis lay back and closed her eyes again. She had been tempted to take a risk with Adam Ashwick, more tempted than she had ever been in her life before, but when pressed she had chosen the familiar ground and opted for safety. She would never know what might have happened had she taken a different course.

There was a splash as Sibella sat up, sloshing much of the precious sulphur water on to the floor. Annis hoped that Mr Thackwray's decorative plaster ceilings were not suffering. Sibella secured the towel about her.

'I am going to rest for a little now before we go to take

a beaker of water at the well. You should rest as well, you know, Annis. The water will have extracted the impurities from your body and you should give it chance to recover.'

'Excellent. My nose in particular needs to recuperate.'

Sibella frowned. 'I do not believe that you take this seriously, Annis.'

'I am sorry.' Annis tried to look suitably repentant.

'There is a chamber through there where you may lie down for a few minutes—' Sibella pointed to one of the doorways that led off the main room '—and I shall be in there.' She pointed to the opposite door. 'The attendant has taken your clothing through and left you some blankets to wrap yourself. Try to rest, Annis! You are always so *active*; I am sure that it must be exhausting for you!'

Annis smiled wryly as she eased herself out of the cooling bath ten minutes later. Sibella did a fine line in indolence, but she had never had that habit. Despite the relaxation of the bath, she felt alert and awake, disinclined to take the rest that Sibella had recommended. She decided to dress immediately and take a pot of tea downstairs in Mr Thackwray's excellent drawing room, whilst she waited for her cousin to come down.

She wrapped herself in a large towel, which was scratchy and none too clean. Annis looked at it doubtfully, wondering if Mr Thackwray had them washed between clients. Really, one way and another, this spa bathing seemed positively dangerous to the health.

She opened the door to the bedchamber and looked around for her clothes. The bed was hidden discreetly behind a screen, but Annis spotted her underclothing and her gown hanging on a hook by the fireplace. She knew that the attendant would return to help her dress, but she had no inclination to lie around in a damp blanket; besides, she

was not a fine lady who could not dress without the help
of her maid. She dried herself briskly, dressed equally so,
and checked her appearance in the spotted mirror. Not bad.
She just needed to pin up her hair, secure her bonnet over
her blonde tresses and then she would be ready to face the
world again.

A sound rather like a sigh stopped her in her tracks.
Annis froze. When she had first walked over to the mirror
she had been intent on her own reflection and had therefore
not noticed the rest of the room. Now she realised that the
angle of the mirror gave a good view of the foot of the
bed, and the foot of something—or someone—else. A bare
foot. She walked to the bottom of the bed. And stopped
dead.

Adam Ashwick was lying there. He was deeply asleep.
He was also naked. Or at least, Annis assumed that he
was, for one of Mr Thackwray's scratchy blankets was
slung low across his hips and thighs, leaving the rest of
him gloriously visible in all his hard, muscular perfection.
Annis's gaze travelled from his feet up the full length of
him, pausing briefly on the tumbled blanket, dwelling con-
siderably longer on the broad, naked chest and moving up
the strong brown column of his throat to his face. The
dishevelled dark hair fell across his brow and sleep had
softened the hard lines of cheek and jaw. His eyelashes
were so long and thick that they gave him an oddly vulnerable look, like a child asleep. Annis swallowed hard.
Her chest felt tight, as though she had a chill. But it was
not cold that was causing her to shiver, nor was it the
effects of Mr Thackwray's spa bathing.

'Lord Ashwick!'

Adam opened his eyes and stared at her in bemusement.
Then he blinked and started to sit up. His blanket slipped
lower. Annis tried not to look and found herself staring at

his thighs before she hastily averted her gaze. The hot colour rushed into her face.

'Annis?' Adam's voice sounded blurred with sleep. His eyes half-opened and his gaze drifted over her thoughtfully, and seemed to linger on the strands of blonde hair about her face. Annis saw a light come into his eyes and thought he was going to smile, but his expression changed, became concentrated. He took her wrist in a negligent grip and pulled her closer to him. Annis's other hand came to rest on his chest and lingered there on the hard warmth of his skin.

'Well, well, sweetheart! What a pleasant surprise this is!'

Adam let go of her wrist and put out a hand and brushed the wisps of fair hair back from Annis's face. His fingers were gentle against her cheek, his expression intent. Annis stared down at him, light-headed and confused. Adam took her chin in his hand and, very gently, drew her face down to his. Not that Annis was resisting. She felt so shaky that she almost tumbled on top of him.

When their lips met, the kiss was light but achingly sweet, drawing Annis deeper into the sensual web that clouded her mind. Her body, already soft and pliant from the spa bathing, grew warm and responsive. She felt Adam's hand at the neck of her gown, his fingers brushing the sensitive skin in the hollow of throat and undoing the tiny buttons one by one. Her lips parted on a gasp of mingled shock and pleasure, but Adam merely angled his head to take advantage and deepen the kiss, touching his tongue to hers. Annis's senses spun. She wanted to sink down onto the softness of the bed, taking him with her all the way. She wanted... Adam's hand slipped inside her bodice to stroke her breast with gentle fingers and the shock finally sent her tumbling beside him on to the bed.

It also appeared to wake Adam from what had evidently been a delightful dream. His black brows snapped together and he frowned at her in a wholly intimidating manner. Annis scrambled to her feet. She looked around, saw another connecting door open and leading to another bathroom, and felt her heart sink. No doubt it was easily done when the hotel was full, but she did so wish that Mr Thackwray had thought to lock some of the connecting doors.

Adam secured the blanket more firmly about his waist, swung his legs over the side of the bed and stood up.

Annis quailed. She had not thought him to be so tall or so intimidating. Nor did she recall him being quite so overpoweringly masculine, but then they had only met previously when he had all his clothes on, which was quite different from being confronted by an angry man who was almost naked. A man who had been kissing her with such passion... She tried to gather her scattered thoughts.

'I do beg your pardon, my lord. I believe one of us must be in the wrong room...'

It sounded ridiculous, as though she was apologising for stepping on his foot during a dance. Unsurprisingly, Adam ignored her feeble apology. He took a step towards her, his grey eyes narrowing ominously.

'Lady Wycherley, what the devil do you think that you are about?'

Annis glared at him. 'What am I about? One might ask what you are about, my lord! You were the one who kissed me, and—' She broke off, blushing.

'And?' Adam raised a brow. Despite his lack of clothes he looked infuriatingly confident, even rather pleased with himself. 'Does this ''and'' have something to do with your gown? It is still unbuttoned.'

Annis looked down. It was true that the row of tiny mother-of-pearl buttons was still unfastened and the bodice was gaping in a way that gave Adam a clear view of the curve of her breast. And Adam was evidently enjoying that view. His appreciative gaze did not falter.

Annis opened her mouth to give him a scathing set-down, her shaking fingers clutching for the buttons at the same time. Before she could say a word, the bathing attendant appeared, carrying a huge pile of towels. The girl screamed loudly at the sight of them, dropped the pile and scrabbled desperately on the floor whilst seemingly unable to tear her gaze away.

'Oh, ma'am, oh, sir…I do beg your pardon.'

'There has been a misunderstanding,' Annis began a little desperately. 'I think—'

'What the deuce is going on?' Mr Thackwray, florid and panting, barged through from the bathroom. He viewed the embarrassed maid and his gaze turned to Annis and Adam. His brows shot up into his hair as he saw Annis still scrambling for those last, telltale buttons.

'My lord!' he began uncertainly, caution warring with a certain man-of-the-world bonhomie in his face as he took in the situation.

'A mix-up over rooms, Thackwray, that is all,' Adam said laconically. 'If you would be so good as to escort Lady Wycherley out and close the door—'

But it was too late. Sibella, swathed in a vast bath sheet, erupted out of the next bedchamber at the same time that other guests, drawn by the maid's shrill scream, pressed curiously through the bathroom and milled in the doorway.

'Oh, good God,' Annis said faintly.

She felt rather than saw Adam's gaze rest on her face in quick appraisal. He touched her arm. 'I will square everything with Thackwray and his guests,' he said, in an undertone. 'Go back with your cousin and I will come to see you as soon as I am able.'

Annis turned her puzzled hazel gaze on him. 'My lord? I am not sure that I perfectly comprehend—'

'I am sure you do, Lady Wycherley,' Adam said, with grim amusement. 'As a chaperon you must have a perfect grasp of social conventions, so you will understand when I say that you have managed to compromise me most thoroughly!'

Adam watched as Sibella shepherded her cousin away protectively. There was a slightly stunned look on Annis's face, as though recent events had moved a little too quickly for her. Adam smiled to himself. He had been awake for a considerable time before Annis had discovered him and had thoroughly enjoyed watching her reflection in the mirror as she dressed. It had been utterly ungentlemanly of him not to alert her to his presence, and the sight of her voluptuous nakedness had done nothing to calm the urgent desire that possessed him whenever he met her. When she had come over to the bed, the impulse to pretend that he was asleep had been too strong to resist, and what had occurred afterwards had been even sweeter. It had strengthened his resolve to claim her for his own.

And now she had played directly into his hands. Adam allowed a small smile to curl his mouth. Annis Wycherley was thoroughly compromised and would have to accept his suit. Adam knew that he was in a fair way to being deeply in love with his delectable Lady Wycherley. He admired her gallantry of spirit as much as he wanted her. She was bright and courageous and kind. He did not intend to let her go.

Adam smiled as he reached for his clothes. It was time to press his advantage.

* * *

By the time that they had reached the neat town house in Knaresborough Square, Sibella was almost recovered from the shock, but still inclined to lament what had happened.

'How excessively unfortunate! It was all Mr Thackwray's fault as well, for all that he tried to shift the blame wherever he could. How they could have made such a mix up with the bedrooms defies understanding. Really, it is too vexing!' Sibella wrung her hands and fixed her cousin with a gloomy gaze. 'Everyone will talk, you know, Annis. There are some vicious gossip-mongers who frequent the spa for that precise purpose!'

Annis unpinned her bonnet and handed it to the maid with a word of thanks. She took Sibella's cloak and gloves, passed them over too and ushered her cousin into the parlour. During the drive home she had had ample time to think about what had happened between herself and Adam Ashwick, and to decide that to play the situation down was the only course of action. It had mainly been her own fault, for staring at Adam like a startled débutante, then compounding her folly by kissing him. Annis fiercely dismissed this as an aberration, and one she was determined to forget.

'Come, I am sure it will not be so bad!' she said now. 'I am sure that Lord Ashwick will be able to sort matters out with Mr Thackwray and his guests. Everyone knows that it was simply a confusion over rooms. Soon it will all be forgotten.'

Sibella settled into an armchair with a heavy sigh. 'I wish I had your faith! Thackwray does not possess an ounce of discretion, and who can speak for his assortment of guests? The story will be all over Harrogate by tonight, you mark my words! What are we going to do?'

'Order some tea for a start,' Annis said, moving to the

fireplace and pulling the bell for the maid. 'Tea is always reviving to the spirits.'

'I will concede that, of course, but I meant what are we to do about the scandal?'

Annis waited while the maid came in with the tea tray, then poured cups for them both before resting her chin on her hand. 'Nothing, dearest Sib. Lord Ashwick and I are agreed that it was merely an unfortunate mistake. It need not concern anyone else.'

'If you believe that then you are naïve,' Sibella snapped, with more acidity than was her custom. 'The scandalmongers will have it that you are having a liaison with Lord Ashwick. How does that idea suit you?'

Annis raised her cup and took a sip of the tea. It was hot, strong and just what she needed. 'I have thought about it and I confess that I do not wish for an *affaire* with Lord Ashwick.'

Sibella gave her a sharp look. 'I do not believe that you take this seriously enough, Annis! Think of the gossip—a tryst in the bath chamber, with Lord Ashwick in a state of undress—why, it is a gift for the gossips and if you try to explain it away you will cause even more scandal!'

Annis sighed. 'I must admit that the whole thing does smell a little dubious—rather like the bathing room!'

Sibella frowned. 'Annis, pray be serious! Your lamentable sense of humour!'

'I am sorry.' Annis sobered at the sight of her cousin's genuine concern. 'I know you think that I possess a levity most unsuitable in an orphan.'

'Yes, well…' Sibella's pretty face was creased with distress. 'Do you not understand, Annis? You are ruined!'

Annis put her cup down with a little click of annoyance. 'Sibella, I believe that you are making far too much of this. It was mortifying, but scarcely damaging.'

'Truly? You consider it only embarrassing? And you standing there with your gown undone?' Sibella jumped to her feet and paced across to the window. 'I believe…I do believe…that Lord Ashwick must marry you, Annis.'

Annis, who had been about to pour herself another cup of tea, put the pot down with a sigh of exasperation.

'Oh, no! Now you do go too far, Sibella!'

'Not so!' Sibella was twisting her fingers together in distress. She took a turn towards the fireplace, and then strode back towards the window again. 'It is the only solution. Lord Ashwick has compromised you. I believe that he must do the right thing.'

'Oh, pish and tish, Sibella!' Annis took a deep breath to hold her temper. 'If you take that line, then *I* compromised *him*! I was the one who walked into his bedchamber when he was in a state of undress! However, I will not press him to marry me as a result. Indeed, if such a suggestion were mooted seriously, I would have to decline the match. Now, will you sit down, if you please, so that we may talk about this sensibly? Your pacing is making me quite dizzy.'

They stared at one another. Annis was determined, but Sibella could be obstinate when her temper was roused. She subsided on to the window seat, but did not abandon her point.

'I am persuaded that Lord Ashwick is a gentleman and as such the thought must have occurred to him as well…' Her gaze sharpened on Annis's face. 'Annis? Did he mention any such thing?'

Annis hesitated, torn. 'He said something to the effect that I…that we were compromised and that he would square the matter with the Thackwray and come and see me, but—'

'You see!' Sibella said triumphantly. 'Ashwick has a

proper feeling even if you do not, Annis! He will call to pay his addresses, you mark my words.'

'Then I shall not receive him,' Annis snapped, losing her temper. 'This whole matter is so unnecessary, Sib. If people are foolish enough to talk, then let them! I shall not regard it. I certainly shall not accept a proposal of marriage on the basis of a misunderstanding!'

'Have you considered, then, the effect this will have on your business?' Sibella viewed her cousin with weary patience. 'What will happen, Annis, if rumour of this afternoon's débâcle gets abroad? You will never gain any further employment. Your future will be ruined!'

This time Annis was silent. In the embarrassment of her encounter with Adam she had all but forgotten her earlier worries about Samuel Ingram and his odious threats. Yet now she could see that Sibella was quite right; this was a gift for Ingram and if he chose to encourage the gossip it could be devastating. She would be branded an unfit chaperon and would never gain any employment again.

She stared at Sibella, torn between a wish to deny the possibility and an impotent anger that such a thing might happen to her. Yet a cold fear was stealing about her heart, a belief that Sibella might be right and that everything she had worked for might be about to be lost.

'I cannot believe that any of this will happen—' she started to say, but even she could hear the note of desperation in her voice.

There was a knock at the door. Sibella jumped up and peered through the window. 'I do believe that Lord Ashwick is here. You may argue the toss with him instead of with me, coz, for, unless I miss my guess, you are about to receive an offer of marriage!'

Chapter Nine

'Lord Ashwick, ma'am.' The little housemaid, thoroughly overawed, opened the drawing-room door and dropped a flustered curtsy.

Annis watched as Adam came forward to greet Sibella. Now clad somewhat more formally than before, in pale fawn buckskins, a coat of green superfine and highly polished Hessians, he looked formidable. Her heart missed a beat.

'Mrs Granger…' The charm was very much to the fore as Adam bowed over Sibella's hand, 'I hope that I find you well. Pray do not concern yourself over the scene you witnessed just now. I am persuaded that your cousin and I may put all to rights.'

Sibella blushed and smiled. Annis watched cynically. Having been on the receiving end of Adam's charm, she knew it took a stern heart to resist him. Nor was his charm superficial, like that of most gentlemen she had met. There was real warmth there to which people responded naturally, in the way that Sibella was responding now. Annis felt cold and unhappy. She was going to need to be very strong to resist Adam's proposals, plus the entreaties of Sibella and the promptings of her own common sense. Although a concern for her future was uppermost in her mind, she was determined not to accept Adam simply to escape from a difficult situation.

His gaze fell on her and Annis saw his expression harden slightly. She raised her chin and met his eyes with a level stare of her own.

'Lady Wycherley.' Adam bowed punctiliously. 'How do you do, ma'am.'

'Well!' Sibella said, with arch brightness. 'I shall leave the two of you alone! Just ring the bell if you require tea…or anything…' She hesitated for a moment, cast Annis a look and made a fluttering gesture with her hands. 'Very well, then…'

She went out and there was a long and slightly awkward silence. Annis was determined not to break it. Adam crossed to the fireplace and stood leaning one arm along the mantelpiece. He turned towards her.

'It seems that we find ourselves in a very awkward situation, Lady Wycherley.' He looked at her thoughtfully. 'The question is, what is to be done about it?'

Annis took a quick breath. 'I am sorry that my actions in not checking the room should have placed us in this position, my lord—'

Adam made a slight gesture. 'Do not apologise, ma'am. It was nobody's fault but that old fool, Thackwray, directing me to the wrong chamber. A mistake easily made in a busy hotel, but one I cannot help wishing had not happened.'

Annis felt a little relieved. 'I am glad that at least you do not think I had contrived the situation to entrap you,' she said. 'It would be the very last thing that I would do.'

Adam's lips quirked into a rueful smile. 'Having shown such a disinclination for my company, Lady Wycherley, I can well believe that!'

Annis blushed. 'Then there need be no difficulty,' she said swiftly. 'It is nothing more than a misunderstanding, my lord, and one that will be quickly forgotten. When you arrived I was telling my cousin that we need not regard it. Whilst the matter is unfortunate, I doubt that it will give rise to much gossip.'

Adam raised one black brow. 'You are misguided, ma'am—or an eternal optimist. I can assure you that when I left the Crown the speculation was already widespread.'

Annis's heart sank. 'Oh, but surely… How foolish!'

'Foolish or not, there is much conjecture about our relationship.' He looked at her. 'Think about it! I was wearing nothing but a blanket, and you…' he appraised her thoughtfully '…you had your hair down and your gown partly undone, you looked slightly flustered—and very pretty. Besides, there is some truth in the gossip, is there not? I had just kissed you, and…' Adam grinned. 'Well…I cannot pretend to forget what happened between us, and everyone saw ample proof that it *had* happened…'

Annis felt more than slightly flustered now. The memory of his hard, lithe body barely concealed by the blanket was disturbing, as was the reminder of his kisses and caresses.

'I suppose…put like that it does seem a great deal worse.'

Adam gestured her to a chair. 'Will you take a seat and hear me out, ma'am?'

Annis sat down reluctantly.

'In such cases as these I believe it is always the lady whose reputation suffers most,' Adam said slowly. 'As a chaperon to young ladies, Lady Wycherley, I am sure that you see the truth of what I am saying. Rumours about your virtue, even unfounded rumours, can be most destructive.'

Annis pressed her hands together in her lap. She was a

little surprised to find that she felt very nervous beneath that cool grey gaze.

'I concede the truth of what you are saying in general terms,' she said, 'but I cannot accept that it applies to my case. I am older and...' her voice faltered and she forced it on '...I have been married. The rules that apply to widows are far different from those that relate to young, unmarried girls.'

Adam inclined his head. Annis did not think that he seemed particularly impressed by her point of view.

'I admit that the rules are different,' he said, 'but the gossip seldom is.' His eyes narrowed. 'I assume that you have a care for your good name, ma'am?'

'Of course.' Annis found she could not meet his gaze. 'Of course I care for my good reputation, but—'

'There is no but.' The incisive tone in Adam's voice silenced her. 'You have taken that good name for granted until now, I dare say, Lady Wycherley, as is your right as a virtuous widow. Now, through no fault of your own, your reputation is questioned. You are considered of shady virtue, perhaps... A widow prepared to indulge in a love affair. People will view you differently because of what happened today. It is inevitable.'

'It is unfair!' Annis could not help herself. 'Why should I suffer censure for something that I have not done?'

A shadow of a smile touched Adam's mouth. 'Dear me, ma'am, do you expect life to be fair? I had not have thought to find that a lady of your mature years would still have any illusions!'

The comment stung Annis. Her hazel eyes flashed.

'I do expect people to think well of me, unless they have a *genuine* reason to think the opposite!'

'Yes indeed.' Adam bowed slightly. 'I am sure that anyone who does know you, ma'am, could not believe anything bad of you. It is of the others that we speak—the people who do not know you, yet are still prepared to rip your reputation to shreds. Besides…' he sighed '…there is some basis for the gossip. I cannot forget that I had been kissing you and it was my fault that your gown was in disarray—'

Annis held up her hand. 'Please! Can we not consider that as an aberration and simply forget it?'

Adam laughed. 'No, I do not think so. It was a mistake that occurs quite frequently, is it not? That should tell you something, Lady Wycherley, although it may be a message that you do not wish to hear.'

Annis sighed. She knew that he was correct. Correct about her reactions to him, correct about the gossips and correct in saying that her reputation was tarnished.

A picture of Samuel Ingram came, unbidden, into Annis's mind. He knew her and he would take every opportunity to blacken her name. This piece of bad luck was a gift for him. Even so… She strengthened her resolve. She would not accept Adam just for the protection of his name and could not compromise her independence over a foolish mistake.

Adam straightened up. 'Annis…' His use of her name, the tone of tender reproach, brought a lump to her throat. 'We have spoken of your honour, Annis, but you must give some consideration to mine. What sort of ramshackle fellow would I appear if I left you to deal with this scandal alone? Come, let us cease this fencing. I would deem it an honour if you were to accept my hand in marriage.'

Annis stood up and moved over to the window. Somehow the conversation had moved to a new level of intimacy with his proposal—and his use of her name.

'I had not thought that you wished to marry again, my lord,' she said. 'You told me yourself that you were sincerely in love with your wife, and I understood that you had no wish to remarry after her death.'

'I was, and I did not. Circumstances alter cases and I would like to marry you.'

'It is most chivalrous of you.'

'Thank you. Your answer?'

Annis turned and met his eyes very straight. 'I am grateful for your generosity, my lord—'

'But you are going to refuse me.' Adam came across to stand before her. 'I do wish that you would reconsider, Annis.'

Annis did not meet his eyes. 'I cannot marry a stranger, sir.'

'We need not be strangers.' Adam took her hands. 'You know that I already I have a feeling for you that is much stronger than mere liking, Annis. And you have confessed—an attraction to me…?' There was a question in his tone.

Annis looked up and met his eyes. And blushed. She could hardly deny it after the wanton way she had responded to him in the past.

'I admit to a certain partiality…'

Adam laughed. 'Thank you for that. We have time to get to know one another better before the wedding—and after.'

Annis risked a fleeting look at his face. 'You are very kind, but I cannot.' She freed herself.

Adam's expression hardened slightly. 'You must not think of it as a betrayal of your first marriage. It may not be the same, but it need not be bad.'

'My first marriage…' For a moment the images flooded Annis's mind: losing her freedom, the stifling propriety, the dreadful sense of being trapped, day after day, without end. She shuddered.

'You are most generous, sir.' She took a deep breath. 'There are reasons why I cannot accept your proposal— matters that you do not understand…'

'Then explain them to me.' Adam walked over to the window. 'You have been open with me up until now, Annis.' His smile did strange things to Annis's already shaky composure. 'Indeed, you have said more than I could have expected. If we already have a regard for one another, where is the difficulty?'

Annis looked away from that compelling gaze. 'Please do not press me, my lord. All I can tell you is that there are reasons why I simply cannot contemplate remarriage.'

Adam sighed. 'I am not a patient man, but I am content to let it wait until we know each other a little better, if that will help you.'

'There is no time.' Annis felt a little panicky. 'If we were to marry on account of this scandal, it would have to be soon. No! It is impossible!' She wrapped her arms close about her. 'I cannot even consider it.'

There was an unhappy silence. 'I presume that you have thought about the effect that this will have on your work, Annis,' Adam said, with what seemed to Annis to be unbearable gentleness. 'It cannot have escaped you that not all guardians will be prepared to entrust their charges to a woman about whose name some unsavoury scandal clings… You might find that your livelihood has been utterly destroyed.'

Annis turned with an angry swish of skirts. 'I know that! I have thought of little else! But even so, the enormity of contracting a marriage, and under such circumstances, is not to be borne!'

An image of Starbeck flashed across her mind, and with it the thought of Ingram. Was everything to be set against her? She closed her eyes for an anguished moment.

'I will leave you to consider my offer,' Adam said, 'and will call on you in a couple of days' time to ask for your answer.'

For a moment Annis considered the cowardly way out— to run to Starbeck and not tell him. However, she suspected that Adam Ashwick was the sort of man who would find out where she had gone—and come straight after her.

'I am leaving Harrogate soon.' The words came out reluctantly.

'For Starbeck. I remember you telling me.'

Annis laughed a little shakily. 'How ironic that you would gain control of Starbeck if you marry me, my lord, and so spite Mr Ingram. Would you go as far as marriage to gain Starbeck?'

Adam gave her a look. It brought the hot colour up into her face. 'My dear Lady Wycherley,' he drawled, 'I would quite like to possess Starbeck but...' he paused '...I ache to possess you.'

Annis drew in a short breath. Her mouth was suddenly dry. 'My lord—'

Adam picked up her hand. 'Let me help you fight your battles, Annis,' he said softly. 'Why must you do everything alone?'

Something caught in Annis's throat. 'I confess it is a habit with me. I have always done so.'

'Then this time allow me to help you. You might find that you like it.'

There was something very persuasive in his tone. They were standing very close to one another. When he drew her closer still she fitted perfectly into his arms; fitted against the entire length of him. Annis's heart began to race.

'After all,' Adam continued, 'you like it when I kiss you...'

Annis quivered. 'My lord—'

Adam bent his head and proved his point. He was very gentle, the kiss light, undemanding and exerting only the slightest of pressure on her lips. Yet when he let her go she could see the conflict in his eyes, the urgent need that he was holding under absolute control. He stepped back very deliberately.

'I will call on you soon, Annis.' He paused. 'By the way, how long were you in the bedchamber before I awoke?'

Annis blushed. 'Only a few moments, my lord.'

'I see. I hope that you enjoyed the view.' Adam gave her a grin and sauntered towards the door.

A sudden, shaming thought struck Annis as she remembered that she had dressed in the same room. 'My lord—' she gave him a look of entreaty '—you were genuinely asleep, were you not? All the time?'

Adam raised his brows. His grin became positively wicked. 'My dear Annis, I would spare you embarrassment and not answer that question! All I can say is that you could not be more thoroughly compromised!'

Sibella's curiosity was such that she left it a very short time indeed before poking her head around the door. Indeed, she might almost have passed Adam in the doorway.

'Well?'

Annis sat down a little heavily.

'He did ask me to marry him.'

'And?'

'I refused. But…' she saw Sibella's moue of disappointment '…I believe Lord Ashwick is not a man who will accept rejection lightly. He suggested that I give the matter thought and told me that he would call on me in a day or two to hear my answer then.' She jumped up. 'Indeed,

Sibella, I am not at all sure what to do. He is…very sure of himself.'

'He is entirely charming.' Sibella gave her a little satisfied smile. 'Confess it, cousin, you like him more than a little, do you not?'

'I do.' Annis gave her a troubled look. 'But, Sib, you know that I could not bear to be married again—'

'Oh, stuff!' Sibella dismissed Annis's scruples with a wave of her hand. 'I know you did not have a happy experience of marriage, but that need not be a barrier.'

'I dislike the restrictive nature of married life.'

'But being married to Lord Ashwick would not in any way be like being married to John Wycherley!' Sibella finished triumphantly. 'Indeed, Annis…' her smile became dreamy '…I think that it might be positively exciting!'

Annis looked alarmed. 'You mean, in a physical sense? I think that you might be correct, but—'

'There is no need to be alarmed.' Sibella's smile vanished. 'If you explain to him about John—'

'I cannot explain anything so intimate! I do not know him well enough for that.' Annis's desperate gaze sought her cousin's. 'It will be difficult enough to explain why I was so unhappy and why I cling to my liberty. How can I possibly broach the topic of my first marriage being unconsummated?'

Sibella sighed. 'I understand your feelings, Annis, but maybe you will find that when you know Lord Ashwick a little better you will have no difficulty in discussing the matter. On the other hand…' she smiled slightly '…perhaps it would be better *not* to tell him. By the time he finds out he will not be in any position to stop and question you, believe me!'

Annis stared at her for a moment, then turned her face away. 'Sib, I am afraid.'

Sibella crossed over to her and sat down. She put her hand over Annis's cold one.

'Trust him,' she urged. 'You already find Lord Ashwick very attractive, Annis, and that is a good start. You already *like* him, and that is even better.'

Annis looked unhappy. 'I suppose so. I do not wish to be married to him, though, particularly not like this. I...am not ready for it.'

Sibella patted her hand. 'Think about it. Give him a little time.'

'There is no time. In matters such as this I believe it is the convention to be married at once.'

'Then do not worry. I cannot believe that Lord Ashwick would behave as a callow boy and force himself on you. Besides, he has been married before.'

Annis shuddered. 'Yes, and that is another thing! He told me quite openly that he had been in love with his wife.'

'That was a long time ago. Besides, it is a good thing, for it shows he is not a man who takes marriage lightly.'

'He may want children.'

'He may indeed. You will have to speak to him about it.' Sibella stretched a hand out to the bell. 'More tea, cousin? You seem in need of it.'

Annis nodded, frowning. 'Thank you. Charles will not like it, you know, Sib.'

Sibella frowned too. 'Because Lord Ashwick is at odds with Mr Ingram?'

'Yes. They are very cool to one another. Oh, dear, this is so very difficult!'

Sibella came across to give her a hug. 'I am persuaded that Charles's first concern will be for you, Annis,' she said loyally. 'Pray do not worry about it any more.'

'I feel so strange.'

'Because you are always the chaperon and never the bride.' Sibella laughed. 'You are accustomed to having the order of things and arranging your own life, and to find yourself in a reversal of that situation is bound to be odd.'

Annis jumped up. 'I need to go for a walk to clear my head. The fresh air might help me.' She gave her cousin a spontaneous kiss. 'I will not take that tea after all, Sibella, but I will see you again soon. Thank you for listening to me.'

'You will tell me what you decide?' Sibella said anxiously. 'May I call tomorrow?'

'Of course.' Annis smiled. 'And if I am to be the next Lady Ashwick you will be the first to know.'

Annis walked until her feet ached, but although the exercise did a great deal to tire her physically it did little to settle her mental state. She could forgive herself for the mistake of walking into Adam's dressing room at the hotel, for that had in fact been Mr Thackwray's fault and was easily done. It might have helped had she not stood gaping at Adam like a green girl until the maid came in, but it was too late to regret that. Annis winced as she thought of the salacious story that was no doubt already going the rounds of the Harrogate matrons. The scandal had all the elements of a perfect piece of gossip—the spa bath, the scantily clad chaperon, the naked lord, and the audience of outraged guests... Annis sighed. She had spent the past three years chaperoning young ladies and keeping them out of scrapes, only to tumble into far worse disgrace herself.

It was late when she returned to the house in Church Row and Mrs Hardcastle was fussing.

'There you are, pet! I was growing quite worried. I sent to Mrs Granger's to see if you had decided to stay for dinner, but they said that you had left hours ago.'

'I am sorry, Hardy,' Annis said wearily. She was conscious that she looked hot and dusty and wanted no more than to take a bath. 'I think that I shall take a tray in my room, if I may, and I am not at home to visitors.'

'Mr Lafoy called already,' Mrs Hardcastle said significantly. 'He seemed quite put out to find you from home and said that he would call again later.'

'Well, I won't see him,' Annis said. She knew she sounded fretful, which was unusual for her, but the thought of receiving a lecture from Charles was too much to bear.

She slept badly and the following morning went into High Harrogate, setting off before the streets became busy. It was another hot morning with a high blue sky and normally this would have lifted Annis's spirits, but not today. She made a few purchases in the shops, went to take a glass of water at the sulphur well and walked briskly on The Stray, and when she returned home her thoughts were still as confused as they had been when she went out.

Mrs Hardcastle was hovering when she reached home, her face working like milk coming up to the boil.

'That Lady Copthorne!' she burst out, when Annis politely enquired about the reason for her agitation. 'She was here earlier, Miss Annis, asking to see you. When I told her you were out she said to tell you that she no longer wished to engage your services to chaperon her Eustacia to London in the autumn.' Mrs Hardcastle's magnificent bosom swelled indignantly. 'Said that you were scandalous and too unsuitable to care for her ewe lamb lest you lead her into trouble! Well!'

'Oh, dear,' Annis said faintly. She sat down abruptly on the chair in the hall. 'I thought something like this might happen.'

'I gave her the right about and no mistake,' Mrs Hardcastle said, with satisfaction. 'Told her you were worth a hundred of her and that Miss Eustacia was fit for Bedlam and would run off with a groom before she was nineteen.'

'Lady Copthorne certainly will not be changing her mind and re-engaging me, then,' Annis said, trying to see the humorous side.

'Ho! I should hope not!'

As Annis toiled up the stairs she reflected that it was only what she had expected. Harrogate was a small community and, like many other small towns, it loved scandal. She had provided the gossip and now her character was in shreds. No doubt Samuel Ingram had assiduously fanned the flames.

It left her with the difficulty of what to do in the future, however. If she did not accept Adam Ashwick's proposal, the chance to re-establish herself as a chaperon looked slim indeed. Similarly she would be given short shrift if she offered herself as a governess or schoolteacher and at present she could not think of an alternative. In a thoroughly bad mood she shrugged off her outdoor clothing and tried unsuccessfully to dismiss her worries at the same time.

The house was very quiet that evening. Annis had been intending to join Sibella and David for dinner, but had cried off at the last moment, pleading a headache. A part of her wished to see Adam and resolve the situation and a part of her shrank from it. He had not called on her and Annis understood that he was keeping his word and giving her plenty of time to come to a decision. She respected him for it, but it made it no easier to decide what to do. Whenever she thought of marriage she felt the panic rise up in her, as though the waters were closing over her head and she could not breathe. Under the circumstances it seemed foolish to condemn them both to so unhappy a match, but Annis was increasingly aware that her alternatives were limited. In fact, at the moment she had no idea of a practical alternative.

She gave the servants the evening off and sat down to a cold collation alone in the dining room. Mrs Hardcastle had put it together before going off to the threepenny seats in the theatre gallery. It was her first opportunity to see Miss Mardyn dance and she had been very excited.

Annis felt tired and gloomy and for once sitting reading alone did not seem an attractive option. Instead, she soon found herself dozing in front of the drawing-room fire. When she awoke the candles had burned down and she felt a little cold and stiff. Her book had slid off her lap and was lying on the floor. And from upstairs came the unmistakable creak of a floorboard.

At first Annis thought that Mrs Hardcastle or one of the other servants must have returned home early, but then she realised that they would have come to greet her had they done so. She waited. There was another stealthy creak. This was definitely not the mice.

Annis picked up the poker in one hand and a candlestick in the other. She crept up the stairs. The bedrooms of Miss Fanny and Miss Lucy Crossley were in darkness now, the doors closed. At the end of the corridor, next to Miss Lucy's bedroom, was the study. Annis had not used it, for she had had no time whilst the girls had been with her. Now she saw that the door was ajar and a faint light flickered beyond. There was the rustle of papers.

Annis pushed the door open and advanced, wondering at the last moment if it was not the most foolish thing she could have done. But it was too late. The figure by the desk was straightening up and turning towards her. His expression was rueful and resigned.

'I fear you have caught me red-handed, Lady Wycherley,' Adam Ashwick said.

Annis put her candlestick down on the table. Anger and disappointment were warring for mastery within her. She had been so close, she thought bitterly; so very close to trusting him completely. And now she saw what a fool she had been.

'I am not surprised to see you here, Lord Ashwick,' she said coldly. 'I suppose you are following Mr Woodhouse's advice and spying on my cousin? How did you get in, by the way?'

'Over the roof and down the ivy. It is not to be recommended.' Adam had the grace to look a little shamefaced.

'I shall not be trying it.' Annis gestured to the door. 'You may leave at once if you wish, without me calling the Watch. You may also leave behind anything that you have found.'

'I have found nothing.' Adam straightened up.

'I could have told you as much. There is nothing to interest you in the desk, Lord Ashwick. It is only a list of my engagements these six weeks past and I could have furnished you with them if you had only asked.'

Adam smiled at her. 'Thank you. As you guessed, it was your cousin, Mr Lafoy, whose movements interested me—'

'I am aware,' Annis snapped. 'It does not take a genius to work out what you are doing here, Lord Ashwick. Have you had time to search the attics? That is usually where people hide things. Or is this your first port of call?'

'I was intending to search the attic next.' Adam came forward. 'I am sorry, Annis. I did not intend to startle you.'

'You did not startle me,' Annis said cuttingly, 'only disappointed me, my lord. I had thought that you would at least have been honest with me. Skulking around here when my back is turned—'

'I had heard that you were from home. My informant told me that you were dining with the Grangers tonight.'

'Careless intelligence work, Lord Ashwick. I was invited but I did not attend. I would not expect you to make mistakes.'

'I appear to have done so this time,' Adam said, a little grimly. 'I would have told you, Annis, but I had so little time—'

'Excuses, my lord.' Annis felt the angry tears prickle her eyes. 'When we spoke at the inn, you promised to consult me before you took any action against Charles. But you did not trust me, did you? First you make me a proposal of marriage and then you demonstrate that you do not trust me one whit! I need not look very far for the reason to refuse you.'

She saw Adam flinch. 'Annis,' he said, 'I appreciate that you are angry with me, but may we please go downstairs to discuss this and would you please put that poker down as well? You are making me nervous.'

He did not look in the least uneasy, but Annis lowered the poker anyway.

'Very well. We shall go to the drawing room. You go first, my lord.'

They descended the stairs in a wary silence.

'You were acting on Mr Woodhouse's tip off, were you not?' Annis asked, when once they were in the drawing room and the poker had been restored to its place by the fire. She watched as Adam kicked the apple logs into a fresh blaze. It seemed comfortable to have him in her drawing room, as though he was in his proper place. Which was all wrong in view of his duplicity. She hardened her heart against him.

'Woodhouse said that you should look for evidence against Charles, did he not, and though you swore to me that you would not do so, that is exactly what you are doing.' Annis shrugged wearily. 'This is not Charles's house and the only connection he has with it is that he took it for me for the season. There is nothing here for you, my lord. You will have to ask Mr Woodhouse to be more precise.'

Adam stepped closer. 'I cannot do that. Woodhouse was found head down in the chalybeate well this afternoon.'

Annis whitened. 'An accident?'

Adam looked sceptical. 'A convenient one. There were plenty of witnesses to say that he was already drunk by midday. Dead drunk.'

Annis shivered and wrapped her arms around her. 'You think that it was no coincidence.'

Adam shrugged. 'I cannot say, but it is expedient for Ingram and damned unhelpful to me.'

He came up to her. 'Annis, much as I would like to find something to Ingram's discredit, that is not what concerns me now. I am sorry that I did not speak to you first before I came here—'

'Why did you not?'

Adam shrugged uncomfortably. 'Because I knew that it would upset you that I was involving Lafoy in my investigations. I thought that you might even say that I should not look for evidence here, in which case I should not have been able to proceed.'

Annis looked at him. 'You are right. It is my house and I should have forbidden it.'

Adam sighed. 'I would have accepted that. So it was easier not to ask you.'

Annis turned away. She felt bruised and tired. 'That is no excuse.'

'No, I agree.' There was a grim set to Adam's mouth, though whether he was angry with her or with himself, and why, Annis could not be sure. 'It was very wrong of me and I understand why you are angry. Do you forgive me?'

Annis frowned. 'No, I do not think so.'

'I understand why you might not believe me, but I swear to share everything with you in future, Annis. *Everything.*'

Annis shivered at his tone. He sounded sincere, but he had just shown her that he did not trust her. Her troubled hazel gaze sought his. Adam took a step closer.

'I am sorry,' he said again. He put his hands on her upper arms and gently rubbed. Annis felt the hairs rise along her skin and trembled with sensual awareness.

'It was an unconscionably stupid thing to do,' Adam said softly, 'and I truly regret it. It was not that I did not trust you, Annis—I would have told you if I had found anything, I swear.'

The soft stroke of his hands was terribly distracting. Annis tried to concentrate.

'I am very cross with you. And disappointed.'

'I understand.' Adam's breath stirred her hair. He slid his arms about her. 'How may I make amends, sweetheart?'

'I have no notion. Certainly not by kissing me. That would be a very easy way out of the situation.'

'I agree.' Adam sat down in one of the armchairs and very gently drew her down on to his lap. Once more he held her close, her head against his shoulder, his arms about her waist. 'If I may, I will simply hold you. That may do a little to convince you that I am sincere and not just a rake.'

'And a deceiver.'

Annis felt Adam wince. 'You are harsh, my sweet. Do you hold grudges?'

'No, I do not believe so.' It felt shockingly comforting

to be in his arms. Warm, intimate, all the things that Annis had trained herself to live without. She burrowed a little closer to that warmth. 'Are you truly repentant?'

'Of course. I knew at the time that it was a foolish thing to do. That is why I was so angry with myself.' He tilted her face up to his. 'I do not want to lose your trust, Annis.'

Annis sighed. 'I think I might forgive you in a few minutes, weak as I am. But only if you promise not to do it again.'

Adam kissed the top of her head. 'I promise not to break into your house again.'

Annis dug him in the ribs. 'You know what I mean.'

'I do. I promise to tell you everything, to share everything with you and only to kiss you when you say that I might...'

Annis pulled away a little. 'That is very handsome of you, I suppose.'

'So may I?'

They stared at one another.

'You may,' Annis whispered.

She saw him smile before he bent closer, too close for her to focus. She closed her eyes. His mouth took hers softly, sweetly. His tongue touched her lower lip before sliding deeper. Annis raised one hand and touched Adam's cheek where the stubble was rough against her palm. She felt as though she was melting, slipping into pure pleasure. His body was hard against hers and she could feel the pounding of his heart against her other hand as it rested on his chest. She felt hot and dizzy, overwhelmed by sensation, confused, all common sense lost. Both her head and her heart were reeling.

Adam eased away from her for a moment.

'You said that you were disappointed in me. Am I disappointing you now, Annis?'

'That was not what I meant,' Annis whispered.

'I know. Marry me.'

He kissed her again, parting her lips, his tongue taking intimate liberties with hers again until she felt weak and clung to him. His hand was on her thigh, warm against the soft silk of her stocking. Annis's clouded mind cleared slightly. His hand was on her thigh *under* her skirts and he was stroking her skin very gently. The desire shot through her like wildfire.

'Marry me,' he said, against her ear.

Annis pulled away a little, still leaning against Adam for support. 'You should not have kissed me so much, for now I cannot think straight. I will give you my answer tomorrow, my lord.'

There was a step on the tiles of the hall and Mrs Hardcastle's voice carolled, 'Miss Annis, are you still awake? I'm back from the theatre. That Miss Mardyn—what a hussy. I thought, she's no better than she ought to be—' She pushed the door of the drawing room open. 'Why are you sitting in the dark, Miss Annis? Oh!' She jumped back.

'Good evening, Mrs Hardcastle,' Adam said, with what Annis considered remarkable aplomb. He loosened his grip on her and allowed her to get to her feet, which she did, albeit shakily. Adam stood up too and put one steadying arm about her.

'If you will excuse me, I was just leaving.'

Mrs Hardcastle gave him a thorough stare. 'That's probably for the best, my lord. Gracious, Miss Annis, entertaining gentlemen callers when you are alone in the house! Whatever next?'

'I was persuading Lady Wycherley to marry me,' Adam said shamelessly.

'I saw your means of persuasion,' Mrs Hardcastle said.

'Not that I'm sure they will work, my lord. My Miss Annis is most obstinate.'

'I should be grateful if you could prevent yourselves from discussing me as though I were not here,' Annis said, recovering herself. She held her hand out to Adam. 'Goodnight, my lord.'

Adam bowed. 'Goodnight, Lady Wycherley.'

'A dangerous gentleman,' Mrs Hardcastle opined when she had shot the bolt behind Adam. 'You make sure you marry him, Miss Annis.'

Annis gave her a startled look. 'It was not very long ago that you were warning me that handsome is as handsome does, Hardy.'

'Aye, well, I've not changed my mind on that.' Mrs Hardcastle smiled grimly. 'There's plenty of men I'd tell you not to touch with a long, sharp stick, Miss Annis, but yon gentleman is not one of them. No, you mark my words. He's a good lad. You marry him.'

'I am glad to have your blessing, Hardy,' Annis said, 'for I think that that is exactly what I shall be doing.'

'No need to sound so mealy-mouthed about it,' Mrs Hardcastle said. 'I saw the two of you just then. You were enjoying his attentions, Miss Annis, so don't pretend you weren't! Either that or you're a better actress than that Miss Mardyn will ever be. The sooner you're married the better.'

As soon as Annis entered the Promenade Rooms the following day she was aware that the buzz in the air came not from gossip about her own doings but something far more exciting.

'Have you not heard?' Sibella demanded, once greetings were exchanged. 'There was the most tremendous riot last night at Mr Ingram's estate at Linforth. The windows were smashed and the outbuildings set alight and the mob delivered a letter that said that unless Mr Ingram desisted from his money-grubbing practices they would not stop until they had burned every one of his properties to the ground.' She gave an artistic shiver. '''Look to thy soul, for we shall deal with thy body,'' the letter said.'

Annis raised her brows. 'How very melodramatic. How has Mr Ingram responded to this warning?'

'He has threatened to have the yeomanry called out and he has offered a reward of a thousand pounds for the capture of the rebel leader,' Sibella said. 'A thousand pounds, Annis! There's many a man would sell his own grandmother for that amount.'

'We shall see,' Annis said. She looked about. Rather than promenading, the good people of Harrogate were gathered in loquacious groups, all discussing the news of the riot. Judging by the laughter and bright-eyed excitement there were plenty who felt that Ingram was getting his comeuppance.

The door opened and Adam, Edward, Della and the Dowager Lady Ashwick all came into the long room. Annis saw Adam excuse himself from the others and quicken his step as he saw her. He came straight over to her and took her hand.

'Lady Wycherley. How are you this morning, ma'am?'

'I am very well, I thank you, sir,' Annis said, her composed tone belying the flutter of excitement his presence always stirred in her.

'Mrs Granger.' Adam smiled at Sibella, who smiled back happily. Annis reflected ruefully that it was good that at least one of her family could get on with the Ashwicks.

'We were just discussing the shocking news of the riot at Linforth,' Sibella said. 'It sounds quite dreadful!'

'Very violent,' Adam agreed. 'I believe the other topic of conversation is Mr Woodhouse's sad demise. Plenty of people are wondering if it is safe to drink the water from the chalybeate well now that it has been polluted by his body!'

Annis's reply was lost as the door opened with a crash that was loud enough to stop all conversation. Samuel Ingram entered, followed by Charles Lafoy, whom Annis thought was looking quite ill. Behind them was Mr Pullen, the magistrate. Annis saw Charles look around and saw his gaze fall on Della Tilney. He winced visibly. Annis met his gaze across the room and she gave him a puzzled, questioning look. Charles shook his head slightly.

A strange silence had fallen in the Promenade Rooms. The chatter, which had swirled up briefly after Ingram's arrival, now died down to an ominous hum before fading away altogether. The three men were walking the length of the room towards them. Edward Ashwick, his mother and sister started to draw closer too as Ingram's party made its way towards Adam.

It was evident to Annis that Charles was deeply discomfited and the fact that she and Sibella were present made matters much worse for him. She moved closer to Sibella and took her arm in a comforting grip.

'Excuse me, my lord.' The magistrate cleared his throat.

Adam looked enquiring. 'Yes, Mr Pullen, what can I do for you?' His gaze moved on to Ingram and his expression hardened. He gave the slightest of bows. 'Mr Ingram.'

'If we might go somewhere more private, my lord?' Pullen looked quite agitated. 'Mr Ingram has laid a matter before us regarding the riot at his estate of Linforth last night and we must ask you a number of questions.'

'Ask me?' Adam raised his brows incredulously. 'Are you implying that I had something to do with the matter, Pullen?'

Mr Pullen looked increasingly unhappy. 'Privacy, Lord

Ashwick. That's the thing. Surely...' he looked around '...you do not wish this crowd to be party to your business?'

Adam's jaw set. 'There is nothing for them to be party to and I have no difficulty in making that clear. I had nothing to do with the riot at Linforth last night.'

Ingram stepped forward. 'Do you own a bay stallion with a white star, my lord?'

Adam frowned. 'Yes, I do.'

'There are witnesses who can testify that the rebel leader rode such a horse last night. That he was a man of broad stature and he spoke like a gentleman.'

Adam looked contemptuous. 'So? That could be any number of people, Ingram.'

There was a loaded silence.

Mr Pullen hopped from one foot to the other. 'Were you at Eynhallow last night, my lord?'

'I was not. I was in Harrogate.'

Pullen said eagerly, 'I am sure that this matter could be cleared up easily if there are witnesses.'

Edward Ashwick shifted uncomfortably. 'My brother had dinner with me last night.'

Ingram looked down his nose. 'At eleven of the clock, Reverend? The damage at Linforth was done late in the night. It takes no time for a man to ride from Harrogate to Linforth on a good horse...'

Once again there was a tense silence.

'My lord?' Pullen said, uncertainly.

Adam shrugged. 'I cannot help you, Pullen.'

Mr Pullen looked as though he wanted to cry. 'Then I have no alternative but to ask you to answer further questions, my lord.'

Annis took a deep breath. She let go of Sibella's arm and stepped forward.

'Lord Ashwick was with me yesterday evening,' she said. She looked pointedly at Ingram. 'At eleven of the clock.'

A ripple went through the onlookers. Annis saw Sibella glance quickly towards her, frowning. Charles took an impulsive step forward, then checked himself. His face was stormy. Annis glanced across at Adam. He looked studiously blank.

'Lord Ashwick called in the evening, after dinner,' she continued. 'We had a glass or two of sherry and spoke for a while. He must have left at about eleven-thirty, I suppose. My housekeeper could verify the time for you, Mr Pullen.'

'I am indebted to you, madam.' Pullen looked as though he was not sure whether to be embarrassed or grateful. Annis wondered whether he had already heard the gossip about her encounter with Adam in the spa bath the previous day and was reflecting that her standing as a reputable chaperon was well and truly done for.

Adam stepped forward to her side. Annis felt his comforting presence at her shoulder although she did not turn to look at him.

'You will appreciate that I wished to keep Lady Wycherley's name out of this matter, Pullen,' Adam said. There was anger in his tone and a tenderness that made Annis tremble. 'However, as she has seen fit to disclose the truth, I can only concur. There is, after all, no law against a man having a glass of sherry with his betrothed...'

This time the gasp of surprise was even louder. Edward Ashwick was the first to pull himself together and stepped forward to clap Adam on the back. 'No, indeed. Hearty congratulations, Ash. I am glad that Lady Wycherley has accepted your suit.'

Lady Ashwick took her cue, pressing forward to kiss

Annis's cheek. 'So am I, my love. I am persuaded that you are just the wife for Adam!'

After that there seemed nothing more to say as Sibella, her face breaking into a relieved smile, came up to hug Annis, and even Charles got himself in hand sufficiently to give her a peck on the cheek.

Mr Pullen, beaming with pleasure, backed off.

'Well, then… Very many congratulations my lord, my lady… Please excuse the confusion, my lord…clearly a case of mistaken identity…'

'Indeed,' Adam said. He gave Ingram a challenging stare. 'You will have to do better than that, I fear, Ingram.'

Ingram's jaw was working. 'I am sure I will do, my lord,' he ground out, turning on his heel and stalking from the room, scattering the onlookers like chaff in the wind.

Adam took Annis's arm firmly in his. 'Ladies and gentlemen, pray excuse us. I would like to take a turn about the room with my fiancée.'

There were murmurs of approval and smiles. Annis, however, was conscious only of the bruising grip of Adam's hand on her arm. He steered her away from the group and over towards the big windows where they might achieve a modicum of privacy. He was frowning hard.

'You should not have done that, Annis.'

Annis glanced at him. 'I did not wish Mr Pullen to cart you off on a trumped-up charge and it seemed you were unwilling to help yourself! Besides, it is the truth.'

'That is not the point. Your good name—'

Annis wriggled. 'My good name was compromised two days ago, my lord, when Mr Thackwray found us together in the spa room. Was that not why you proposed to me?'

Adam gave her arm a little shake. 'Yes…no! You had no need to make matters worse!'

'I do not see why you are objecting. Mrs Hardcastle can

vouch that you left and she is the very acme of respectability.'

Adam sighed sharply and let her go. 'Am I to take it then that you have accepted my proposal?'

Annis felt a small pang of guilt that the matter should have been resolved in this manner. It was not how she would have chosen and somehow it seemed to set everything off on the wrong foot. 'I...yes, I thank you. Has there ever been a more public plighting of troth?'

Adam did not smile. 'You do not really wish to marry me, though, do you, Annis? You are only accepting out of necessity!'

Annis's face crumpled up with a misery that reflected the unhappiness inside. 'It is not like that, my lord. It is not that I do not wish to marry you; it is that I had not wished to marry at all—' She broke off, aware of listening ears. 'We cannot talk about this now.'

'No.' Adam glanced at his watch. 'Devil take it, I have an appointment in ten minutes that I cannot break. Do you still travel to Starbeck this afternoon?'

Annis glanced across at Charles, who was clearly only waiting for his chance to pounce on her. 'Oh, yes. I would like to get away from Harrogate for a space.'

'I hope that the house is habitable.' Adam looked irritable. 'Damn it, I do not like this, Annis. It is not wise for you to be alone at Starbeck with a rioting mob on the loose. I have a better idea.' He looked across at his mother and Edward and Della. 'Why do you not come to stay at Eynhallow for a few days? It will give us time to discuss wedding arrangements and I would feel happier to know that you are under my roof. We may ride over to Starbeck together and decide what is to be done with it.'

When apprised of the plan, Lady Ashwick seemed pleased to offer hospitality.

'Indeed, Lady Wycherley—Annis—that would be delightful. Edward, Della and I are travelling home immediately and you are welcome to ride with us, but if it suits you better to join us later…'

'I will do that, I think, ma'am,' Annis said. She was feeling a little panicky at the way in which the Ashwick family suddenly seemed to be taking charge. Her precious independence was disappearing faster than moorland mist. She felt quite hopeless—on the one hand she realised that she had no option now other than to marry Adam, and quickly. On the other, she felt trapped and afraid. She hoped that Adam could not tell how reluctant she was, but when she looked at him she saw that he was watching her and she realised that her fingers were grasping her reticule so tightly that the tortoiseshell clasp was almost bending under the pressure. She quickly loosened her grip, but she knew that he had noticed, and when she looked into his eyes all she could see was regret.

Chapter Ten

It was getting dark as Annis's coach passed the gibbet at Welford Hill and started up the steep incline out of the Washburn Valley towards Eynhallow. The countryside was bathed in the purple of twilight as the sun sank behind the hills. They were a mere fifteen miles from Harrogate and yet it was like another world. Gone were the bandbox-neat town houses and tidy streets, gone the order and comfort of civilisation. This was a landscape that could kill the unwary, with its empty hills and sudden mist rolling down from the moors. This was a countryside where men scraped a living. The contrast with the town had always fascinated Annis, especially as night closed in and the true wildness of the moors was revealed.

The trees beside the track were etched black against the paling sky and Annis, who was leaning forward to look out of the window, shivered suddenly, although the summer air had not yet lost its warmth. There was something so free about the hills, something that called to her. Her spirit wanted to be free, yet now she felt boxed in, trapped by convention and necessity. It was exactly the feeling she had had at seventeen when, having married John Wycherley out of a desperate need for security, she had found out that she had made a terrible mistake.

The coach lurched to a halt and Annis almost fell off her seat. She opened the window.

'Barney? What is the problem?'

'Fire up ahead, Lady Wycherley,' the coachman replied. 'I thought it safer to stop and find out what is happening.'

Annis craned her neck. Some fifty yards ahead there was a building on fire. All she could see was the blazing silhouette against the darkening sky. The moon had not yet risen.

'It is the tollhouse! Mr and Mrs Castle may need help! I will go and see what is happening.'

Annis grabbed the carriage pistol from its holster and jumped down, ignoring the objections of the coachman. There was a chill in the night air now and a cold breeze from the hills. It fanned the flames and they hissed and cracked, dancing wildly. As she drew closer, Annis could see that the tollhouse had been completed and what had been a fine little building of wood and stone was now crumbling to ash in the leaping flames. There was a crash as a roof spar fell and set up a shower of sparks.

Annis hesitated, for she could see that the house was beyond saving and there was no possible way that she could even get close enough to discover whether the Castles had escaped. She prayed hard and fervently that they had not been trapped inside.

Another light flared further up the road and suddenly the air was rent with shouts and the roar of flames taking hold. There was another shout closer at hand and Annis spun round to see Barney whipping the horses up the road towards her.

'Lady Wycherley! Get in the carriage, ma'am! They are coming!'

It was too late to run and the carriage was still too far away. Annis saw the mob spill into the road, a seething mass of men, shadowy, outlined by the firelight. Some were armed with sledgehammers, others with pistols and blunderbuss. All were masked and in the firelight they looked like mummers depicting a scene from hell as they swarmed over and around the ruined building, fanning the flames, hastening the destruction.

The air sizzled with the sound of cracking timbers and flying sparks; it was alive with the shouts of the rioters and it crackled with the excitement and atavistic pleasure of the men as they went about their destructive work. Annis pressed one hand against her mouth and flattened herself against the hedge, feeling the twigs stick into her through the thickness of her cloak, trying to efface herself in the darkness. This was a very dangerous place for any witness to be, let alone a woman on her own armed only with a pistol that, suddenly, she could not remember whether she had loaded.

Not all of the rioters were on foot. As Annis watched, a rider came down the road on a skittish bay stallion. He turned the horse expertly in front of the tollgate itself, which still blocked the road in all its five-bar splendour. Annis remembered Charles saying that Samuel Ingram had been very pleased with the design and construction of his tollhouses. Some of the structures on the roads were a flimsy affair, but Ingram had had his built to last and to bring in maximum profit. Instead they had kindled rebellion.

The leader on the horse raised his voice above the sound of the wind and the flames.

'This tollgate has no right to be here, does it?'

The crowd roared its defiance. 'No!'

The leader turned his horse again as it skittered away from the flames. 'What shall we do with it?'

In reply, a man ran forward from the ragged crowd, swinging a sledgehammer. A ripple of a sigh ran through the mob as the hammer made first contact with the wood, then a shout rang out and the men were all in there, hacking, trampling, reducing the pretty little gate to a pile of matchsticks ready for the burning. Someone thrust a torch forward and the makeshift bonfire leapt into life. A cheer rang out.

The mob was on the loose now, wild, unpredictable and masterless. As the flames jumped high in the wind they illuminated the road and the bulk of the carriage some fifty yards distant. A shout went up and the crowd rushed forward.

Annis gave a little, terrified squeak. She had the shelter of the hedge and a rough stone wall, and she had the dubious protection of the pistol, but they were scant comfort if the mob were looking for scapegoats. By the light of the flames she saw Barney jump clear of the carriage and drew in a short breath of relief. She took a step back, stumbled down a small bank and felt herself pitch over and over in the hay, stopping with the wind knocked out of her.

She was in a small hollow beneath the bank and above her head the riot roared past. Someone slithered down the slope and almost stepped on her, and Annis struggled up, raising the pistol.

A hard hand closed about her wrist and a voice she knew well said, 'At least you remembered to bring it on this occasion.'

The relief was intense. Adam's arms went about her and Annis clung to him and all she could say was, 'Thank God you are here,' over and over, until she finally turned her face into his chest and all was quiet.

* * *

'Annis? Annis, are you hurt?'

It was minutes rather than hours later, and there was a note of urgency in Adam's voice. Annis raised her head a little and blinked. The pressure of his arms about her eased slightly.

'No. I do not believe I am hurt.' Annis moved and stretched. She felt bruised and a little stiff, but otherwise uninjured.

'I must get you away from here,' Adam said. He pulled her to her feet. 'They will not harm us, but it is not good to linger.'

'Will not harm us?' Annis' voice rose incredulously. 'Adam, did you not see what was happening? That was a riot! These men are dangerous!'

'I know, love. All the same, I do not believe that we are in danger. The Washburn Men do not hurt their own.'

Annis started to brush the hay from her skirts. 'I wish I could share your confidence. And are we their own? I do not like the sound of that.'

'Most certainly we are. Anyone Washburn born and bred...' Adam let the sentence hang. 'All the same, we should not wait around. They are looking for another target. Come along.'

His hand slid down her arm, tightening about her wrist as he drew her behind him along the line of the wall, away from the road. The firelight flickered behind the hedge and the cries of the rioters faded on the wind. They walked quickly and he was sure-footed in the dark. Annis felt the waves of shock and relief flow over her. As ever, Adam's presence was comforting. Yet it was exciting as well. She was reminded of the time they had met in the garden, except this time the danger and the relief combined in a much headier brew. The feel of him beside her, the scent of him, turned her stomach into knots.

After they had gone a little way Annis was obliged to stop to shake a stone out of her shoe. She leaned one hand against the wall for support and bent down carefully to remove her pumps. Her cloak caught of the rough edges of the wall and almost pulled her off balance and she reflected ruefully that she was hardly dressed for walking on the moors. They were high up here; she could see the fields falling away into the valley below and above them crouched the dark edge of the hills. The stars were out but there was no moon, and the summer breeze nevertheless had a cold cutting edge.

'I have to hurry you—'

There was an edge of urgency to Adam's voice. He took the pump from her hand and bent down to slide it back onto her foot. For a second his hand was warm against the silkiness of her stocking and Annis almost fell over again. She heard him make a noise of mingled disgust and resignation.

'You will not get more than a hundred yards in those shoes. This will slow us up.'

'I was not dressing for a walk on the hills, my lord,' Annis said, a little tartly. 'If we could go back for the carriage—'

'Impossible.' Adam was short. 'We will find your carriage again in the daylight—if we are lucky.'

They started to move again, more slowly, more carefully. At one point Annis was obliged to accept Adam's help over a wall and took the opportunity to lean against the rough-hewn edges for a rest. She was hopelessly out of breath.

'Please…my lord…may we not rest just a little?'

Adam gave an irritable sigh. 'Very well. And you called me Adam just now. Does this mark a return to formality between us, my lady?'

'I was very discomposed just now,' Annis said. 'I said the first thing that came into my head.'

'I realise that.' There was an odd note in Adam's voice. 'You seemed very pleased to see me.'

'I was.'

'You clung to me.'

Annis drew in a sharp breath. She did not need to be reminded. It had been more than relief. It had felt right. 'That is consistent with the fact that I was pleased to see you, my lord.'

'Are you trying to imply that you would have embraced anyone who was fortunate enough to rescue you?' Adam laughed. 'I am sorry that I was obliged to grab you in the darkness for a second time, Annis. I suppose I should be grateful that this time you did no damage to me.'

'Perhaps if you did not lurk about at night you would not run that risk.' Annis paused, curious. Up until now she had had little time to think amidst the panic of flight. Now she had some questions. 'Whatever are you doing here, my lord? Surely you are not mixed up in this riot?'

'You think me a renegade and a criminal?' Adam's tone was amused. 'You have a low opinion of me, my lady.'

'You have not answered my question.'

'No. What about you, Annis? Were you there with a purpose?'

Annis frowned. 'Certainly not. Do not be ridiculous. The penalty for burning a tollhouse is death.'

'That is the penalty for being caught, certainly. But you have a grudge against Samuel Ingram—'

'And so do you—'

'So either of us could be suspects. It is not wise to travel after dark around here, Lady Wycherley. I thought that I had told you that before. We expected you at Eynhallow long before this.'

Annis looked at him closely. She could not see him clearly in the darkness but she knew him well enough by now to read every nuance of his voice.

'You are trying to distract me, Adam. I think that you had some purpose for being here tonight.'

There was a sharp silence, then Adam laughed. 'A shame that Pullen does not have you working on this case, Annis, or he would have solved it before now. How did you know that?'

'I am not sure,' Annis said cautiously. 'Something in your voice, I think. And when you first found me you came down the bank, from the direction of the road. That was why I wondered if you had been with the rioters all along. You came from the same direction as they did.'

'I was not a part of the riot.'

Annis paused. 'I believe you. But… You came to warn them, didn't you? You knew that the yeomanry were to be called out and you came to warn them that they were in danger.'

She saw Adam grin. 'How I wish you had not guessed that, Annis! Now you know far more than is good for you.'

Annis drew a deep breath. 'Then it is true?'

'It is true. Ned knew what was planned for tonight. When we were in town earlier, we heard that Ingram had called out the yeomanry. We were…anxious…that the men should not run straight into a trap. Many of them are known to us and can only do themselves and their families harm if they are caught, condemned, transported or hanged.'

Annis studied him closely. 'Then Mr Ingram was not so far from the truth. You may not be the rebel leader, but you have aided and abetted the rioters. Perhaps you even know the identity of their leader.'

Adam shook his head. 'It does not work like that. That

is the beauty of their system. Because all the men are masked and messages are passed purely by word of mouth, no one knows who else is involved. I must admit to a certain curiosity, though. I would like to know the identity of the mysterious rebel leader, the man who rides a horse so conveniently like mine that I may end up hanging for him!'

Annis frowned. 'Did you see him tonight?'

'Of course. As did you, I imagine. Who do you think it is?'

Annis was silent. 'I do not know.' Even she could hear the hesitation in her tone. 'It could be you, for all your protestations of innocence. I did not see the two of you at the same time!'

Adam laughed. 'Please keep that theory to yourself. Do you suspect any other candidates?'

Annis hesitated again. 'I saw several horses stabled at Starbeck when I was there last. One was a bay with a white flash. That is all I know.'

'At Starbeck…' Adam sounded thoughtful. 'That is interesting…'

Annis clutched his arm. 'It could be a mere coincidence.'

Adam's laugh was cynical. 'I doubt it. You see how easy it is to become involved, Annis. Already you are keeping information quiet, protecting someone. Tom Shepard… Your cousin Charles… It could be either of them!'

The shock hit Annis hard. 'Charles? You think that Charles might be the leader of the rioters? No, that is impossible! Besides, you said yourself that he is hated here. As well suspect your brother Edward!'

Adam laughed. 'Ned has a different role to play.'

Annis stared. 'I did not expect to find you excusing violence, my lord.'

Adam's voice hardened. 'Generally speaking, I do not, but Ingram has caused nothing but hunger, misery and death through his cruelty. He sowed the wind and now he is reaping the whirlwind.'

He pulled her to her feet again and with a sigh Annis complied, pulling her tattered cloak about her. Adam looked behind them. 'Come into the shelter of the wood,' he said abruptly. 'They are burning the coach.'

Annis pressed a hand to her mouth. 'But Barney—the coachman! I saw him jump down, but if he has come to any harm I shall never forgive myself.'

'If he has any sense he will have run away before they arrived. I will send to look for him as soon as it is safe.' Adam urged her onwards, down a bank and into the wood. 'Besides, they will not hurt him. They are rioters, not murderers, and their argument is with Ingram, not with one of their own.'

Annis took several more steps, then stopped again. 'The horses! Surely they will not have harmed the horses!'

This time Adam laughed. 'Certainly not, my lady! These are countrymen. In a fire they would save the horses first.'

Annis sighed. They were walking along a path through the trees now and once again Adam seemed sure of his way. The bracken crackled underfoot and, every so often, thorns would catch at the trailing edges of Annis' cloak. She ruefully reflected that it would be fit for nothing in the morning. The trees grew close here, arching overhead, providing a dense canopy through which the starlight barely penetrated.

'We are almost safe at Eynhallow now,' Adam said, in an undertone. He turned to Annis and pulled her close. 'There is something I wanted to ask you, Annis. When you clung to me before—'

Annis shivered. 'Pray do not remind me, my lord. It was most improper of me.'

'Would you also say that it was improper for your body to soften against me so sweetly, as it did then—and as it is doing now?'

There was a silence beneath the trees, but for the rustle of some night creature scuttering through the undergrowth. Annis could not think of a single, helpful prevarication.

'You smell of honey and apricots and wood smoke and your skin is smoother than velvet...' Adam's tone was conversational, as though the air between them was not hot with the sparks of a different fire. His fingers moved from her wrist to touch the back of her hand in a light caress. 'I have been thinking about you ever since we parted this morning, Annis. In fact, I seem to spend the majority of my time thinking about you these days.'

Annis's breath caught in her throat. 'I do not believe that you should say such things to me, sir.'

'No? We are betrothed.'

'That may be so, but this is not the time or the place.' She cast a glance over the hill at the tollhouse fire, burning lower now. The rioters had gone and the night was still.

Adam's hand came up to cup her chin, the thumb stroking along the line of her jaw. 'You do not find danger an aphrodisiac, Annis?' His voice was a little rough. 'You do not feel the excitement like a fever in the blood?'

'I have never done so before.'

'And now?'

Annis was trembling. It would be easy—and wise—to deny it, but there was something about this man...

'I admit that something attracts me—'

His mouth took hers with unerring accuracy and without gentleness. Her lips parted instantly under the pressure. He was demanding, overpowering, and the shock and the ex-

citement hit Annis in one irresistible blow. The blazing
heat of his body, the sheer intimacy of his caresses... Annis swayed and his arms went about her tightly. When she
pulled away a little, overwhelmed, one of his hands came
up to cup her head, tangling in her wind-blown hair, tilting
her face up to his so that he could explore her mouth again
at will.

Eventually he had to let her go, for neither of them could
breathe.

'If I had done that the night we first met—'

Annis's breath caught at the raw undertone to his voice.
'I would have run away from you.'

'Do you want to run now?'

'There is nowhere to run to.'

Some of the tension eased between them. She heard him
laugh. 'That is true. You will just have to trust me then.
Damnation. That puts certain obligations on me.'

'Such as?'

'Such as not to seduce you.'

'What, out here?' Annis could not keep the incredulity
out of her voice. Here, in the woods, with the smoke on
the air and the touch of the breeze on her skin... She shook
violently at the thought.

'Yes, here. I will show you one day.'

This kiss was gentle, heavy with promise. It still stole
her breath. Annis sighed. She knew marriage to be a stifling trap for a woman and yet this sweet seduction told
her otherwise. And tonight she did not want to be sensible.

She raised a hand and traced the lines of his face. In her
mind's eye she could see his features: the thick, dark hair,
the straight brows, the hard planes of his face. His cheek
was a little rough. She rubbed it enquiringly.

'Annis, you are treading on dangerous ground.' Adam's

voice was husky, his fingers hard about her wrist as he restrained her marauding hand. Annis drew back a little.

'I am sorry. I was curious.'

Adam turned his mouth into the palm of her hand. 'About what, Annis?'

'About what it felt like—what you felt like. I have…so little experience.'

She felt him smile against her skin. 'Is that so? Yet it is not physical intimacy that you are afraid of, is it, Annis?'

Annis stood on tiptoe to run her fingers into the tousled softness of his hair. 'No, I suppose not. I am behaving very badly, I know. I am not sure why. It has not happened to me before and it feels a little like drinking too much wine.'

Adam laughed. 'I cannot imagine you doing that either, Annis.'

'No, indeed.'

'Chaperons do not become tipsy.'

'Nor do they kiss strange gentleman in the woods at night. I cannot think what has become of me since I met you.'

His arms about her were as warm and reassuring as they were demanding. His breath tickled her ear. 'I am a bad influence on you. Plus tonight it is the effect of the release of tension. It weakens one's inhibitions and the darkness does the rest.'

'Yes, there is something unreal about this.' Annis pressed closer to him. 'There is something anonymous about the dark.'

Adam's arms tightened about her. 'You imply that I could be anyone? I am not flattered by that thought, Annis.'

Annis laughed, but part of her felt sad. 'I only meant that everything will seem different in the morning.'

'I know. I shall want to speak of wedding arrangements and you will have that hunted look in your eye that tells me you are afraid to proceed...' His lips brushed the line of her cheek, sending quivers of sensation along her nerves. 'What are you afraid of, Annis?'

Annis almost told him, but drew back at the last moment. 'I do not want to speak of it tonight,' she said in a small voice. 'It will spoil things.'

'Very well.' Adam sounded patient, almost indifferent. 'We may leave that until the morrow as well.'

Annis thought that he meant to let her go then, but instead he tightened his grip. The whole, hard length of him was pressed against her and a shiver went down her spine at the sense of delightful helplessness it engendered. She was accustomed to fending for herself. She was not accustomed to feeling so powerless, nor was she expecting it to be so enjoyable.

His mouth engulfed hers, provoking a heated pleasure. The kiss deepened, his tongue exploring, the feel and the taste of him filling her senses. He felt frighteningly familiar and deliciously tempting. Annis slid her arms about his neck and kissed him back.

Adam's hand came up to rest just beneath her breast, languidly stroking the underside, caressing gently. Annis squirmed, wanting more. Much more. Her senses were alight. When he eased the neckline of her gown down to free her breasts from the confines of the bodice, Annis gasped with mingled pleasure and relief, needing to feel his hands and his mouth against her bare skin. He stopped kissing her and slowly traced his tongue down her breast, flicking the hard, pink bud. Annis thought she would explode with passionate need. Her knees were giving way and her blood was racing. She wanted nothing other than for Adam to take her there and then, beneath the trees with the smoke on the air and the touch of the breeze on her skin.

Adam raised his head. With a deft movement he rearranged her bodice. Annis almost screamed with frustration.

'In the morning,' he said in her ear, 'pray remember that—along with all your scruples about getting married.'

He let her go, taking her hand to guide her through the wood. Annis walked by his side, scarcely noticing where she was going, aware only of the touch of his hand on hers, the ache in her body and the memory of his kiss. The twigs and bracken crunched beneath her feet and the brambles caught at her clothes, and once Adam had to stop to disentangle her, his hands lingering for a second on her waist, tightening, before he sighed and let her go. They did not speak again.

Eventually he scrambled down on to a metalled road, where a pair of iron gates led to a wide drive. The moon was rising now, clothing everything in silver.

'I do not like arriving at Eynhallow with nothing but the clothes I stand up in,' Annis said. 'It makes me feel like a beggar bride.'

Adam laughed. 'Nonsense, my love. Della will be able to lend you anything that you may need and in the morning we shall send to Harrogate for the rest of your belongings.'

They started up the drive, hand in hand.

'My lord,' Annis said, a little shyly, 'how soon did you intend for us to wed?'

'I thought very soon. As soon as the banns may be read.' He smiled at her. 'I have always been impatient to wed you, Annis, but I believe that tonight has made things worse rather than better.'

Annis hung back. 'My lord—'

'Adam. You called me Adam earlier on.'

'If you wish. Adam, physical intimacy is not a good

basis for marriage. Not at all. Sometimes the reverse is true and it completely obscures the reality.' Annis hesitated. 'I do not want this to confuse me…'

'I understand.' Adam bent his head and his lips brushed hers. 'But sometimes, Annis, physical intimacy is just another, wonderful aspect of being married, along with the friendship and the shared experience.'

Annis felt a huge sadness fill her heart. 'Is that what your first marriage was like?'

'It was. And I feel sure that with you it could be the same.'

He was kissing her again, but Annis could not lose herself in the kiss as she had before. She envied him the easy intimacy he had had with Mary. She had never experienced such a love match. A part of her that she was ashamed to admit to was both jealous of his previous happiness and afraid that he would be disappointed in his second choice.

The following morning was bright and sunny once again, with the promise of heat in the air. Adam rode out early, taking no groom with him, which caused no speculation since he made a habit of riding alone. He took the track through the woods and out on to the hillside, where he allowed the bay stallion his head and galloped along one of the old drovers' tracks that criss-crossed the moor, sending the peat flying from its hooves.

Eynhallow lay below him, curled in a fold of the hills, the sight of the manor, the church and the village bringing an ache to his throat. It had stood there for time immemorial and he was only a small part of that pattern. He felt that very strongly this morning, perhaps because he had chosen to marry again and so the sense of continuity struck more strongly than usual.

When his first wife had died, he had thought that he

would never want to remarry and that Edward would have to be the one to marry and to provide an heir. Then he had met Annis and, almost immediately, the decision was made. His instinct was strong; he wanted her. More than that, he wanted to marry her. He was convinced that she was the right wife for him.

Adam reined in to pause and appreciate the view. Perhaps it had been arrogant of him, but the last thing he had expected was that he would find the lady he wished to marry only to discover that she was reluctant to marry him.

At a softly spoken word from him, the horse moved off again, trotting downhill at a more sedate pace. Adam smiled a little as he thought about Annis. Her refusal to accept his suit had been a salutary lesson. When he had first proposed, he had assumed that her reluctance to accept him stemmed from their short acquaintanceship, and that perhaps she had happy memories of her first marriage that she was afraid she would be betraying. He had been self-confident, he realised now, assuming that a penniless chaperon would be happy to accept the proposal of an eligible lord, especially given that she had been compromised. Yet Annis's reluctance had gone deeper than that. She had admitted as much, whilst refusing to confide in him. There was something that frightened her.

Adam frowned slightly. Any notion that Annis was afraid of the physical side of marriage had been banished last night, when he had held her in his arms. She might have been inexperienced, but she was neither cold nor afraid. Rather she had seemed intrigued by the possibilities of physical passion. He had been warmed to find that with many of her inhibitions gone, she had felt the same overwhelming need for him as he had for her. It was not logical, it was not even sensible, but it was there.

As for Annis's fears, Adam knew they must stem from

something else, something he had yet to discover. Of one thing he was certain. He would overcome her scruples, allay them. Nothing would take Annis from him now, just as he would never surrender Eynhallow to Ingram, nor see it lost in debt. He could be very stubborn when he chose and he chose to be now.

He turned off the track on to the turnpike road and increased the pace towards the ruined tollhouse. The ruins were still smoking and made a strange sight in the bright daylight. The gate was smashed to pieces and nothing was left but a scatter of ash and debris across the road. Further down the road, the burnt-out hulk of a carriage squatted, looking like a malignant toad.

There were men already busy about the tollhouse, sizing up the damage and discussing what should be done. Adam recognised Ellis Benson and a number of men from Ingram's estate. Bad news had travelled quickly, then. No doubt Ingram himself would be here soon to assess the damage and rail against the criminals, demanding they be caught. Adam had already sent a messenger to Harrogate to acquaint Charles Lafoy with the news that his cousin was safe, even if his carriage was not. He smiled a little. He suspected that Lafoy would already be on his way.

A small crowd had gathered, as crowds do when there has been some sort of incident. There was nothing in particular to watch, but they were watching anyway. Adam recognised some of the villagers from Eynhallow and the surrounding hamlets. A few of the men were there, but it was mostly the womenfolk and children. All had identical expressions of surly blankness, leavened occasionally by unholy glee. Mr Ingram had got his come-uppance and no one was sorry.

Adam allowed his horse to idle up to the ruined tollhouse and exchanged a few, short words with Ellis Benson.

The man's gaze was not friendly. Adam paused for a few words with the villagers, then turned at the sound of another horse approaching up the road. It was Edward, looking benign and vicarly, and deploring the damage in unctuous tones.

'How dreadful! How truly shocking!'

Ellis Benson turned away, scowling, and Adam brought his own mount alongside his brother.

'Doing it too brown, Ned!' he said in an undertone. 'Everyone knows that you are on the side of the rioters!'

Edward looked suitably disapproving. 'I have no idea what you can mean, Ash!'

'Indeed? Cast your mind back to last Sunday's sermon—the one about the houses of the ungodly being scattered like dust in the wind…'

A smile tugged Edward's mouth. 'That was rather a good one, wasn't it?'

'Yes, and see what it has done!'

'Benson is looking as sour as stale wine,' Edward observed.

'Can you blame him? No doubt Ingram will—for this unholy mess. Benson should have stopped it, Benson should have seen what was happening…' Adam shook his head. 'Ingram will blame everyone but himself.'

'It is fortunate, then, that he has such willing place men to shoulder the blame.'

'Benson, Lafoy…' Adam sounded thoughtful. 'He does rather surround himself with the gentry, does he not?'

'Snobbery,' Edward said comfortably. 'It makes him feel superior that he has bought them.'

'You are harsh.'

'I merely observe, Ash. What happened last night?'

The horses picked up speed away from the smouldering ruin and down the valley towards Eynhallow. They were far away enough from the crowd now not to be overheard, but Adam still glanced over his shoulder.

'It was as you suspected it would be. Roughly forty men, armed. They burned the tollhouse, then set about Lafoy's coach. It was fortunate that Lady Wycherley was clear of it by then or it would have been the devil of a job to get her out of there safely.'

Edward grimaced. 'The coachman turned up safe and sound. He's at the rectory. I told him to go straight up to the house as soon as he was ready. Lady Wycherley will be glad to know he is safe, I think. The whole experience must have shaken her quite badly.'

Adam nodded. 'She will be glad to see him.'

Edward grinned. 'Did Lady Wycherley ask you what you were doing there?'

'Yes.'

'Did you tell her?'

'Of course.'

Edward looked alarmed. 'You told her that you had gone to warn the men?'

Adam grinned. 'She guessed that I had gone out with a purpose. Annis is no fool.'

Edward frowned. 'I did not think it. But this is dangerous, Ash. She is still Lafoy's cousin, and the more she knows…'

Adam shrugged. 'Annis knows that I have an interest in seeing Ingram brought down, but then, so does she. She is not sympathetic to his cause.'

Edward sighed. 'Are we no nearer to discovering the identity of the rebel leader?'

'No. You know as much as I, Ned. He spoke like a gentleman and rode a very fine, bay horse similar to mine. Do you have any ideas who he might be?'

Edward shook his head slowly.

'What were you doing last evening?'

Edward shot his brother an appalled look. 'I?'

'Why not?' Adam quirked a brow. 'You are a gentle-man—and a fine rider—and you have a grudge against Ingram as much as I do, or indeed as much as Lady Wych-erley. She and I can speak for each other since we were together. But you?'

Edward goggled at him. 'You know as well as I that I do not possess a bay stallion! Damn it, Ash, surely you don't suspect your own brother?'

'Why not?' Adam said again. He saw Edward's appalled look and grinned. 'No, I do not really suspect you, Ned. All the same, it is odd. Horses are expensive. I won-dered...'

'Yes?'

'If Ingram might be setting the rioters up. You know how difficult it is to prosecute the villagers, for they will not testify against each other. He might have thought that the easiest way to capture the ringleaders would be to in-filtrate the gang.'

Edward frowned. 'It is a cunning plan, Ash, but I don't think the men would fall for it. They all know each other and they know who the leaders are—'

'*You* know who the leaders are!'

'Yes, some...' Edward looked uncomfortable. 'Mar-chant and Pierce are behind a lot of the trouble, but I know of no one with the means to keep a fine stallion.'

'Except Ingram. Could he have bought some of the men, then? Bribed them, I mean.'

'Unlikely.' Edward winced. 'They hate him like hell's pains.'

'Then there is no one else hereabouts. Ingram's estate, and Eynhallow and Starbeck are the only estates big enough to support that kind of income. Annis has seen horses stabled at Starbeck, but swears she does not know who purchased them.'

Edward whistled under his breath. 'Interesting. I had forgotten Starbeck. Ingram and Lafoy are going to hate you even more for gaining possession of it, Ash!'

'I know. There is no denying that it would be useful to control Starbeck, but I should not wish Lady Wycherley to think that that was why I wanted to marry her.'

'I thought it was because you had compromised her?'

'It is true that is why I made a formal proposal...' Adam hesitated '...yet I should not want Annis to believe that was the only reason.' He made a slight gesture. 'I am... very much attracted to her.'

Edward leant over to unlatch the gate that led into the Eynhallow deer park. 'You have known her all of two months,' he pointed out mildly.

'Sometimes it takes two days. Or two minutes.'

'I suppose so. If you are sure—'

'I am.'

'And Mary?'

Adam sighed. 'I loved Mary. But loving once does not prevent a man from loving again.'

'Have you told Lady Wycherley this?'

'Not yet. We have had little opportunity for intimate conversation since we became betrothed.' Adam frowned. 'Also there are her feelings about her first marriage to consider. I formed the strong opinion that it has set her against marriage, but I do not know why.'

Edward frowned. 'If Wycherley was the martinet we have been told, there may be your answer. A bully, a tyrant... Your Annis will need gentle wooing.'

'Yes.' Adam smiled. He felt warm at the thought. 'That is precisely what I shall give her.'

Chapter Eleven

When Annis went into the library after breakfast, Adam was standing by the windows in a patch of sunlight. Seeing him now in the daylight, after all that had happened between them the previous night, Annis was beset by such conflicting emotions that she could barely speak. She had known that Adam could move her to a passion that she had never experienced before, but the most difficult aspect to believe was that she had been so uninhibited with him. Not since she was seventeen in Bermuda had she felt so free from inhibition. In those days her behaviour had been prompted by innocence. Last night… She blushed to think of it. Last night she had been almost overwhelmed by her desire for him. Now, in the clear light of morning, she felt utterly tongue-tied.

Adam came forward to greet her, and when he smiled Annis felt her heart trip, missing a beat. For some reason she had thought that the effect Adam had on her would be reduced in the daylight as well. That had been a mistake.

'I trust that you are feeling well this morning, Annis,' Adam said, gesturing her to sit on a long gold sofa before the fireplace. 'I imagine that you have heard that Barney

Thompson is safe? Edward said that he had sent a message over from the rectory.'

Annis nodded. 'I am greatly relieved. The loss of Charles's carriage is unfortunate, but nothing compared to any loss of life.'

'There is the loss of the horses as well.' Adam's lips twitched. 'I doubt that Lafoy will ever see them again. Or if he does, someone will swear blind that they are completely different animals from his carriage horses! I fear the events of last night have cost him dear, assuming that you were correct and he is in no way connected with the riots.'

'Have you been up to the Skipton Road this morning?' Annis enquired. It was, in part, a genuine concern for the welfare of Mr and Mrs Castle that prompted her enquiry, but it was also an attempt to avoid the conversation moving on to more personal matters.

Adam nodded. 'I have. The tollhouse is ruined, but Mr and Mrs Castle are safe. As yet no one appears to have come forward to name the suspects and...' he gave her smile '...no one was captured last night. The militia sprang their trap, but by some mischance the rioters were already apprised of their plan...'

'How lucky for them,' Annis said, smiling back. 'Of course, you know nothing of that, my lord.'

'Nothing at all. And neither do you, should your cousin ask. I imagine he will be travelling over from Harrogate at this very moment to check on your welfare.' Adam came across to sit beside her on the sofa. 'I have been speaking to Ned about the marriage banns,' he said. 'They will be read for the first time of asking tomorrow.'

A huge panic welled up in Annis. She stood up quickly and moved over to the long windows that looked out across the parkland.

'Must it be so soon?' She sounded stifled.

When she looked back at Adam, she saw that his face had set in hard lines. He too got to his feet. 'I have the strong impression that you do not wish to marry me.' His tone was clipped. 'Such unwillingness is not flattering, my sweet, particularly after your…enthusiastic response to me last night. Can it be that you are having second thoughts?'

Annis swung round to face him properly. Adam's body was tense and his expression unreadable, but there was something in his face, a tiny hint of vulnerability, that made her wonder if she had hurt him. The thought upset her. It felt like a dreadful thing to do.

She felt something snap within her. 'I told you in Harrogate that it was not that I did not want to marry you, Adam,' she said quietly. 'It is marriage itself that I have always sought to avoid. And now that I cannot avoid it, I am afraid.'

Adam did not move towards her and the light in his grey eyes was brilliant. They threw her a challenge. 'You have no cause to fear me, Annis. Surely you know that?'

Annis struggled, with herself, her thoughts and her fears. 'Marriage is too important for me to embark upon it without the expectation that it would work.' Her tone rose with feeling. 'Yet I know so little of you, of your reasons and expectations! I do not know you well at all! This attraction we have between us…this affinity…simply makes matters more difficult.'

The panic was rising in her and she tried to crush it down, seeking Adam's gaze, desperate for him to understand. 'I have told you that my first marriage was unhappy. It made me resolve never to repeat it again—'

She found she could not quite put into words her fears of being trapped once again in marriage. The horror of such a prospect was so huge that it literally closed her throat. On the one hand she knew that not all men were alike. A small part of her even whispered that Adam would never bully her or make her ill, as John Wycherley had done. Yet somehow she could not get past that mistrust and give him her heart. Not yet. It was too soon and she was too unready.

She saw the anger go out of Adam's face and the hard lines soften, and she thought that he was a better man than she deserved. Perhaps in time she would be able to explain the whole to him—but for now this was the best she could do.

He took her hands in his. 'Annis, as for my hopes and expectations, they may be summed up quite easily. I truly wish to marry you, and not just to save your reputation or put matters to right in the eyes of the world. If you consent to our marriage, we will have the time to discover more about each other and then your fears may be put to rest.'

Annis could have wept at his gentleness. She looked up at him. 'I do not know…' The words were wrenched from her. 'I am so very bad at relinquishing control…'

His eyes filled with tender laughter. 'You are bossy, my sweet. That is why you were always so good at marshalling those tiresome girls.'

'And then there is your previous marriage to Mary…' Annis's voice faltered. She did not wish to forever live in Mary Ashwick's shadow.

Adam let her go. 'One day soon I will tell you about Mary, just as you will tell me the whole about your marriage and the reasons you are so chary to commit to another match.' He kissed her cheek. 'Do not look so doleful, my sweet. I am sure that everything will resolve itself in time and for now we had better get on with this business of arranging a wedding.'

Annis did not say anything else. Adam had offered her

his understanding and his patience and she knew that he was being generous to her. It was more than she could have expected. But as for time, that was the one thing that she did not have.

It was a strange couple of weeks. The banns were read for the first time that weekend and after that Annis felt that there was no going back. Adam had intimated that he would like to invite a few of his closest friends from London to attend the wedding service, and, although Annis was quaking in her boots at the prospect of meeting them all, she agreed that it was only appropriate. Her side of the church would be sparsely populated, with only Sibella, David and their family, Charles, Mrs Hardcastle and the Shepards attending. Lady Ashwick had called her own dressmaker from Harrogate to fashion Annis's trousseau and the time seemed full of fittings, re-fittings and the choosing of dress materials, from the diaphanous négligées that brought a blush to Annis's cheek to the day dresses, walking dresses, riding habits and all the other outfits that seemed so essential to a lady. Soon all of Sir Robert Crossley's money had gone, but Annis was determined not to allow Adam to pay. He had little enough money in all conscience, and Annis was determined that she should not be the one to push him further into debt.

Eventually, one fine afternoon, she and Adam found the time to play truant from their duties and ride over to Starbeck. Mrs Hardcastle had already been drafted in to wage war on the dirt and the mice and this was the first time that Adam had the opportunity to inspect the property closely.

'It is not so bad,' he said encouragingly, as together they inspected the broken window frames and peeling walls. 'Much of the damage is superficial and I am confident that we shall find a tenant once the structural improvements are made and Mrs Hardcastle has had the opportunity to clean it up.' He smiled at her. 'Or we could keep it as a love nest for when we wish to escape from Eynhallow...'

Annis blushed and smiled, but a part of her felt frightened. Starbeck had been her refuge; now that it was to go to Adam on their marriage, it felt as though she had nothing left, no place to hide. She was very quiet as they accepted a tankard each of Mrs Shepard's cider and wandered outside to drink it in the shade of the garden.

'I hear that the Pensioners were called out again last night to deal with the latest riots,' Adam said, as they walked slowly down the path into the walled garden, past Starbeck's small sulphur well and the beautiful brass sundial that Captain Lafoy had brought back from his travels. 'Apparently they were so old and out of condition that the rioters managed to overpower and disarm them! Ingram is threatening to call the regular troops next time.' He looked closely at Annis. 'You are not attending, are you, my love? I could have been speaking a different language for all the sense I am making.'

Annis sat down on a stone bench in the shade of the apple tree. There was an old summerhouse leaning against one of the walls and in front of it a pool of water supplied from the same spring as the well. The garden was very overgrown now, with roses and cornflowers and honeysuckle all tangling together in the profusion of high summer. It was warm, scented and very peaceful. She stroked the furry head of a snapdragon.

'I beg your pardon, Adam. I was thinking.'

'Of Starbeck?' Adam came to sit beside her. 'You will not be losing it, Annis.'

His quick understanding both impressed and alarmed

Annis. She cast him a look under her lashes. 'No, I know. But it will not be the same.'

Adam took her hand in his. 'You are worried because you will have nowhere to run to,' he said acutely. 'Why do you think that you will want to run away, Annis?'

Annis looked at him. His gaze was very deep and dark and she felt a shiver of apprehension. She could not tell him that she could not yet trust herself to him. That would be too hurtful when he had been so patient with her. Besides, the problem was not in him, but in her. And it was not her only concern.

'I know that you were in love with Mary and I am afraid that you will be disappointed in your second choice,' she blurted out. 'I could not bear it if our marriage was a pale imitation of what went before.' She locked her shaking fingers together. 'Perhaps it is a fault in me, wishing not to be second best, but I would rather we never wed than that we be haunted by memories.'

The words were out. She waited, trembling inside, for Adam's reply.

He did not answer at once, then he stood up and moved a little away from her. 'I should like to tell you about Mary, if I may, and then you will understand me, Annis. It is very important that there is no misunderstanding.'

Annis waited.

'I ran away with Mary when she was seventeen and I was eighteen.' Adam smiled faintly. 'We knew that my father would never have approved the marriage and neither would Mary's family. Everyone said that we were too young to know our own minds and that it was a most unsuitable match.' He shrugged. 'We knew well enough what we wanted. We ran away to Gretna and our families simply had to accept what we had done. It was uncomfortable at first, but matters soon settled down.'

A butterfly settled on a flower by Annis's cheek. She stared fixedly at its jewel-bright colours.

'We were very happy for five years,' Adam said softly. 'There were no children, but we always thought that we had plenty of time. Then Mary contracted scarlet fever. Within two weeks she was dead.'

Adam got up and walked across to the sundial, resting a hand on the warm stone of the rim. 'I could not accept it at first. We had been so young and I suppose we had never been tried. Apart from our elopement, which had seemed little more than a romantic adventure, nothing had ever gone awry for us. And suddenly I was left with nothing.'

Annis did not speak. Adam's voice was expressionless, but she knew that it must be hurting him to talk about this. She wanted to touch him, to comfort him, but she did not dare to get up and go to him. He seemed far away from her, wrapped up in the grief of years, beyond her reach. She was afraid that if she went to him he would reject her.

Adam rested his booted foot on the base of the sundial and looked away across the gardens.

'Such heartache does not last forever. Inevitably the initial sharpness will ease, although one does not ever forget.' He shrugged. 'I went abroad and fought the French. I came home and—' he smiled a little '—I confess that I played the part of a rake about Town. It is perfectly possible to survive on one's own. It is simply that one feels… unfinished. The years passed and I never met a lady I wished to marry. Until now.'

He came back to the bench with a swiftness that took Annis by surprise, and took both her hands in his.

'Annis, I love you. From the very first I was attracted to you and I quickly realised that I wanted to marry you. There is nothing to say that a man cannot love—sincerely love—more than once.' He gave her a little, loving shake. 'What I felt for Mary was a boy's passion that I believe would have mellowed into something deeper with age. What I feel for you cannot be compared with that. I am a man now, not a boy of eighteen, and I feel for you everything that a man can feel.'

His arms went around her and he pulled her hard against him. Annis clung to him, her face turned against his chest, hearing the thud of his heart, breathing in the scent of him. He was offering her everything that she could ever have asked for and she could not quite believe it. In a few moments, when he felt the warmth of her tears drench his shirt, he held her a little away and scanned her face.

'Sweetheart…why are you crying?'

Annis shook her head slightly. Her heart was too full for her to speak. 'I am sorry,' she managed to say. She freed herself from his grip. 'You are so generous and I…' Her words failed. *I cannot tell you that I love you…* The words hung in the air, unspoken between them. She wanted to say them; wanted to believe them. She was so close to it…

'I suppose that I am envious,' Annis said in a moment, 'which is no very admirable thing. My own marriage was such a poor thing in comparison.'

There was such a tender light in Adam's eyes that she almost cried again. 'That need not matter one jot, Annis. It does not mean that we cannot be happy. I am confident that when you are ready, you will tell me what happened to you. In the meantime, I can wait.'

There was a week to go before the wedding. The house in Church Row had been emptied and all Annis's meagre possessions moved to Eynhallow. Mrs Hardcastle was established at Starbeck and suddenly it seemed that there was nothing for Annis to do.

'It is very odd,' she confided in Della Tilney, as they sat together in the drawing room one morning. 'I am so accustomed to being busy that I cannot settle. I feel as though I am suddenly become useless.'

Della looked up from her needlework, a light of understanding in her grey eyes.

'It is only until the wedding, Annis. At the moment you are in that state of anticipation where you are simply waiting for something to happen. Afterwards…'

'Yes?' Annis cast her needlework aside restlessly and jumped to her feet. 'Afterwards I may do what?' She spread her hands appealingly. 'It is so long since I have been a lady of leisure, Della, that I cannot remember what to do!'

Della laughed. 'Why, there are endless things for you to do, Annis! If you do not care for the usual pursuits of reading and needlework, then you may walk or go out riding, or visiting. There are plenty of good causes for you to embrace and besides…' Della cast her a smiling look '…Adam will want to monopolise you for plenty of the time!'

'He does not seem to want to do so now,' Annis said gloomily. Adam and Edward had gone out hunting that morning and she imagined that they would be away for the whole day.

Della gave her a shrewd look. 'I rather suspect that Adam finds your company too much temptation prior to the wedding,' she said, with a wicked smile. 'Last night he was watching you all the time during dinner. I asked him the same question three times and he cut me dead! He is fathoms deep in love with you, my dear!'

Annis was spared an answer by the arrival of Tranter.

'Excuse me, Lady Wycherley.' The butler bowed low. 'Mrs Hardcastle is here to see you, ma'am. She seems in some distress. I tried to encourage her to wait for you in the library, but she insisted on staying in the hall. She is out there now.'

Annis got to her feet in some surprise. The thought of Mrs Hardcastle in distress was difficult to imagine, for that redoubtable lady had been a tower of strength for years.

'Excuse me, Della,' she murmured. 'I think I had better go and investigate. In the hall, you said, Tranter?'

Mrs Hardcastle was occupying one of the hard, straight-backed chairs that stood beside the long pier glass at the bottom of the stairs. She was looking straight ahead and was clutching in her hands what looked like a piece of old sacking. When she saw Annis approach she got hastily to her feet and Annis saw that she was not so much distressed as agitated. She launched into speech at once.

'Oh, Miss Annis! I found this yesterday when I was cleaning at Starbeck and I thought I should bring it straight over to you! I've been awake all night worriting.'

Annis took her arm. 'Come into the library, Hardy. Tranter, a pot of tea, if you please.'

'Couldn't drink a drop!' Mrs Hardcastle puffed. 'I'm that distraught, Miss Annis!'

Annis urged her to a seat and Mrs Hardcastle again sat bolt upright, the piece of sacking clutched in her hands. She seemed to recall suddenly that it was there, for she held it out to Annis and said again, 'I found this yesterday, ma'am. I was cleaning the end bedroom, the one where the gable is coming down. Anyway, that's nothing to the purpose. Proper mess it was in there, with the floorboards loose and the paint peeling. I got young Tom Shepard to bring a hammer and nails to settle the floor, but before he did I just stuck my head down. Disgraceful mess there was down there, Miss Annis, with paper everywhere, and mouse droppings and this disgusting sack…' Mrs Hardcastle paused to draw breath. 'So I bundled it all up and took it down to the fire and when I was about to throw it in I suddenly saw this!'

She thrust the sack at Annis, who looked at it dubiously.

'Yes, Hardy? It is a sack.'

'Look inside, ma'am,' the housekeeper said, in tones of deep foreboding.

Annis inserted her hand into the canvas bag.

'Careful now,' Mrs Hardcastle said, reverting to her usual practical tone. 'Mind the mouse droppings!'

Annis's fingers closed on a scrap of paper that was left in a corner of the bag. It was larger than the rest and had escaped the destruction of the mice. She pulled it out.

The first thing that she saw was the image of Britannia, then the words one thousand pounds, ripped across by sharp little teeth. She felt a little faint.

'But this…this is one thousand pounds, Hardy!'

'You mean it was one thousand pounds, Miss Annis,' Mrs Hardcastle corrected heavily. 'There was ever so many of them papers as well—banknotes, I suppose they'd be—all nibbled to destruction by those pesky mice! I've been worriting and worriting all night about what they was doing there. Tom and me, we searched all under the floor, but there was nothing left but shreds. So this morning I put on my bonnet and got Tom to bring me over here in the cart because I knew you would know what to do, Miss Annis.'

Annis frowned. She had no idea what to do. Whoever had hidden the money in the first place had clearly not banked on Mrs Hardcastle's obsession with hygiene, and whoever had hidden it must have gained it by criminal means. No one could have so many banknotes sitting under the floorboards for a legitimate purpose.

Annis got to her feet and walked across to the window, staring out at Eynhallow's beautiful gardens bathed on the afternoon sunlight. The sensible thing would be to wait until Adam returned and discuss it with him, but he and Edward had indicated that they might be away until dinner. Besides, Annis was accustomed to taking action of her own accord and she was feeling very restless. She rang the bell decisively.

'I think that it would be best if I came back to Starbeck with you now, Hardy,' she said. 'I shall leave a note for Lord Ashwick and explain where I have gone. We must instigate a search of the house, for who knows what else may be hidden on the premises? And then we must alert the appropriate authorities, whoever they are.'

Within ten minutes the matter was settled. Tom Shepard brought the cart round to the front of the house, looking appalled when he was informed that both Annis and Della Tilney would be accompanying Mrs Hardcastle back to Starbeck. Della was there because she had insisted that it was not appropriate for Annis to go on her own.

'I never have any excitement,' she said, a twinkle in her grey eyes as she drew on her cloak and gloves and following Annis out to the cart. 'Besides, Adam will be very displeased about this, dearest Annis, so it is better that he should have two of us to vent his bad temper on. You see what a staunch sister-in-law I shall be to you! I think that we shall deal together extremely well.'

They searched all afternoon, but found no more money and ended up dusty and thirsty for their pains. Della declared that she had seldom enjoyed an afternoon more and that Mrs Hardcastle's elderflower cordial was marvellously refreshing. Mrs Hardcastle beamed.

When the time came for them to return to Eynhallow, they hit a snag. Tom Shepard refused to take them. He stood in the hall, twisting his cap in his hands and looking bashful but determined.

'Sorry, ma'am, but I can't allow it. There's word out that it's dangerous to travel tonight.'

Annis looked at him. He fidgeted and looked away, his handsome face slightly flushed but set in stubborn lines.

'Tom,' Annis said, with ominous calm, 'are you telling me that you refuse to take the cart out? Can you possibly be afraid of the Washburn Men?'

Tom's gaze jerked back to hers. She saw him smile. 'No, ma'am. But I have my orders. It's more than my life's worth to go against them.'

Annis looked out at the bright summer evening. The sun was still high in the sky. 'It will take us all of an hour to get back to Eynhallow and it will not be dark even then. I cannot see the problem.'

'Sorry, ma'am.'

There was a tense silence.

'Why do we not drive ourselves?' Della suggested. 'I am sure that either of us could manage the cart, Annis.'

'Sorry, ma'am,' Tom said again. 'I can't let you do that. There's pickets on all the roads already and tonight is going to be fierce. So…you're to stay here. Master says so.'

'I would like to meet this Master of yours,' Annis muttered. 'Of all the high-handed, arrogant nonsense!'

'Yes, ma'am.' Tom grinned. He gave an awkward bow. 'Don't think to set off walking either, ma'am,' he added as an afterthought. 'There's men on the end of the drive that would bring you back!'

'Of all the ridiculous situations!' Annis said, after Tom

had gone out. She took an angry swish about the room. 'Here we are marooned for the night in a scarce-habitable house, with no food, mice in the rafters and a restless mob outside! I am almost inclined to walk back to Eynhallow and damn their impudence!'

'Why do you not come into the drawing room and sit down?' Della suggested soothingly. 'I am sure that Mrs Hardcastle can scrape together something for us to eat and she mentioned that at least two of the bedrooms are fit for human habitation. Although, Annis…' she hesitated '…I would prefer to sit up tonight with you, if you do not object. I am unlikely to sleep a wink, knowing that there is a rabble of rioters outside!'

In the event they dined royally by candlelight on ham, cheese, bread and apples, with some of Mrs Shepard's cider to accompany the meal. Annis had tried to persuade Mrs Hardcastle to join them, only to be put in her place by the housekeeper, who said that she had work to do turning down the beds, heating the water and warming the bricks to put in the ladies' beds. In vain did Annis and Della protest that they would not be able to sleep. Mrs Hardcastle went away muttering that she had her house-keeping duties to fulfil.

'I hope that Adam understood your message,' Della said, pouring more cider into their beakers. 'He is going to be unconscionably worried when we do not arrive back.' She looked at Annis, her grey eyes bright with mischief. 'He will be angry as well, but I am certain that you may talk him around. I believe you could wrap him about your little finger, he loves you so much!'

Annis blushed and disclaimed. 'All the same,' she said, 'I know Adam is a good man.' Her voice dropped. 'Better than I deserve.'

Della narrowed her eyes. 'Why do you say that, Annis?'

It was dark outside now. Beyond the uncurtained windows the moon was rising and the sky was black. The moon was shining through the mullions and pooling on the wooden floor. On the makeshift table the remains of the meal sat between them. The candlelight was warm and a small fire burned in the grate. Annis drank some more of her cider.

'I do not deserve Adam for I know that he loves me, yet I am unable to trust him and love him back. I *want* to love him,' she added, with a fierce vehemence, 'but my first marriage… My husband was a bully who would browbeat me into submission. Oh, not physically,' she added hastily, as she saw the shock mirrored in Della's eyes, 'but sometimes other methods are just as bad. He would lock me in my room when he went out and he would open my letters to see who was writing to me… He dominated every aspect of my life in and in the end I thought I would run quite mad, and I was so ill that I wanted to die to escape him.' She looked up. 'That is the reason I find it so difficult to trust any man again—and the reason I cannot tell Adam why I am so cool with him.'

She blushed a little, for coolness was not precisely the word to describe their relationship. Yet for all their physical intimacy, for all the delight that she took in their kisses, there was a part of her that she always held back. It was a barrier between them. She knew it and Adam knew it too.

Della was shaking her head. 'I am sure that love and trust will come in time, Annis. I think that you do love Adam. You are just afraid to let yourself give in to it.' She laughed and drained her beaker. 'Hark at me! I was hardly such a pattern card of marital bliss myself!'

There was a bitter note in her voice. 'Humphrey was a

weak man and I could not give him my respect. At least you do not have that difficulty, Annis.'

'No,' Annis agreed, thinking that Adam could hardly be described as weak. She drank some more cider. It was extremely delicious. Della evidently thought so too, for she pushed her beaker across to be filled and leaned one elbow on the table. Annis's lips twitched. It was perhaps fortunate that she was no longer a chaperon, for her recent behaviour was far below the standard that was acceptable. Shamelessly embracing a gentleman in the woods, getting tipsy on cider... She felt warm and pleasantly at ease.

'Your cousin, Mr Lafoy,' Della said casually. 'Is he a man a woman could respect, Annis?'

Annis hesitated. 'I used to think so. I love Charles and Sibella dearly, for they are my only family and have always been there for me. Yet recently Charles has changed.' She frowned. 'It is not so much that he has fallen under the influence of Mr Ingram, but more that he seems a different character... All his good qualities have been distorted. I cannot quite explain it.' She looked at Della, who was now pillowing her head on her folded arms. Her dark hair was tumbled about her face and there was a dreamy look in her eyes. Annis suddenly remembered the scene in the Promenade Rooms and the night at the theatre. The words came out before she could stop them.

'You like Charles, do you not, Della? Like him a great deal, I mean?'

Della raised her head and for a second Annis could see her heart was in her eyes. 'I love Charles,' Della said slowly, almost defiantly. 'I have loved him since before Humphrey died. We were lovers, Annis. There! I have shocked you—'

The shock was in fact almost enough to sober Annis up.

She stared, her hazel eyes as wide as an owl. 'Della? But how…'

The tears trembled on Della's lashes. 'It was just the once. I do not know… It happened so slowly, yet so inexorably, somehow. We had known each other for an age and then I began to realise that my feeling for Charles had changed and then, one day, I was out riding and met him here…' She smothered a little sob. 'Humphrey was a weak man and, as I said, I could not respect him. But that is no excuse, no excuse…' She covered her face with her hands again, but when she looked up a second later, her eyes were dry. 'So I told Charles that it must end. It had not really begun, and since then we have barely spoken.'

Annis put a hand out to her and after a moment, Della clasped it hard, before letting her go. She took another draught of the cider and gave a watery giggle.

'Oh, Annis, look at us here like two topers drowning our sorrows in drink! I declare we must be the most outrageous sight!'

Annis started to laugh too. 'Oh dear, this is all too melancholy to be true. I cannot bear it…' She dissolved into giggles and after a moment, found she could not stop. She reached for the pitcher of cider and saw that it was almost empty. 'And as if that were not the outside of enough, we have run out of drink! I must ask Mrs Hardcastle for some more…'

She lurched none too steadily to her feet, then sat down again heavily as the door opened with a crash that shook it on its hinges. Della was still laughing, her face flushed pink, her eyes bright.

Mrs Hardcastle appeared in the doorway, carrying a candle. 'Miss Annis, his lordship is here.'

Annis waved the pitcher at her. 'Hardy, we should like some more cider, if you please.'

'It is quite clear that you have had enough,' Adam said. He strode into the room and his gaze fell on Della, now almost asleep on the table. 'Both of you,' he said, 'what the devil is going on here?'

Chapter Twelve

'Oh dear,' Annis said. She blinked at him, feeling ever so slightly cast away. 'You received my message then, Adam.'

Adam gave her a look. 'I did. However, you neglected to mention that the two of you would be carousing on cider at Starbeck with a restless mob of rioters less than a mile away. What the deuce are you doing here, Annis?'

Annis went up to him and put a hand against his chest. He looked stern and unyielding, yet she could have sworn that there was a gleam of amusement in his eyes.

'I am so glad to see you,' she said conversationally.

Adam laughed. His arm went about her. 'Do not try to gammon me, Annis! When Ned and I got back we found nothing but Mama in a state of high excitement and a cock-and-bull note from you saying that you were looking for treasure at Starbeck and would be back by nightfall! Ned and I got over here as quickly as we were able.'

The door opened and Edward came in. His gaze took in Annis, standing within the circle of Adam's arm, Della asleep on the table and the two empty beakers of cider.

'I see,' he said, with a grin.

Annis turned towards Adam. 'Tom Shepard said that the

men were blockading the roads. How did the two of you get through?'

Now it was Adam's turn to grin. 'We talked our way past them.' He gave her an old-fashioned look. 'Surely you did not imagine that we would leave the two of you here unprotected but for Mrs Hardcastle? Although I concede that it would be a brave man who tried to take her on.'

'I suppose that you have come to take us back to Eynhallow.' Annis moved away and went over to take her cloak from the back of the chair. 'If we have your escort we should be quite safe.'

Adam shook his head. 'It is not safe for anyone to be out tonight. The gang are but a half-mile from here. They are tearing down the fences Ingram put up to enclose Linforth Common.'

'And the troops,' Annis said quickly. 'Have the regulars been called out?'

Adam and Edward exchanged a look. 'I heard so,' Edward said.

'And you have warned the men?'

Adam laughed. 'Annis, do not ask! Now, what is this about treasure?'

Before Annis could reply there was the sound of a horse approaching up the drive, and fast. Edward turned back into the hall for a lantern and they all hurried to the main door. The cool night air was sobering. By the light of the moon Annis saw the bay stallion with the white flash. It was carrying a double load. One man dismounted and the other slid from the saddle to crumple on the gravel sweep. Annis started forward.

'Charles!'

Her cry was echoed by another from behind them. Annis swung round to see Della hurrying down the shallow stone steps to join them on the drive.

'Charles! Are you injured?'

In the candlelight Annis saw that her face was paper white, her eyes huge.

'Devil a bit,' Charles Lafoy said cheerfully. He straightened up. 'I did not expect to see you here, Della—nor the rest of you.' He nodded to Adam. 'Servant, Ashwick. Can't talk for the time being. Can you help me?' He gestured to the prone figure, whom Annis saw was Ellis Benson. She went down on her knees beside him on the gravel.

'Is he much injured, Charles?'

'He took a bullet in the shoulder,' Charles said. 'He has lost some blood, but I think he will be fine.'

'A bullet?' Annis said.

'The troops are out,' Charles said tersely. He glanced over his shoulder at Adam. 'We are indebted to you for sending word, Ashwick.'

'Let us get him inside,' Annis said quickly, as several ideas quickly rearranged themselves in her head. 'We may talk later.'

Adam nodded. 'I'll help you carry him inside, Lafoy. Ned, could you take the horse around to the stables? Della, would you and Annis be so good as to search out some bandages and water and whatever else we might need? I do not suppose there is much here, though Mrs Hardcastle may have some ointments.' He turned back to Charles. 'Are we to expect a visit from the militia, Lafoy?'

'I hope not, but one never knows.' Charles shifted a little to support Ellis Benson's weight. 'I do not think that we were followed, but I cannot be entirely certain.'

'Then the most difficult thing to explain will be the horse. We can hide Benson and it is not surprising for you to be visiting your cousin, but it is known that I only have one bay stallion.' Adam cast Edward a glance. 'See what you can do, Ned.'

They carried Ellis Benson across the threshold and up the stairs, laying him on the bed in the first chamber they came to, which was the one Mrs Hardcastle had prepared for Della. There was a hot brick in it and the chamber was warm.

'There are no bandages,' Della whispered to Annis. 'I suggested to Mrs Hardcastle that we might tear up some sheets, but she told me it was a waste and to make do with my petticoats!'

Annis smothered a laugh. 'We may use mine too, although I think that Hardy's would be best. She wears flannel, even in summer!'

They ripped some strips off their underclothes and then Mrs Hardcastle arrived with the hot water and she and Della set to work cleaning and binding the wound to Ellis Benson's shoulder. Annis looked across at Charles and saw that he was watching Della intently as she worked. She glanced at Adam, who met her look with a faintly questioning one of his own. Annis smiled faintly and shook her head. That was another explanation that must wait until later.

Ned returned from the stables. 'All's quiet outside,' he announced. 'How goes it here?'

'He'll survive.' Mrs Hardcastle spoke briskly. 'Tough lad, is our Ellis.' She turned accusingly to Charles. 'What do you think you were doing, Master Charles, lettin' him get beat up like that?'

Charles grinned. 'Sorry, Hardy. I did my best. I brought him here to you, didn't I? I just didn't expect you to be entertaining a house party!'

'Well, give the lad some air,' Mrs Hardcastle said, steering them all towards the door. 'I'll fetch you all some tea and then I'll sit up with him.'

'I'll get the tea, Hardy,' Annis said. 'You had better stay

with Mr Benson, since you seem to know exactly what is going on here!'

The housekeeper turned a little pink and looked a little shifty. 'One hears things, Miss Annis…'

Annis looked at her cousin. 'I am sure that Charles can put the rest of us in the picture,' she said pointedly.

Charles, Edward and Della went back into the drawing room whilst Annis went along to the stone-flagged kitchen. The huge copper kettle was already hissing on the fire and she made a pot of tea with quick efficiency.

'I would rather have some brandy,' Adam said, following her in, 'but I do not suppose that there is any in the house. Just cider, I suppose?'

Annis laughed. 'I assure you that I am quite sober now, my lord. Dramatic events have a habit of having that effect!'

Adam nodded. He leaned against the table and folded his arms. 'Did you know about any of this, Annis?'

Annis raised her brows. 'Which bit? That Charles and Ellis Benson were mixed up in the riots? Of course not. I thought that *you* knew!'

Adam shook his head. 'I confess that I wondered about Benson, but I had no idea about Lafoy. He has played his hand with an admirably cool nerve.' He gave her a searching look. 'Did you know about his feelings for Della? Good God, I could not believe my eyes when I saw her come flying out of the door to save him!'

Annis smiled a little. 'I knew about that five minutes before you and Edward arrived. We were sharing confidences in our cups…'

Adam's eyes narrowed. He pushed away from the table and took a step towards her. 'I see. And what were you telling Della in return, Annis?'

Annis busied herself fussing with the teapot and the

cups. She leaned over the tray, allowing her hair to fall forwards to hide her face. 'I? Oh, not a great deal… She…I…'

'Yes?' Adam said. He took the tea cloth from her nerveless fingers and put it aside. 'What were you saying?'

Annis turned away. She wondered if perhaps some of the cider was still in her blood, or whether perhaps it was simply a night for taking risks.

'Della was saying that you loved me.'

'That is no great secret,' Adam said dryly. 'Go on.'

'And that she thought that I loved you too,' Annis finished in a rush. 'She thought that I was simply afraid to admit the truth.'

'Are you?' Adam said, after a pause. A hint of impatience came into his voice. 'Will you please put that teapot down and answer me, Annis?'

Annis turned and looked at him. There was an expression in his eyes that made her heart turn over. 'No,' she whispered.

She saw the hurt on his face before his expression turned studiously blank. 'I see,' he said dully.

'I am not afraid to admit it.' Even as she spoke, Annis was aware of the lie. She was afraid, very afraid. Her heart thudded and it was all that she could do to speak the words. 'I do love you, Adam. I love you very much.'

She thought later that she had never seen anyone move as quickly as Adam did then. One moment he was standing staring at her and the next she was in his arms, held closer than she had ever been before. His kiss was overwhelming, passion and tenderness rolled into one. Annis pressed closer and gave him back kiss for kiss, without restraint. After a time, she freed herself a little.

'Adam, I want to explain to you why—'

'Some other time.' Adam's voice, husky with desire,

was barely recognisable. 'My darling Annis, I do not want to talk just now...'

Some unquantifiable amount of time later, Annis was aware of the kitchen door opening.

'I wondered if you needed any help—' Edward began, then stopped. 'Evidently not,' he said, and closed the door.

'I scarce know where to begin, Charles,' Annis said. A fresh pot of tea had been made and Annis, Adam, Edward, Charles and Della were seated in the drawing room. Charles and Della were holding hands. Della looked flushed and starrily happy and there was such a look of incredulous contentment about Charles that Annis could have cried. She herself was sitting close within the circle of Adam's arm in a quite improper manner, but nothing could have separated them at that moment. She could not bear to be far from his side.

'Is it you, or is it Ellis Benson, who has been leading the rioters against Mr Ingram's property?'

Charles looked relaxed and tousled in the firelight. 'It is Ellis who has been one of the leaders, although I do believe that he shares that privilege with Tom Shepard. All the rioters are masked and they take it in turns to raise the men, so it is more difficult to identify who is involved.'

Adam nodded. 'We knew about Shepard and we suspected Benson, but what about yourself, Lafoy?'

'The horse is yours, is it not, Charles?' Annis said suddenly. 'I saw it on my first visit here and I knew that the Shepards could not afford to keep a stable.'

Charles laughed. 'So you knew about that, did you? I thought you might have seen it, though Tom Shepard swore you had not.'

'I did glimpse him. A fine stallion. I had a very nasty

feeling when Pullen started looking for someone who possessed such a beast.'

Charles looked shifty. 'Well, I assure you that I have not been riding him. I have had a hand in some of the planning, but the execution has been down to Ellis.'

'A difficult task,' Adam said drily, 'when trying to control an unruly mob of forty men.'

'Yes indeed.' Charles turned back to his cousin. 'Ellis has had some bad moments where your safety was concerned, Annis, not to mention my property. Since it was imperative that no one knew that I was working against Ingram, it was inevitable that I should be a target.'

Annis laughed. 'How unfortunate that your carriage should have been destroyed,' she said unsympathetically.

'Ellis was more concerned for your safety,' Charles said. 'He knew that you were not in the coach, but he did not know where you had gone. You gave him a fright that night, Annis. Until we received Ashwick's message we were scouring the countryside for you.'

Annis sighed. 'I am sorry. Though why I am apologising to a pair of law-breakers I am not certain! I am shocked, Charles. I had both you and Ellis down as Mr Ingram's most loyal supporters.'

'That was the idea,' Charles said drily. 'Do not judge Ellis too harshly, Annis. He has his reasons for what he did.'

Della spoke for the first time. 'What are his reasons, Charles?'

'He loves Venetia Ingram,' Charles said flatly. 'They care for each other. Ingram found out and made life a misery for Ellis, taunting him, tormenting him until he was nearly mad with the strain of it all. It changed him completely from being Ingram's man to being so set against him that I believe he would do almost anything to bring him down.'

There was a silence. Annis saw Della tighten her grip on Charles's hand. None of them, knowing Ingram as they did, could find it in themselves to condemn Ellis.

Annis sighed. 'What of your own motives, Charles?'

Charles shifted a little. 'I have known for a while that Ingram has been involved in some very questionable deals, but the man is as slippery as a fish and cannot be caught. I felt that he had to be stopped.'

'I see. Why not simply refuse to work with him any longer?'

Charles met her eyes very straight. 'That is not good enough, Annis. He has to be stopped.'

Annis saw Della smile, as though Charles had confirmed something for her. She felt the same. Both of them had thought Charles a man of integrity and neither of them could understand how that fit with his work for Ingram. Now, at last, he was free to tell the truth.

Charles frowned. 'I am sorry for deceiving you, Annis, particularly over Starbeck. I wanted to help you so much—or at the least to reassure you—but too much was at stake. I almost cracked that day you came to Ingram's offices and as good as told me you would never speak to me again. Yet I could say nothing to you, for not only was it too dangerous but I could never risk Ingram finding out what I was up to.' He looked at Adam. 'There were several occasions on which I thought you might be a useful ally too, Ashwick, but I could never risk Ingram guessing the truth. I apologise for my apparent hostility.'

Adam's arm tightened about Annis and he smiled at her. She knew that he was remembering the time she had told him how gloomy it was to be estranged from her cousin. Her heart lifted and she gave Adam a dazzling smile back.

'Perhaps there is still time for us all to unite against Ingram,' Adam said slowly.

Della yawned. She practically had her head on Charles's shoulder by now. 'Do you know anything about banknotes hidden here at Starbeck, Charles? Is that part of Mr Ingram's duplicity?'

Everyone looked at her. Annis, who had completely forgotten about the notes in the canvas bag, jumped up. 'Oh, yes!' She turned to Adam. 'This was why we originally came to Starbeck today, my lord. Mrs Hardcastle found this when she was cleaning the house…'

She picked the remains of the canvas bag up from the side table and held it out to him. Adam turned the bag over in his hands, studied the scrap of banknote and handed it over to Charles.

He squinted at it, then recoiled, his shock showing on his face. 'Good God! I have been looking for this everywhere!'

Now it was Annis's turn to feel shock. 'You mean that you knew? Charles—'

'I mean that I suspected that the *Northern Prince* had never gone down.' Charles looked at her. 'Did you not wonder why I was so edgy when you mentioned it the very first day you were back in Harrogate? I was afraid that you might alert Ingram's suspicions if you asked difficult questions!'

Edward, who had sat a little apart during the whole discussion, now leaned forward. 'You suspected that Ingram had saved some of the cargo from the ship, but you did not know where it was?'

'Exactly,' Charles said. 'Ellis and I looked everywhere. He certainly searched here. It was one of the reasons that we kept the house empty, Annis, for we were certain that

Ingram was using it. It was conveniently isolated. Ellis will kick himself that he never found this, though.'

'I wonder why Ingram did not come back to take it,' Edward said thoughtfully. 'Or perhaps he did... If he had embezzled the cargo of the *Northern Prince* he might be helping himself to it little by little.'

'And I would guess that he wished the hue and cry to die down before he started to spend too lavishly,' Adam said. 'Is this all that there is, Annis?'

'I fear so. The mice have eaten all the rest, or shredded it into pieces so small that it cannot be identified.' Annis sighed. 'Della and I searched all day, as did Mrs Hardcastle, but all we found was a mouse nest. Whilst Ingram may not benefit from his ill-gotten gains, unfortunately we cannot pin anything on him.'

Adam picked up the scrap of bank note again. 'The Bank of England may be able to trace this note. If so, the insurers may be interested.'

'If the ship did not go down,' Annis said, 'where is it?'

Charles shook his head. 'I have spent many fruitless hours trying to discover precisely that, Annis. The *Northern Prince* sailed from Whitby and was supposedly lost shortly afterwards, but there are any number of rocky inlets where it might be possible to unload a cargo under cover of darkness and then...' Charles made a gesture '...the boat sails elsewhere. It is repainted, re-named. The ocean is a vast place and tracing one ship, proving that it has been re-named, would be a tricky business.'

'What of the crew?' Annis said, frowning. 'Surely there is someone who would give the game away?'

'Someone did,' Adam said grimly. 'Woodhouse knew what had happened, did he not? Either he knew, or he suspected. Maybe he even tried to extort money from Ingram for his silence and ended up head first down the chalybeate well for his pains!'

Charles sighed. 'The crew were hand-picked by Ingram and I imagine that they were well paid. Very well paid.'

'So Ingram pockets the insurance money and the cargo as well, and he still has a ship left at the end of it,' Adam said. 'Very neat.'

'Very risky,' Edward said. 'He pocketed your thirty thousand pounds as well, Adam. Humphrey never incurred that debt. He was cheated.'

Della raised her head. She was looking absolutely furious. 'Oh, Adam! I cannot bear it! The man gets away with all that money and we can prove nothing!'

They all looked dolefully at the scraps of mouse-eaten money.

'There is still the gold,' Charles said slowly. 'Ellis is convinced that Ingram secreted some bags of that as well. Do not forget that he was still Ingram's man at this point and was deeper in his confidence than I. The only thing he does not know is where it is hidden—or even if it is still hidden. Ingram may have spent it by now.'

'I do not think so,' Annis said thoughtfully. She turned to Adam. 'Remember what Woodhouse said, my lord. It was like a riddle and no doubt it gave Woodhouse a sense of power to taunt you so. He mentioned sunken treasure, and suggested that you look to the skies and into the depths. Supposing that the skies are Starbeck, then the sunken treasure is in the depths—at Starbeck.'

'Sunken,' Edward repeated. 'Can it be buried in the cellars, Lafoy?'

Charles shook his head. 'We have searched there. Several times.'

'Sunken, not buried,' Adam said. There was a blaze of light in his eyes. He turned to Annis. 'There is a well here at Starbeck, is there not? I saw it that day we came to inspect the property.'

'It is a natural sulphur well,' Annis confirmed. 'There are many hereabouts, as you know, my lord.'

Charles's face was a picture. 'A fine pair Ellis and I have been! Ingram hides his paper money in the house and his gold down the well right under our noses—and we cannot even find it! Of all the damned nerve!'

Annis laughed. 'We will have him yet, Charles.'

Adam stretched. 'We may check in the morning, I suppose.' He glanced at the clock. 'I do believe that it is almost the morning already.'

'Then all we have to do is think of a way to lure Ingram into giving himself away,' Annis said softly. 'Which is easier said than done, I suppose.'

There was a gleam in Adam's eye. 'I have a plan,' he said.

Some two days later, Annis and Della were both at the Starbeck once more, concealed in the summerhouse in the garden on the night that Adam intended to put his plan into action. 'I am beginning to regret this, Annis,' Della Tilney said. 'Adam and Charles both insisted that we should not stir outside the house all evening and who is to say that they were not right? We have no guarantee that Ingram will come. We might be immured in this summerhouse the whole night long and see nothing and achieve nothing but to be tired, hungry and aching! I am tempted to go back to the house.'

'Well, I am not.' Not for nothing had Annis defied Adam's instruction to stay safely indoors until the danger had passed. Starbeck was still hers, she thought fiercely, and if Ingram had been using it for his own nefarious purposes she wanted to be in at the end of it all when he was caught. She pressed closer to the summerhouse window and stared out into the starry night. Tonight there was no moon and the gardens were all in shadow.

'I am glad that you and Charles appear to have settled your differences, Della,' she said. 'I hope that the two of you will be happy.'

'There is nothing like a shock to bring one to one's senses,' Della said. 'When I thought that Charles had been injured I could think of nothing but all the time we had wasted.' She sighed. 'I shall always feel guilty for what happened between us when Humphrey was alive, but I cannot carry that regret forever. And one has to live.' She smiled at Annis. 'It is your wedding in two days' time. Do I imagine it, or have you and Adam resolved all your differences, Annis?'

'Almost all.' Annis gave her a smile. 'I have only to explain to him the reasons why I was so reluctant in the first place. I feel I owe that to him—' She broke off. 'Della, look! Is that not a light? There, coming down the path—'

There was indeed the light from a lantern skipping down the path from the house, through the neglected topiary garden, dodging the bushes, faint but clear. The two girls pressed closer together. They watched as the figure came on, dark against the darker background, until it reached the walled garden and put its lantern down on the stones beside the well. There was the faintest creak of a chain and the splash of water.

'He is here!' Della clutched Annis. 'I did not believe that he would come.'

'Adam said that he would,' Annis whispered. 'He said that if Ingram were given a hint that his banknotes were found he would come to retrieve the rest. Charles dropped the hint. Ingram trusts him, so he did not guess that he was being tricked. That was all that was needed…'

'Look!' Della pointed. Beyond the walled garden, out on the drive, a column of light flared.

'They are coming!'

Annis was gripped by the same primitive fear that had caught her up on the night she had first witnessed the riot. Suddenly the air seemed alive with it. Straining her ears, she heard the insistent beat of a drum on the night air. It had a ragged, savage rhythm, an undertone of violence.

The man in the garden heard it in the same instant and raised his head to sniff the air like a hunted animal. He scrambled to his feet, turning towards the gateway. There was only one way out of the walled garden and it was already too late. Already the procession was flooding through the gateway into the garden, torches blazing, and the barbaric rhythm of the drum filling the air. The light and shadow flickered over the faces of the masked men as they lined the walls.

Annis drew in a sharp breath. She could feel Della beside her, tense as a bowstring. There was something primitive here. In this seething crowd it was not possible to tell which was Charles, or Adam, or Edward or Tom Shepard. The masks were on, the tricorne hats drawn down over the eyes, the men dressed all in black tonight.

There was a clatter of hooves and the crowd parted with something like a sigh. The drumbeat died down. The magnificent bay stallion sidled almost gently up to the cowering figure by the well. The rebel leader raised his voice a little.

'I told you that we would come for you, Ingram.'

Samuel Ingram struggled to his feet and immediately two masked men came forward to take up their stance on either side of him. They did not touch him. There was no need. He was almost expiring with fear where he stood.

'Why do you not take your money?' The leader said gently. He turned the horse. 'Take it, Ingram. Pull it out of the well.'

Ingram fell to his knees, grappling feverishly with the chain of the well, half his gaze on the horse's circling hooves. No one moved to help him. Everybody watched him. The torches flared in the breeze. The men stood like sentinels.

Eventually Ingram managed to haul up the bucket and dropped a dark, dripping canvas bag onto the grass.

'Open it,' the rebel leader said.

Ingram scrabbled at the neck of the bag. A few golden coins rolled out to lie amidst the grass and to sparkle in the torchlight. There was a rumble as the rest of the money fell out in a huge pile.

For a moment there was absolute stillness, then Ingram gave a high, keening cry of pain and loss and started to clutch hopelessly at the piles of tarnished coins. There was no gold here, only a mound of blackened metal with a greenish tinge. There was a strong smell of sulphur.

'Take your money, Ingram,' the leader said. He turned the bay stallion and Ingram flinched away from its hooves. 'Take your ill-gotten gains and run away. Spend it, Ingram! Spend all the money you have stolen from the poor and the dispossessed and the weak! Take it and run, before we come after you.'

Ingram scrabbled in the grass for the few golden coins that still sparkled there, shoving them in his pockets, staggering to his feet. The crowd parted silently for him. He cast a feverish look around, from masked face to masked face, reeling from one to the other as he tottered towards the gate. No one moved to stop him. No one moved at all.

Ingram looked back once as he reached the gateway, then took off into the night. Five long, slow seconds passed then, and with a roar, the mob suddenly poured through the gateway after him, the primeval beat of the drum in the air, the torches blazing. Ingram took to his heels and the rabble raced after him, spilling across the gardens and fields until the night was still.

Two men only remained in the walled garden. Charles Lafoy pulled off his mask, his eyes bright, laughing. Della opened the summerhouse door and tumbled out into his arms.

Annis stood waiting in the shadows, then came forward more slowly. The man on the bay stallion turned his horse unhurriedly and brought it alongside. He looked down at her for a long moment, eyes brilliant behind the mask, then, as he had done once before, he bent down and swept her up onto the saddlebow before him.

Annis turned into his arms. 'Adam,' she said, her mouth very close to his, 'swear to me that that was the first time you did that. Swear to me that you were never the rebel leader before tonight.'

She saw Adam grin, saw the blaze of triumph and satisfaction in his eyes. 'What do you think?' he said.

Chapter Thirteen

'There was gunpowder in those sacks originally,' Charles said as, later that night, they sat once again in the drawing room at Starbeck. 'Ellis told me that he had used canvas bags like that one and the one in the attic when he went hunting on the Linforth Estate. One of them must have held his bread and cheese and the other his gunpowder. An unconscionable piece of bad luck for Ingram.'

'I am no chemist,' Adam said, frowning, 'but I assume that the gunpowder and the sulphur water combined in some way to tarnish the silver—'

'Except for the coins at the very top of the bag,' Edward finished, 'which were undamaged.'

'Poor Mr Ingram,' Annis said. 'His whole ill-gotten fortune mouse-eaten and tarnished. He may be a ruthless businessman, but he is a hopeless criminal.'

There was a pause whilst they all tried to look suitably sober, then everyone burst out laughing.

'Are you certain that he got away?' Della asked. 'For all that I detest the man, I could not bear him to be torn to pieces by the mob.'

Adam's smile faded. 'He is safe,' he said shortly. 'We

chose the men carefully tonight and they had their instructions.'

'What will happen to Ingram now?' Annis asked. 'Will he be prosecuted?'

Charles nodded. 'I believe so. There is sufficient evidence from the bank note and the gold for a number of difficult questions to be asked. The insurance companies will be very interested. And the Admiralty will probably put a watch out for a ship answering the description of the *Northern Prince*. Even if Ingram escapes prosecution he is ruined. I imagine he may well run away abroad.'

'I am sure he will,' Edward said quietly. 'He is a laughing-stock. The whole of Harrogate society will dine out on this for weeks.'

Annis shivered. 'It was very humiliating for him, was it not? I confess to feeling not quite comfortable seeing a man brought so low.'

Adam's face was hard. 'Annis, even when the man was at his lowest ebb he was scrabbling in the grass for his money! That was all that mattered to him.'

'You are too forgiving, coz,' Charles agreed. 'Remember how he threatened to take Starbeck from you.' His voice was bleak. 'Think, if you will, of the people who were thrown off their land by him, the men who could no longer scrape a living, the tolls that were too high... People have almost starved and died through Ingram's greed and cruelty.' He laughed shortly. 'I thought you were remarkably measured tonight, Ashwick.'

There was a little silence.

'What of the rioting?' Annis asked. 'Do you think that that will be at an end now, Charles?'

'I imagine so. Ellis Benson stirred much of that up; now that Ingram is brought down, Ellis will be much more at peace. Besides, without Ingram to impose his harsh rents and tolls, I imagine that the unrest in the countryside will die away.'

Charles looked at Adam. 'I am sorry that you are the loser from this case, Ashwick, having paid Lord Tilney's debt to Mr Ingram. If he has embezzled money from the sinking of the *Northern Prince*, all debts must be null and void, but I doubt if you will see your money again. We will have to see what we can do.'

Adam held out his hand. 'It is enough to know that Ingram is brought down, Lafoy.' He grinned. 'Although the money would come in handy as well!'

After Mrs Hardcastle had taken Charles and Della and Edward up to their improvised bedchambers, Annis turned to Adam.

'I must go up in a minute, for I am sharing a chamber with Della and would not wish her to imagine that I am staying down here with you, Adam.' She looked dubiously at the hard couch. 'Will you be quite comfortable? I seem to remember that this sofa was lumpy even in my father's day!'

Adam sighed, rubbing his cheek against her hair. 'I have no doubt that I shall be very uncomfortable, my sweet, not least because I shall be imagining you sleeping so close by! As for Della, I hope that you find she *is* in your chamber! I should hate to have to call Lafoy out when I am starting to like him so much!'

Annis smiled. She rested her head briefly against his shoulder. 'I am so glad, Adam. And I do believe they shall be very happy.' She yawned and stood up. 'I am for my bed. As for the proprieties, we should not worry. What could be more respectable than having a vicar in the house?'

'The rabble-rousing vicar of Eynhallow!' Adam laughed. 'Sometimes I think that Ned was born in the wrong century!'

The wedding guests arrived from London the following day and despite Annis's qualms about meeting Adam's friends, she had to admit that for the most part they seemed harmless. The Duke of Fleet was indeed so thoroughly charming that Annis could quite see why Miss Mardyn had chosen him as her protector. The Earl of Tallant, despite being one of the most handsome man that Annis had ever met, was pleasantly self-deprecating and so utterly in love with his sweet little wife that it brought an ache to Annis's throat to see them together. Only Lady Juliana Myfleet, the Earl's sister, was a different matter. She kissed Adam far too lingeringly for Annis's taste, purred that Annis had caught the man she had always wanted to marry, then went on to entertain the company with malicious observations about various mutual friends. Since Annis had never met any of these people she felt pointedly excluded and certain that Juliana was doing it on purpose. She felt herself becoming quieter as dinner wore on that night, answering only briefly the questions put to her, her insecurities threatening to come back and swamp her. After the scene with Adam in the kitchen at Starbeck she had not had the opportunity to speak with him, for first there had been the matter of trapping Ingram and then all the wedding guests had arrived, taking all Adam's time and his attention. Consequently there had been no moment for private discussion and there was still one matter left unspoken between them.

'You must not mind Juliana,' Amy Tallant said shyly that night as she accompanied Annis upstairs after dinner. 'She is not happy and so she sharpens her claws on other people. She is particularly sharp with those who have what she does not—love.'

Annis grimaced. 'Adam has intimated that she has had an unhappy past.'

Amy nodded. 'In the same way that Adam loved Mary, Juliana was sincerely in love with her first husband, but whereas Adam has found love again, we despair of Juliana ever being happy.'

When Amy had left her, Annis felt too wakeful to go to her room. Tomorrow was her wedding day and she knew that she should try to sleep, but she felt too restless. She took up her cloak, intending to go for a walk in the gardens. She knew that Adam would be busy entertaining his male guests, but she needed some reassurance, some element of him to hold to her. She went out of her bedroom and, on impulse, pushed open the door of Adam's dressing room. After a moment's hesitation, she slipped in. The clothes that Adam had been wearing before dinner had not yet been put away and, succumbing to temptation, Annis went over to the bed and picked up his jacket, slipping her arms into the sleeves. It was far too big for her. She wrapped it about her and turned her face against the collar, rubbing her cheek against the rough twill, inhaling the scent of him. It smelled of smoke and sandalwood and Adam. It turned her knees to water.

Annis closed her eyes. She loved Adam so much and she knew she did not have to be afraid of anything. This was no marriage trap and with the right man she was as free as she chose to be. She could fly but she would never fly away, for she did not want to. Adam had taken her on trust, not forcing her to tell him what had happened to her but giving her all of the time she needed to reach the point where she would choose to trust him too.

There was a step in the doorway. Annis opened her eyes.

Adam was standing there, watching her. His face was in shadow, his expression hidden. Annis suddenly realised that she was still wearing his coat. She slipped it from her shoulders and dropped it on the bed.

'I was coming to look for you,' Adam said. 'You were so quiet at dinner that I was worried about you.' His voice was a little rough. His gaze went from her to the discarded jacket and back again. 'Annis?'

'I would like to talk to you, Adam,' Annis said softly. 'May we? Not here.' She gestured around the candlelit room. 'It is a pleasant night. I should like to talk outside.'

Adam stood back wordlessly to allow her to precede him through the door. They went down the stairs in silence and out into the night. The lighted windows of Eynhallow Hall faded into the dark behind them. The stones of the carriage sweep were sharp through Annis's slippers. She crossed on to the soft grass and made for the edge of the wood, slipping under the arch of the trees and into the heart of the forest. She could hear Adam's footsteps behind her, the crack of the twigs beneath their feet, the sound of his breathing. Neither of them spoke.

Annis reached a small clearing where the moon spun patterns through the trees and turned to face him.

'That night when we were in the kitchen at Starbeck…I was going to tell you then what I had been afraid of, Adam—the reasons that I held back from marriage. I am sorry that I could not tell you before.'

'Do not be. It was not the right time.'

'And now it is? You have been very patient with me, Adam.'

She saw the shadow of his smile. 'I told you before that I was prepared to wait for what I wanted. You have not kept me waiting very long at all, Annis.'

Annis sat down on the stump of a tree.

'I never wanted to marry again. You knew that—I told you from the first. It was not because I was afraid of intimacy, or…or that I had had an unpleasant experience in the past, at least not in any physical sense.'

Adam took her hand. 'I never thought that. At least, I wondered if that was the case at first, but then I realised that you were not repulsed by my touch, nor were you afraid.' He entwined his fingers with hers.

Annis gave a shaky laugh. 'I must beg you not to touch me yet, or I shall never finish the story.'

'Very well. I can grant you a few moments at least.'

'It was another sort of intimacy I dreaded.' Annis hesitated. 'I married at seventeen, immediately after my parents died.' She sighed. 'I suppose that they had spoiled me. The time I spent in Bermuda that summer had been the best of my life. I ran wild in the sand and the sunshine, I was unsuitably tanned, and I knew I was frowned upon by the ladies who had transported English society rules out to the Indies with them, but I did not care.' She smiled at Adam. 'I was heedless and a hoyden, and then my father was killed in a naval action and my mother went into a decline and died, and the whole structure of my life came crashing down.' She looked away. 'I had not realised until then how gravely I had transgressed. The whole weight of a disapproving society seemed to be resting on me, forcing me to conform. I was left almost penniless and there were rumours… Oh, unfounded ones, of course, but the kind of gossip that circulates when a girl is different and a little wild.'

She jumped to her feet and took a few paces away.

'Sir John Wycherley offered me security. He was older and comfortably off, and he had the gallantry to offer me the protection of his name. I was in a haze of grief and loneliness; I had no money…I took the offer.'

'That is understandable. Your parents had both died and you were left with nothing.' Adam's voice was rough. 'You cannot blame yourself for such a decision, Annis.'

'Yes, but I had no notion what it would mean!' Annis turned to him. 'Oh, Adam, I was seventeen and I was trapped into a domesticity that almost swallowed me alive! I had no time to myself, no money of my own, no identity! I was Annis, Lady Wycherley, not Annis Lafoy any more, and I had to eat, sleep and behave as my husband demanded. Why, John chose my clothes and my friends and if I were to go out alone, he would demand that I account to him for every second that I spent away!' Annis put both hands up to her head. 'Worse, he would lock me up if it suited him, and dictate my every move! Before long I thought that my very identity would disappear, utterly submerged beneath the woman that Sir John Wycherley had fashioned. I felt so trapped that it made me ill.'

There was a silence.

'No wonder that you had no wish to submit yourself to a husband ever again,' Adam said quietly.

'No.' Annis swallowed hard. 'I tried to disregard my fears, but I could not quite do it. But it was marriage that I wished to avoid, Adam, never you yourself.' Annis hesitated. 'Deep down I think that I knew it would not be like being married to John. I knew that you and he were completely different people. Yet I was so afraid. I had worked so hard to achieve some freedom. That was why I could not bear to give up Starbeck even when I could not afford to keep it. That was why I found it so difficult to agree to marriage even when I had no way out.'

Adam put his arm about her and pulled her against him. 'And now?'

'Now I realise that marriage to you will not be a cage

but…' Annis smiled a little tremulously '…an adventure, perhaps?'

Adam kissed her.

'I swear I shall never bully you, or tyrannise over you, or tell you what to do.' He spoke into her hair. 'I love you, Annis. I love you exactly as you are and I would never want to change you.'

Annis played with one of the buttons of his coat, suddenly shy at what she was about to say. 'Adam—'

'What is it, sweet?'

'I love you, Adam. Will you make love to me? Here, in the woods, with the smoke on the air and the touch of the breeze on my skin…'

There was a moment of absolute stillness, then Adam's grip tightened on her with bruising intensity.

'Annis, are you sure? For once I have done that I shall never let you go.'

Annis stood on tiptoe to kiss him. 'I do not want you to let me go. Please…'

The pent-up feelings between them could no longer be denied. Adam's kiss was violent in its intent and its effect, seeking, searching, demanding everything. Annis pulled away a little, tilting her head back, a hot triumph racing through her blood. The kick of excitement was like a fever.

Adam found the ribbon that tied her cloak and gave it a tug, so that it unfurled and the velvet slid to the ground in a slippery pool. The night was warm but Annis still noticed the loss. It was as though some part of her had been stripped away, some protection had gone. There was no going back.

Adam's hands were hard on her waist, holding her still as he kissed her again, his tongue tangling with hers. One of his hands came up to her breast, pulling apart the bodice of her gown, sending buttons flying. His warm fingers cupped her breast through the thin linen of her chemise and Annis crumpled to the ground. The leaves of a previous autumn and the soft, dry bracken provided a makeshift mattress, but neither of them was really noticing. All Annis was aware of was the cold breeze against her heated skin and the wood smoke in the air... She was naked to the waist and Adam had taken one nipple in his mouth, sucking, biting, teasing until she thought she would dissolve with blind need. She moaned aloud and he covered her mouth with his in a deep, possessive kiss. Her skirts were up around her waist, her legs parted, the cold night air against her skin. And then he was bending over her, his lips again roughly demanding as he spread her arms wide, entangling his fingers with hers on the bed of bracken as he slid hard and fast inside her.

There was a momentary pause—she felt it, he felt it too. Then he started to move, the sleek friction dragging a whimper from her as she felt the desire shudder through her body. So soon, so quickly. She felt herself tumble over the edge of mindless pleasure, powerless to help herself.

Some semblance of normal thought returned and she tried to pull away from him, belatedly aware, wanting to cover her nudity. But Adam was desperate too. He held her arms apart, his gaze feasting on her nakedness as she writhed with pleasure, beneath him in the moonlight. Hot and hard, the relentless rhythm would not let her go. Annis thought she would faint from the very sensation of it. Then he gave a shout that would have raised all the birds from the trees, and drove into her with all his urgent need, finally reaching his release. And Annis, astonished and bewitched at the power she had over him, felt the same sensual desire capture her again and send her spiralling down into bliss.

For a while they lay still, wrapped in the velvet cloak.

Adam's arms were about her. He refused to let go. After a while he said softly, 'Why didn't you tell me?'

Annis wriggled a little. His body felt warm and hard against hers and she could not remember a time when she had felt so happy and so absolutely free.

'Tell you what? That I had never been with a man before? I did not wish you to make a fuss. You would have insisted that we be all decorous the first time, in bed...' Annis laughed and moved languidly. 'This was much better. This was what I wanted.'

'How did it happen?'

'You mean how did it *not* happen?' Annis laughed. 'My husband was not interested in women.'

'You mean—'

'I do not know if he was interested in men instead. Possibly so. At first I thought it was me.' She paused. 'Then I observed him with other ladies and realised that they did not interest him at all. In fact, I believe that he held a very low opinion of our sex. There are plenty of men who do.'

'You never wished to take a lover?'

'Never, until now.' Annis rubbed her hand along the line of his jaw. 'And now it is too late, for I am about to be married to him.'

Adam kissed her again, softly. 'Do you wish to go back inside and make love again?'

'Again?' Annis smiled, her face dreamy in the starlight, her tone bemused. 'May we?'

Adam laughed. 'Annis, you delight my soul. We may, if you wish it. I swear it will be better next time.'

'It is difficult to imagine, but if you will show me...' She caressed his cheek. 'Must we go back inside?'

'Not if you prefer it here.' Adam's voice had roughened again. He spread the cloak under them and stripped her of her remaining clothing. The moon had risen. She was edged in silver, tip-tilted breasts, smooth skin and shadows.

'Your clothes too…' She sounded dreamy.

'Of course.'

He lay beside her, half-covering her, his hands smoothing, stroking. They kissed, languid and warm where they touched. It was gentle and urgent. Annis, running her hands over the planes of his body with love and wonderment, could not quite believe that it could be true. Or that she could know such ecstasy. Adam bent his head to her breast and his fingers stroked the inside of her thigh. Annis squirmed.

'Open your eyes,' he said. 'I want to look at you.'

She looked into his face and saw all the love and desire and tenderness fused in the blazing passion in his eyes.

'I love you,' he said.

The feeling of him inside her was exquisite and she rose to meet him, dazzled by sensation, consumed with pure love. And then they slept, intertwined, Adam's head against Annis's breast, both wrapped together closer than close inside the cocoon of the velvet cloak.

Annis woke as the birds started to stir and the first light filtered down through the branches into the wild wood. She felt a little stiff and chilly, but she pressed closer to Adam for warmth and rubbed her cheek against the silky softness of his hair. He made a sleepy sound of contentment and her heart melted.

'Adam… It is the morning and we should go back to the house…'

Adam made another sleepy sound, this time of agreement. He did not move. Annis smiled a little to herself. 'Adam…'

She ventured a small caress. Adam made another sound,

though this time it was more like a groan. His eyes opened. 'Sweetheart, if you do that we shall not be going any-where.'

Annis gave him a wicked little smile. 'I fear I may have developed a…a partiality for making love in the woods…'

Adam tumbled her into his arms. 'So have I, sweetheart. So have I. It is fortunate that I own such a great tract of woodland where we may not be disturbed…'

Eventually they strolled back lazily to the house in the morning of their wedding day. The sun was coming up and it was going to be a glorious day. Annis had her head on Adam's shoulder and his arm was close about her waist.

'Speaking of love,' she said, 'did you see how Ned was watching Lady Juliana during dinner last night? He was so distracted I thought that he would forget to eat. I do believe he has a *tendre* there, Adam.'

Adam laughed ruefully. 'Poor Ned. He has been in love with her this age, but I fear he is wasting his time there. Juliana is way beyond his star.'

'Yet she is not very happy,' Annis said presciently. 'For all her beauty and her glamour, I do believe true happiness eludes her.' She looked up at Adam's face.

'And then there is poor Ellis Benson,' Annis went on, 'languishing for love of Venetia Ingram. I wonder what will happen to her now that Ingram is disgraced?'

'Must you be so melancholy on our wedding day?' Adam grumbled. 'All this talk of unfulfilled love…' He paused, then laughed. 'Actually, my love, you have re-minded me. I fear you must include Seb Fleet on your list of thwarted lovers, for he told me yesterday that Margot Mardyn has run off and left his protection.'

Annis raised her brows. 'Has she, indeed? With whom?'

Adam looked at her expectantly. Annis narrowed her eyes. 'Not Lieutenant Greaves?'

'No, no, it is more piquant than that!' Adam smiled. 'I always suspected that Margot would exchange a life on the stage for the respectability of a wedding ring if only she could find a man willing to offer one. I understand that she is the new Lady Doble.'

Annis stared. 'Lady Doble? But Sir Everard... But Fanny Crossley...'

Adam grinned. 'I told you that it was piquant! There you were, assuming that Miss Crossley was the flighty one, when in fact it was Sir Everard who made the runaway match.'

Annis pressed her hand to her mouth. 'Oh, no!' She looked at him suspiciously. 'Did you have any inkling, Adam?'

'I confess I did.' Adam laughed. 'I mentioned his name to her on the very first day we were in Harrogate, after I had rejected her advances myself!' He cast Annis a look and saw she was frowning at him fearsomely. 'I thought it would help her,' he added apologetically. 'After that, I saw them together a couple of times, but when I heard that Sir Everard was betrothed to Miss Crossley I assumed it was just an *affaire*...'

'You men are disgraceful!' Annis said.

Adam smiled. 'Sweetheart, you have nothing of which to complain. I told you that I had rejected her advances!' He drew her unyielding body closer. 'I have no interest in any woman but you, as I have just demonstrated.'

'So I should hope,' Annis said, struggling half-heartedly to be released. 'And Fanny has received her come-uppance, I suppose. It is just a shame that everyone is in love with the wrong people!'

'Not everyone.' Adam bent to kiss her.

'It is supposed to be bad luck for the bridegroom to see the bride on the night before the wedding,' Annis said.

Adam laughed. 'It is fortunate that it was dark then, for I cannot feel luckier than I do now.' He turned to smile at her. 'I hope that you will still meet me in church later, Annis?'

Annis felt a smile curve her lips. 'I shall be there.'

'That is good, for I was afraid that you might have changed your mind. You always said that matters looked very different in the morning.'

Annis snuggled closer to him and turned to face the rising sun. 'Oh, they do, my love. They look better. In fact, they look perfect.'

They were married six hours later.

* * * * *

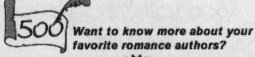

HEAD FOR THE ROCKIES WITH

Harlequin Historicals®
Historical Romantic Adventure!

AND SEE HOW IT ALL BEGAN!

**Check out these three historicals
connected to the bestselling Intrigue series**

CHEYENNE WIFE
by Judith Stacy
January 2004

COLORADO COURTSHIP
by Carolyn Davidson
February 2004

ROCKY MOUNTAIN MARRIAGE
by Debra Lee Brown
March 2004

Available at your favorite retail outlet.

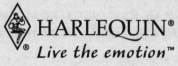

HARLEQUIN®
Live the emotion™

Visit us at www.eHarlequin.com

HHCC

COMING NEXT MONTH FROM

HARLEQUIN HISTORICALS®